Praise

P9-DHF-136

When She Said I Do

"Bradley puts her unique touch on Beauty and the Beast when a devil's bargain flings an innocent into a demon's den. Brimming with her signature depth of emotion, delightful characters, and perfect pacing, this sexy love story tugs on the heartstrings and makes you smile." —*RT Book Reviews* (Top Pick!)

And Then Comes Marriage

"I am looking forward to reading the rest of the books in this series. They will definitely be on my auto-buy list." —*Night Owl Romance,* 5 stars

And these other novels from
New York Times bestselling author
CELESTE BRADLEY

Rogue in My Arms

"Bradley doesn't disappoint with the second in her Runaway Brides trilogy, which is certain to have readers laughing and crying. Her characters leap off the page, especially little Melody, the precocious 'heroine,' and her three fathers. There's passion, adventure, nonstop action, and secrets that make the pages fly by." —*RT Book Reviews*

"When it comes to crafting fairy tale–like, wonderfully escapist historicals, Bradley is unrivaled, and the second addition to her Runaway Brides trilogy cleverly blends madcap adventure and sexy romance."

—*Booklist*

Devil in My Bed

"From its unconventional prologue to its superb conclusion, every page of the first in Bradley's Runaway Brides series is perfection and joy. Tinged with humor that never overshadows the poignancy and peopled with remarkable characters (especially the precocious Melody) who will steal your heart, this one's a keeper."

—*RT Book Reviews*

"Part romantic comedy, part romantic suspense, and wholly entertaining, *Devil in My Bed* is a delight!"

—*Romance Reviews Today*

"Laughter, tears, drama, suspense, and a heartily deserved happily-ever-after."   —*All About Romance*

Duke Most Wanted

"Passionate and utterly memorable. Witty dialogue and fantastic imagery round out a novel that is a must-have for any Celeste Bradley fan."   —*Romance Junkies*

"A marvelous, delightful, emotional conclusion to Bradley's trilogy. Readers have been eagerly waiting to see what happens next, and they've also been anticipating a nonstop, beautifully crafted story, which Bradley delivers in spades."   —*RT Book Reviews*

The Duke Next Door

"This spectacular, fast-paced, sexy romance will have you in laughter and tears. With delightful characters seeking love and a title, [this] heartfelt romance will make readers sigh with pleasure."

— *RT Book Reviews*

"Not only fun and sexy but relentlessly pulls at the heartstrings. Ms. Bradley has set the bar quite high with this one!"   —*Romance Readers Connection*

Desperately Seeking a Duke

"A humorous romp of marriage mayhem that's a love-and-laughter treat, tinged with heated sensuality and tenderness. [A] winning combination."

—*RT Book Reviews*

"A tale of lies and treachery where true love overcomes all."   —*Romance Junkie*

With This Ring

CELESTE BRADLEY

St. Martin's Paperbacks

This is a work of fiction. All of the characters, organizations, and events portrayed in this novel are either products of the author's imagination or are used fictitiously.

WITH THIS RING

For information address St. Martin's Press, 175 Fifth Avenue, New York, NY 10010.

ISBN: 978-1-250-01614-0

Printed in the United States of America

St. Martin's Paperbacks edition / July 2014

St. Martin's Paperbacks are published by St. Martin's Press, 175 Fifth Avenue, New York, NY 10010.

10 9 8 7 6 5 4 3 2 1

Prologue

England 1818

*"Here's a juicy tidbit from your very own Voice
of Society, gentle reader! A confidential source
has informed your Voice that now returning triumphantly from a wealth-building sojourn in the
Bahamas, Lord Aaron Arbogast, who will soon
assume the title of the Earl of Arbodean, has a
secret motive—he has, in fact, come home to find
himself a proper English countess!"*

Inside a ferociously fashionable carriage lacquered in
green so dark as to be nearly black, drawn by a perfectly
matched pair, rolling down Bond Street at a purposeful
clip, a man handed his companion a news-sheet folded
open to the tattle page. "Will that do it, do you think?"

The second man peered at the passage indicated.
"Hmm. Wealth-building sojourn?"

The first man shrugged. "Well, I do think the term *banishment* should be discouraged for the nonce."

A soft chortle rose from the second man.

"Welcome home, Lord Aaron Arbogast!"

In a feminine but genteelly shabby chamber in a house located in a once-but-no-longer-fashionable neighborhood in London, a dainty fingertip tapped thoughtfully on a portion of the gossip column. Then the girlish hand reached for a quill and dipped it into the inkwell on her escritoire. Upon the desktop lay a sheet of foolscap on which was inscribed a very short list of names—wealthy, titled, *eligible* names.

The pen rested for a moment at the bottom of the list.

Then slowly and thoughtfully, the quill tip rose to the top of the list, where it wrote a new name.

It underlined the name. Twice.

<u>Lord Aaron Arbogast</u>

In a breakfast room, not too far off in distance but miles away in aristocratic standing, a man forked eggs into his mouth as he perused a folded news-sheet with sleepy boredom. His half-raised eyelids suddenly widened in horrified disbelief. The fork clattered down to the fine china plate, spattering xanthous yolk onto the snowy tablecloth. The hand holding the news-sheet drew tightly into a white-knuckled fist.

"Lord Aaron Arbogast!"

Chapter One

"No need to fret, Zander," Elektra Worthington had assured her brother Lysander when he'd silently protested her strategy. "What could possibly go wrong?"

She ought to have known better than to jinx matters by saying such a thing. Worthington plans, no matter how well-laid, had a way of twisting ever so slightly sideways.

Now she sat in a dripping ruin at midnight, with her elderly but functional—mostly—pistol on her lap, staring at the suntanned and handsome—if a bit on the shaggy side—bound and furious fellow for whom she had risked her reputation, virtue, and any chance in hell of ever lifting her family from their penury, and found herself at a loss for the first time in her determined, single-minded existence.

Bloody hell. I've kidnapped the wrong man.

Twenty-four hours earlier . . .

Muddy water spattered high onto the chipped and scratched enamel of the carriage's exterior. Punishing rain immediately washed the majority of it right back down onto the sodden, rutted road. Though the sun stood only a few hours after noon, one could not tell time because there was almost no daylight at all piercing the heavy black clouds.

Lord Aaron Arbogast, grandson and heir of the Earl of Arbodean, drove the carriage through the storm with capable, callused hands. How strange to remember that when he'd left England nearly ten years previously, he'd never driven himself in anything but a sporting curricle. He certainly wouldn't have dreamed of exposing his lazy highborn hide to actual weather!

Now he thought nothing of the torrent beating down on his drooping hat, borrowed from his manservant Hastings, except to wistfully recall that the rainwater in the Bahamian Islands was never this cold.

His oilcloth driver's cape was borrowed from Hastings as well, for his own wool finery was wrapped around his shivering, feverish servant, who was tucked up safe and warm inside the once luxurious but now somewhat scruffy-looking carriage.

It had taken far too much of his savings to purchase the conveyance in London, but once his ship had reached port Lord Aaron had wished to escape the city of his youthful downfall as quickly and as surreptitiously as possible.

Everything had cost more than it ought to—the two passages on the not-terribly-comfortable freight ship for himself and Hastings, the posh togs that had ended up wrapping the wiry Hastings to keep him warm, the aged carriage and the not-quite-matched, not-quite-shiny pair of horses to pull it.

Behind the conveyance there even plodded a "gentleman's mount," a rangy bay gelding of dubious descent and sullen temperament, but with long legs and a surprisingly fine gait, who, because of his problematic outlook on his servitude to mankind, had cost Aaron little more than meat market coin. Literally. The beast had been on his way to the knackery when Aaron had noticed the aristocratic lilt to his equine step. Outbidding the butcher at that point had been a matter of a few farthings.

In the last ten years, Aaron had come to believe in the reformative power of the second chance.

All of this was purely intended to make a good impression on his grandfather, whom he'd not seen since the day "Black Aaron" was banished from England for his poor judgment years ago.

Is that what we're calling it now? Poor judgment? The girl died!

Aaron flinched at the accusing voice in his own mind. He had paid for that terrible mistake over the last decade, although even ten years in the sweltering tropics could not bring Amelia back to life.

Such enforced exile had been his grandfather's only recourse. Aaron knew that. The crime that had driven his only family to reject him across three continents had been so unforgivable that it had taken every day of those ten years to slowly and steadily rebuild his personal sense of honor.

His reputation, sadly, remained unsalvageable.

If the old earl were not so ill, Aaron might not have drummed up the courage to return even then.

However, if his grandfather was indeed as ill as

Aaron's aunt's message stated, this would be Aaron's last opportunity to plead his case and claim his full heir status at last. For the title and estate were entailed, and none could take them from him, no matter his social odor—but try managing all those square miles without the wealth or standing that his grandfather's forgiveness would give him.

If he could get to Derbyshire in time, he might, just possibly, perhaps, prove to his grandfather that he was a changed man. He had brought letters of recommendation from respectable gentlemen, his grandfather's steward on the isles, and the local magistrate. Those missives, safely wrapped in oilcloth and tucked deep into Aaron's baggage, were his proof and his talisman. Perhaps all his hard work at redemption had not been in vain.

During a lull in the slashing rain and booming thunder, Aaron heard another explosive sneeze from his suffering servant. He flipped open the trap and gazed down into the carriage from his high seat. Hastings blinked miserably up at him, a pale face splotched with feverish cheeks and a spectacularly red nose visible in the wildly rocking light of the interior lantern, and sniffed pitiably.

"I need soup, ye rotten toff," Hastings informed Aaron in thick Cockney tones. "Soup and a bed, one wi' real blankets and all!"

Lord Aaron Arbogast, a man who in his decadent youth had once knocked a footman unconscious for a barely audible snicker, merely nodded in sympathy at his loyal, ex-thief servant. "You'll have it, my friend, as soon as we find that inn. Are you certain it is on this road somewhere?"

"Aye!" Seized by a fit of coughing brought on by his vehemence, Hastings dissolved into petulant mutters. "Good thing 'e's a toff, for he'd never last a moment as a workin' bloke!"

Aaron let the trap fall closed, for the rain had increased and he didn't want Hastings to get any wetter or any colder than the poor man already was. Gripping the reins more tightly in his hands, ignoring the gasping chill of the rain hitting his body, he gently urged the weary horses just a bit faster.

When the inn emerged from the gloom, its windows glowing yellow and welcoming through the blue English dusk, Aaron let out a yell of pleasure and gave the horses one last lick of the reins across their backs. The pair scarcely needed it, for they well knew where good grain and warm hay came from. The carriage rattled into the cobbled yard of the inn, and Aaron was grateful to see the groom's boy run into the rain to take the horses by the lead.

Gesturing to a stout fellow he took to be the innkeeper, Aaron drew in his assistance in getting Hastings from the carriage. The innkeeper shook his head at Hastings's illness.

"Oy, your poor master looks bad, lad! Want I ought to send for the village physic? He isn't much, just a tooth-puller, really, not near good enough for a fine lord, but he knows a fair bit about a fever."

Aaron hesitated at the innkeeper's mistake, then nodded, tugging the brim of his dripping hat in a respectful gesture. "Aye, sir. I'd be right grateful if ye did." In Aaron's coat of fine dark wool trimmed in gold braid, fit for the Prince Regent's Court, Hastings looked the very picture of an ill nobleman. Aaron's boots were finer, but both men were mud to the knees so it wasn't likely anyone would note it. Hastings would get the best of care if the inn staff thought him a wealthy gentleman.

Together the innkeeper and the boy began to carry the limp and shivering manservant indoors. Aaron let out a deep sigh as he gazed longingly up the muddy road.

So close. The Arbodean estate was a mere half day's journey north. There was no help for it. He could not abandon Hastings until he was sure his man was well set. Once he found them rooms, he would send a message to his aunt that he would be delayed.

Aaron went back to the carriage to retrieve their baggage, little though it was. Then, as he turned back toward the inn, he glanced upward into the most beautiful green-blue eyes he'd ever seen.

Elektra Worthington glanced up from her novel as her brother Lysander entered the private dining room they'd overtaken at the Green Donkey Inn. The innkeeper hadn't offered it for their use. He likely didn't even realize they were using it, but Ellie knew from long experience that a smile and an assumption were as good as permission. Especially out here, nearly to the wilds— relative to London—of Shropshire.

Now, after they'd finished their beef and greens, her brother Lysander had become restless as usual. Zander couldn't be still if he wasn't eating or sleeping—and even then the entire Worthington household was sometimes woken by his nightmares.

Not as often now, of course. He was much better than the mostly silent, sometimes howling, shell of a man who had returned from the war against Napoleon. He wasn't nearly so thin for one thing, though his restlessness did tend to keep him well honed. And he did speak now . . . at least, occasionally.

At the moment, however, he simply gazed at her meaningfully. Fortunately, as a Worthington, Elektra was a native speaker of the Cagey Clue. "Something I should know?" Saving her place, Ellie set aside her book and gave her beloved older brother her full attention, just as if he'd clamored for it, which he would never do.

Lysander's dark eyes shifted toward the casement window that looked out onto the inn-yard below. Ellie stood, crossed the room, and leaned one hand upon the window frame to look out. Through small, diamond-shaped panes separated by wooden muntins, she saw a rainy, muddy yard, the same one they'd driven into earlier that day on this ridiculous errand that she'd have given anything to skip—

"My goodness!" She leaned closer, peering down at a limp form even now being lifted from a dark, unmarked carriage. "Is that man dead?" She glanced back over her shoulder in time to catch Zander shaking his head. She rose to tiptoes and pressed her forehead to the chilly glass to watch as the burdened men passed directly below her on their way into the inn. When she noted the horizontal gentleman rolling his head in feverish protest, she let out a breath of relief.

Then she noticed the other man, still out in the rain, pulling two satchels from the carriage. She wasn't sure why her gaze was pulled to him.

The fellow turned at that moment and lifted his gaze to meet hers, almost as if he'd known she stood there, watching him. A jolt of something exhilarating shot through her and fixed low in her belly. Elektra caught her breath in surprise, then blinked at her own reaction.

Then the stranger lifted one hand to his dripping hat and tipped it, all the while gazing at her boldly. Cheeky fellow!

Her eyes narrowed as she cataloged the curious fellow's person. Years of practice taking note of appearances had bestowed a lightning ability to accurately sort and label everyone she met according to wealth and rank.

His build was tall and fit, at least as far as she could tell beneath his oilcloth cape. He moved like a man prepared for anything—a little like the Worthington siblings' old fencing master, combined with the determined intent of a pugilist and a dash of the head-up awareness of a . . . highwayman?

His clothing marked him as a servant or driver. She could not make out his face clearly through the wavy glass spattered with raindrops, but he looked road-worn and unshaven, and far too disreputable to be gazing boldly at a lady as if she were a barmaid.

Do I look like a barmaid?

Well, wavy glass twisted the light in both directions, didn't it? Likely he wasn't even looking at her.

The flutter in her belly told her a different story, but she ignored it.

Never mind the driver. What of the first man, the ill one? Tapping her fingertip on her bottom lip, Elektra drew his image from her memory.

"That was a fine coat," she mused aloud. "Though it is from several seasons ago . . . real gold thread, I'd say, from the shimmer . . . it fitted a bit loose, but if he's been ill . . ." She let her assessing gaze encompass the carriage as the horse boy led the team out of the rain. "The carriage is well made, though it is almost as old as the one in our mews. Could be he can't replace it, or could be the frugality of the wealthy, buying good and keeping it up." She squinted as she tried to peer between raindrops at the disappearing horses. "His team is matched, but they are too covered in mud to tell if they're fine."

She set back on her heels with a sigh, her curiosity wriggling like a hooked fish. "I would have liked to have seen his face, but it wouldn't look proper for me to run out and gawk." Though she had taken a good long look at the driver, hadn't she? She turned to Zander. "Go on, will you, and tell me if he's dying? And if he's young or old? Ask the innkeeper—well, try to catch his name, at any rate."

Zander nodded indifferently and left the room.

Elektra glanced back through the rain-streaked glass, but the yard had inconveniently been emptied of evidence. The impudent driver was gone as well.

With a huff of impatience, she stomped back to her chair and sat with a flounce. She was bored out of her mind, stuck in this room, waiting for a cousin she'd never seen—never even heard her parents speak of, for pity's sake!—the previously unknown Bliss Worthington. They were meeting her halfway from her home in Shropshire, the seat of the Worthington name, where apparently she had long been living with a foster family

far from London. Their mission, in the end, was to bring
Miss Bliss Worthington to London to share in Elektra's
hard-won victorious first Season.

*I, as one might imagine, am less than thrilled at the
prospect.*

Not that Elektra was looking forward to the journey
back to London, particularly. It had been a slow, dreary
ride—where she'd been mostly alone inside the coach.
Lysander rode his horse alongside, since he was still
quite unable to be confined in a small space. No one in
the family knew what had happened to Lysander in
those months when the world had thought him dead behind enemy lines, but the tense stranger who had come
home was every bit as beloved as the laughing boy who
had gone away soldiering.

He was simply not as well understood.

The assumption was that Bliss would join her in the
coach home. Doubtless she would come supplied with
luggage after all.

The foul weather that had made Elektra and Lysander's
journey a slow and tedious one had apparently delayed
Bliss's arrival as well. The only interesting thing to happen in the past tedious hours of waiting was the arrival
of a dead man. Well, almost dead.

Elektra pondered the possibilities, uncomfortably
aware that she was being quite heartless.

Well, a girl in her position couldn't afford a heart,
could she?

Folding her arms, she allowed herself to slouch back
into the seat and glare around at her private little do-
main. If the new gentleman were of any social quality
at all, he would likely claim this room for himself,

contingent on his survival, of course. The Worthington name was old and well connected, but not terribly high in rank—and the innkeeper would doubtless prefer to be paid in something more substantial than Elektra's radiant smile.

The only thing more boring than being stuck in this dingy sitting room would be to languish in her own tiny closet of a private room. Even her best smile and a demurely cleavage-focusing curtsy hadn't been able to upgrade her accommodations above what she and Zander could afford. At least they had separate rooms. She loved her brother with a deep and terrible pity, but she couldn't tolerate his wakeful restlessness for long.

If only her blasted cousin would hurry along!

Elektra snarled slightly as she recalled her parents' request three days before.

Papa had acted as if he were offering her a treat. "It will be lovely, dearest! She's a darling girl, just wonderful—at least, she was when we saw her last—"

"She rode on your shoulders, Archie, while you played the gallant steed!" Iris, as all the Worthington siblings called their mother, had fluttered her trailing handkerchief flirtatiously at her husband. "And she called you 'Uncle Artsy'! It was adorable. Just wonderful."

Elektra had stared at her parents. "Let me understand fully. You wish for me to miss Lord Orwell's revel, for which I have been preparing for weeks, in order to tromp across the countryside to pick up a cousin I have never even heard of, so that I can bring her back to London to share in *my* Season?" Her Season, her first and probably only Season? The Season she had lied and scraped and sold her soul to have?

Thinking of the endless work, the decade of preparing for this year, the dance lessons paid for with egg money from the garden hens, the begging of gowns from a family friend, the endless work trimming and retrimming said gowns so that she never looked the same yet always looked stunning, the forged correspondence from her "mother" begging invitations from everyone who was everyone, the outright theft of invitations from the overflowing side-tables of her own wealthier friends—

Her belly had gone cold at the loss. "I won't do it! I won't! If this Bliss creature thinks she can horn in on *my* Season, she can bloody well—"

She hadn't been able to continue when her dear, foolish parents had turned to her with hurt incomprehension in their eyes. Iris and Archie loved her, she knew that. They might be utterly useless in every other respect, but their love was unconditional and warm and true. Beneath her sarcasm, hidden under her pragmatism, down deep in her cynical heart Elektra violently adored them both. She couldn't bear to disappoint them.

Helpless to do anything but agree, she'd scowled darkly. "She'll not borrow any of my things. Ever." Only her Season. Only her one chance to fix everything that was broken in her family with a single brilliant match. Only her family's best and only hope for the future.

Damn you, Bliss.

Just Wonderful Miss Bliss Worthington. Ellie despised her already.

Ridiculous name, Bliss. Really, the things some people named their children! With a motion of her fingertips, she figuratively brushed aside her own family's tendency toward grandiose classical names: Daedalus,

Calliope, Orion, Lysander, Castor, Pollux, Atalanta—and of course, Elektra. They had all at least managed to boil those extravagant monikers down to Dade, Callie, Rion, Zander, Cas, Poll, Attie, and Ellie.

Bliss? What was she supposed to do with a name like that? What in heaven's name was she supposed to call her cousin? Bly? Lissy? "*Bliss*, fix your bonnet," Ellie caroled facetiously to the silent room. "*Bliss*, your petticoat is showing!"

Bliss, give me back my bloody Season!

Idly, Elektra wondered if her cousin was pretty. Worthingtons generally were. Iris, though gone a bit plump and prone to wearing her long silver hair in outlandish, off-center knots, often shot through with paintbrushes, was still radiantly lovely. Elektra's married elder sister, Callie, was very attractive. Little Attie, while still a bit unbaked at thirteen, threatened to outshine them all—if anyone could ever get her to wear a bonnet or put a bit of lemon juice on her freckles.

Born with symmetry of facial features and a pleasing figure, Elektra worked a keen fashion sense and a bold confident flair for all she was worth, giving the impression that she was more beautiful than she truly was—but not, as most people thought, out of vanity. She viewed her looks the way some people viewed their bank accounts. Ruthlessly, with frank calculation. It was the only true currency she had, and she meant to make the most of it. A title, absolutely, and not an impoverished one, either! She meant to spend her single advantage wisely, and her final purchase would mean the restoration of the Worthington family to their former glory.

And with the widespread and quirky reputation of her peculiar, madcap clan, for that she'd need an insanely wealthy earl—a spotless earl, truly above reproach!—at the very least.

Of course, her virtue she guarded with zealous care, for it was value added, but she wasn't some ignorant schoolroom miss. She had seen clearly the mechanisms of the world since a tender age, and she meant to utilize those gears to save her family, by God!

She was, in her own opinion, the only Worthington who inhabited the tangible world. Her family cared nothing for the swirl of petty gossip and stabbing of backs in Society. Worthingtons walked blithely through it all, secure in their important friends and their ancient name. "Older than Stonehenge" was Archie's stout assertion.

Unfortunately, that mighty ring of stones remained stubbornly silent on the topic of who would pay the butcher's bill, or repair the ancestral manor, or provide a decent dowry for Attie. Those tiny little concerns were apparently left to Elektra.

Zander entered the room, interrupting her wandering thoughts. "Lord Aaron Arbogast," he told her shortly. "Fever. Not dying, not yet." Then he turned and left again without ceremony.

Elektra sat up straight, her quick mind flipping back through the gossip sheets stored in her memory. *Lord Aaron Arbogast . . . wealth-building sojourn . . . assuming the title . . .* and, saving the best for last, savoring the words on her tongue, she spoke aloud.

" . . . to find himself a proper English countess!"

Elektra's fingers twitched as if eager to get her hands on such a fellow. This was it. The intimate setting of the inn . . . the ill lord . . . Zander hadn't mentioned if he were old or young, not that it mattered, really . . .

And the best of it all was that he had just arrived *from out of the country*! Had she actually found a man who had never heard of the Worthingtons? A singular, elusive creature indeed—a veritable unicorn!

And she was just the virgin to snare him.

By her presence, in this place and in this moment, she had finally been handed an advantage in a game unjustly weighted to the wealthy and powerful.

Bless you, Bliss!

Chapter Two

Later that evening, as Aaron gazed down at his bed of hay in the stable loft with dismay, he decided that his sacrifice almost—*almost*, mind you—repaid his debt to Hastings. The man might have saved his life, but at this moment he was ensconced in a heavenly soft bed, being doted on by angels . . . well, voluptuous chambermaids, anyway.

But not her.

That moment in the inn-yard, standing in the rain gazing up at the princess in the tower . . .

Restless at the memory, impatient with himself for dwelling upon it, Aaron threw himself down upon his straw pile in an uneasy sprawl. It was always thus, was it not? A fellow thought he was on the right road, doing the proper thing, minding his own matters—only to encounter one of *them*.

Her presence had struck him like an arrow. He'd known instantly by the arch of her long neck, by the insubstantial touch of her fingers against the glass, by the haughty tilt of her head, that she was no chamber-maid.

Ah, the English lady, the most refined and delicate creature in the world—and the most dangerous.

She had marked him as well, he reckoned, though he knew not as what. He'd stood there, like an idiot, practically daring her to look at him, to find him out, to tell the world that the most evil of blackguards, Lord Aaron Arbogast, was back in England—everyone, bring out your stones!

It only proved his point. Women like that one made a fellow lose his mind, lose his soul, lose his honor. If Miss Amelia Masterson had only had a little honor of her own—

No. He could not blame Amy. She had been a silly, overwrought sort of girl, prone to melodrama and fantasy, but she had been an innocent in need of safeguarding. Whatever Amy had done, whatever anyone involved had done, Aaron himself had most certainly failed to perform his gentlemanly duty in protecting her.

Who carried the most blame for the tragic end of Miss Amy Masterson was not at issue any longer. The fates had chosen him for that role. Nonetheless, he would someday become the Earl of Arbodean and inherit the estate. He needed to convince the old earl that he, Aaron, had changed. He was no longer the careless spoiled boy who had been driven from his home by scandal and public outrage. He had become a responsi-ble, dutiful man—one well accomplished in land management, one who would be a good master to Arbodean.

If he inherited the wealth needed to keep his home from falling into ruin. He needed to remain on course, to stick to the straight and narrow, as he had for the past ten years. If only he could, his grandfather might just come to believe, if not in Aaron's honor, at least in his stability as an able lord.

The twist of guilt and loss in his belly made Aaron writhe on his lumpy bed of straw. Sometimes he thought he only cared about securing the accounts, which were not entailed to him as the estate was. Other times, the memory of his grandfather's shocked and revolted gaze burned through him like lava.

Then, as always, he would hear Hugh's pleading voice. *"You're the heir to the Earl of Arbodean. He'll never turn against you. But I have no one, no one but you."*

"You! Driver!"

Aaron lifted his head just in time to catch a face full of rough wool. He yanked it down to see the groom's boy grinning at him from across the loft. A sharp word nearly made it to his lips before he realized that the young man was sharing one of his own blankets with him. Gravely, he nodded deeply in gratitude. "My thanks, lad."

"Too right, your thanks." The freckled young man snorted. "Airs and graces. Driving gents about is makin' you into a right lady."

Aaron found himself snorting a small laugh, his spirit warmed by the boy's easy generosity. Brooding would get him nowhere. In the end, he still walked the earth and he knew himself to now be a good man, though he was resigned to the fact that the world might never agree.

So he rolled himself up in the horsy-smelling blanket and let himself sink deep into the golden, summery hay. He had never slept better in his life.

In the morning, just after cock's crow, Aaron freshened himself at the horse trough alongside the stable-boys, scrubbing his face with the cold, green-tinged water pumped from deep underground.

Yet another activity he could not imagine his young, arrogant self performing.

The hour was too early for the guests at the inn, so he joined the boisterous lads as they breakfasted on bread and cheese, washed down by watered beer. He enjoyed their cheerfully rough company. When they sent him off, laughing, to tend to his "toff," he left them with a smile on his face and headed indoors to visit his servant.

Hastings was ensconced in lordly comfort in the best room in the inn, the one, Aaron had been informed, with the freshly stuffed mattress and the window overlooking the meadow instead of the muddy cobbles of the inn-yard. "Ye can't even smell the stable from that'un!" the innkeeper had stated proudly.

Aaron took this information without grinding his jaw at the time he had spent picking straw from his hair that morning. He felt quite proud of himself. Hastings's room was toasty warm and filled with solid furnishings and draped in protective maidservants. It took some time for Aaron to free his man from all the feminine pulchritude hovering tenderly over "his lordship."

Finally, they were alone. Aaron pulled a chair up to Hastings's bedside. The man lay very still, clad in Aaron's last decent nightshirt and worn but still-fine velvet dressing gown, his covers tucked about him as neatly as a crust surrounding a meat pie. A lordship pie. His face was pale as parchment but for the twin spots of fever glowing on his cheeks.

Aaron poked him in the chest with one fingertip. "You can open your eyes now."

Hastings let out a gust of held breath and cracked open two reddened eyes. "Blimey, them girls is meddlesome!"

Aaron found himself unsympathetic. "Have you figured out the game yet?"

"Aye." Hastings snorted damply. "Though I'm ashamed to say it weren't till the tenth time one of 'em 'lordshipped' me. Me head's a sodden cork!"

Aaron smiled. He knew his stalwart companion wouldn't slip, even in the flights of feverishness. "You're going to be fine. All you need is a bit of rest. But ..." Aaron tilted his head. "You know I have to go on without you."

"But you haven't—" Hastings began to raise himself onto his elbows, then dissolved into a fit of coughing. Aaron handed him a mug of water to sip and then eased him back down onto the pillows. "Ye—ye can't go yet," Hastings managed to croak. "I'll be on me feet in no ti—" The cough commenced once more.

Aaron shook his head. "You can't finish this journey right now. You can scarcely finish a sentence! It's not even another day's drive to Arbodean, unless the roads give out entirely under all this mud. I'll be there and back before you know it."

Hastings glared at him, obviously dying to say a great more on the subject. However, although Aaron allowed the man many liberties, Hastings knew who was master and who was servant. Hastings might have saved Aaron from certain death, but Aaron had saved Hastings from a life behind bars. Just ask Hastings which end was worse.

Frowning down at the top button of his nightshirt, Hastings shrugged. "Figured you'd scrape me off one day," he mumbled. "Heartless toff."

Aaron gave him a mild blow on the shoulder and a rueful smile. "Worthless piker." He stood. "Enjoy your stay, 'Lord Aaron.' I'll be back soon to pay the landlord—I hope. Keep the dodge going as long as you can, at any rate. Get well."

"Go on then." Hastings nodded. "I'll be right glad to stay out of that cursed damp weather!"

"I shall think of you when the cold rain runs down my neck." Aaron absently reached for the folded newssheet on the breakfast tray.

Hastings's eyes widened in alarm. "Oy, I be readin' that!"

Startled, Aaron blinked and let the paper drop to the bedcovers. "You can read?"

Hastings snarled and obviously would have liked to deliver some blistering retort, but his customary insubordination deteriorated into coughing before he could respond further. The relapse brought his nurses bustling back into the room. Aaron stood back and let them tend his friend. Seeing that Hastings was in good hands, Aaron turned to leave, but stopped at Hastings's hoarse call.

"You there!" Hastings commanded in passably posh tones. "You must go ahead of me and tell the Earl of

Arbodean not to fret! I be—I shall be along soon enough!"

Aaron turned and bowed exaggeratedly, tugging at his forelock. "Aye, me lord. Ye will be done." He even managed to make it fully out the door before he snickered.

As he left "his lordship's" room, Aaron felt the pull of urgency drawing him north once more. Hastings might very well take a fortnight or more to recover—a stay that Aaron most certainly could not afford. He couldn't even pay for the simple bread and cheese he had been fed as his lordship's servant! His only recourse was to leave Hastings behind and allow him to run up the account while Aaron continued on to Derbyshire. There, he was in hopes that his bright new relationship with the old earl would extend to covering the bill.

Now Aaron must set out under cover of bad weather in his lordship's empty carriage, hoping to make it to Arbodean before he ran out of stolen grain for his horses.

Lost in thought, Aaron was only vaguely aware of another person in the hall. A womanly figure wafted toward him. The English lady whom he'd allowed himself to be distracted by. He suppressed a sudden urge to see her face clearly, forcing his eyes down. Recalling his "place," he ducked aside as she passed, so that his dirty boots would not brush her hem in the narrow hall, and in that motion brought the brim of his hat down over his face as well.

Her politely distant "good morning" wafted pleasantly on his ear. Although females, particularly the dreaded subspecies of "ladies," were on his list of dangerous creatures best avoided, he had to admit that he'd missed the cool crisp accents of an educated Englishwoman. He was home again.

Almost.

The last ten years of his life had been spent in a different place, a balmy palm-studded chain of islands redolent with sensual and carnal delights—and he'd not sampled a single one in his quest to improve his character and gain back everything he'd so carelessly thrown away.

His sense of smell, however, he'd secretly indulged to the fullest. Now, oddly, he found himself recalling those exotic aromas. He realized that the lady's scent lingered in the hall, bringing to mind nights of dark warmth and sweet, juicy fruits that left sugar on his lips.

Jasmine.

How . . . unexpected. Not rose or lavender or even tart lemon verbena, but jasmine—a wickedly sweet and tempting bloom, as white as snow, as tender and moist to the touch as the petals of a woman's center.

Despite himself, he turned his head, but the lady had gone into one of the other rooms and had shut the door on a mud-spattered servant without another thought—as well she should.

He ought to be going himself. It wasn't going to be easy travel for the carriage down these sodden country roads. He'd originally bought the conveyance to make a good impression. The alternative was to ride a second-rate horse up to the gates of Arbodean. Aaron flinched at the thought. It was bad enough that he had to wear his third-best suit, since his gold-trimmed finery still lay soaking in the inn's laundry and his second-best he'd carefully set aside to greet his grandfather on the morrow, hopefully not covered in the region's ubiquitous clay mud.

No, he needed the carriage to further his good impression. He would find another driver somewhere between the Green Donkey and the estate of Arbodean. A driver who wasn't much interested in immediate payment. Who could fit into Hastings's livery. And who could, of course, drive. Actually, Aaron was willing to overlook any lack on that last requirement, if only he could find someone to fulfill the other two!

Elektra entered "her" private dining room and crossed to where her tea tray awaited her. With the inn's maids twittering about his lordship's door like brown feathered pullets, she was surprised she'd had any service from them at all!

Despite the distraction of the staff, her tea was brewed most properly and accompanied by two dainty iced cakes. The pot was still warm, and she poured herself a cupful gratefully. Her brilliant plan to catch his lordship's eye had been completely dismantled by the fact that he had yet to leave his room.

You caught his servant's eye easily enough.

Elektra firmly put the rugged driver from her mind. She had no business thinking about anything—or anyone!—but her goal. She would find a way to introduce herself to Lord Aaron somehow.

In the interim, she'd had to satisfy herself with a fact-seeking visit to the innkeeper's wife, which by chance had given her opportunity to peruse the woman's surprisingly comprehensive collection of recent gossip sheets, although they were riddled with clipped holes, as if a flock of moths had been at them . . . with scissors.

Now, with some reliably exaggerated information at hand, Elektra set about a bit of research.

Curling into her chosen throne by the fire, she spread her cadged collection out before her. Lord Orwell's ball had been held last evening. This morning's gossip rags would not yet have made it as far as the Green Donkey. She wondered if anyone she knew had been mentioned for dressing well.

If it were not for her "wonderful" cousin, Miss Bliss Worthington, Elektra would have been there herself. Securing a brilliant match was the task at hand, and being seen was the first step toward that goal.

Privately, she thought the night had likely been an overheated bore. The ballroom would have been badly lit and more than one young lady would have sacrificed a dearly bought hem to the young gentlemen's overeager, overstepping, overlarge shoes.

However, any opportunity to catch the eye of just the right sort of not-too-old, not-too-hideous, not-too-stupid set of title and estates—and yes, the fellow himself— was not to be missed. She might be pretty enough and her connections might be good, but there were only a handful of such prizes on the market and there were many dozens of young ladies vying for those few.

Elektra's tea was growing cold, as was the room, thanks to a fresh spit of rain. Elektra crossed the chamber to close the window, but not before a gust tossed the last news-sheet onto the coals. It fluttered as it fell and opened to a page she'd not bothered to read. Announcements.

"Returning triumphantly from a decade-long wealth-building sojourn in the West Indies, young Lord Aaron Arbogast, soon to be the Earl of Arbodean, has come home to find himself a proper English countess!"

Arbogast.

Bending quickly, she deftly rescued the smoldering page and efficiently smacked the scorched folds on the hearthstone. It wasn't the first time in her life she'd had to reach into a fire to retrieve something of value. Five brothers, after all.

The account was just as she remembered it.

Young Lord Aaron Arbogast.

The man in the next room was (1) wealthy, (2) young, (3) eligible—and (4) heir to an earl!

Elektra's excitement increased as she read the page over and over. Arbodean—wasn't that up north somewhere? It certainly wasn't in Shropshire, or the Worthingtons would be more familiar with it. Elektra had the vague notion that she'd heard of it and that it was vast. An estate like that would go a long way toward undoing the Worthington repute of quirky destitution further stained by the rigorous application of outrageous conduct.

An entire decade out of England?

A decade away from the increasingly mad antics of her mad family making the rounds of London gossip? Even better.

And looking for a proper English countess?

Elektra had spent her last decade becoming precisely that!

Now all she needed was the opportunity for a little quiet time with Lord Aaron . . .

Lysander entered the room. "No Bliss."

Rather than believing that brief utterance to be a description of Zander's emotional state, Elektra took it to mean that their cousin, the Just Wonderful Miss Bliss Worthington, had not arrived on the morning coach as they'd hoped. There was another due in the evening, the innkeeper had informed them.

Elektra waved a hand carelessly. "Bliss may take the rest of the week to arrive if she wishes." There was work to be done here!

Lysander wandered to the window. "The corpse is leaving."

Elektra's head snapped up. "What? He's leaving? Are you sure?" She joined him quickly, for if having five brothers taught one anything, it was to confirm all rumor and implication.

Zander, however, was usually inclined to brief, unvarnished truth. Elektra's fingers tightened on the windowsill. "That's the same carriage. I'd know it anywhere." She couldn't allow this. Lord Aaron Arbogast was perfect.

There was only one thing to be done. It wasn't so much a plan as a moment of superbly imaginative panic. She turned decisively to Zander. "We cannot allow him to get away!"

Chapter Three

Zander Worthington, bless him, didn't even blink. He simply turned and left the room. Elektra knew that her brother would have his horse ready in moments. She dashed toward her own room to don something a bit more appropriate for her half-formed plan. Then, on impulse, she diverted to Zander's quarters instead.

She threw on a pair of Zander's trousers and cinched them tight. He was still so thin that they almost fit anyway, despite his height. She added one of his shirts, left untucked to hide the revealed curves of her hips and bottom. Her bosom she concealed with one of her brother's weskits, buttoned up and tightened snugly in the back. Her own sturdy traveling boots with her own stockings would have to do.

Done! Having taken a bare seven minutes to dress herself—possibly a lifetime record—Elektra opened Zander's door and flung herself into a run before she'd even fully entered the hallway.

And ran directly into one of the maids walking down the hall with a covered tray.

Elektra bounced back into the wall. The smaller girl was flung right off her feet. Her salver tumbled through the air, scattering its contents over both of them.

Elektra was at the girl's side before she'd managed to right herself. "Let's see there." She ran a quick sisterly inspection, just as she would for Attie after a tumble. No cuts, no head wound, stand her up, brush her off. "Now, see? Right as rain."

When she looked into the girl's face, she realized that the petite, dark-haired maid who stared back at her was at least her own age. Elektra dropped her hands. "So sorry. That was pure habit. I have this younger sister who is always falling out of trees and such."

Thinking about time and escaping almost-earls and Zander waiting downstairs, Elektra dropped to her knees to quickly gather the fallen items back onto the tray.

"Oh, no, miss! You mustn't!"

Elektra snorted. "Well, I knocked it down, didn't I?" It was all quickly sorted. The clunky pottery water jug had a new chip or two, but the lidded pot of something smelly remained solid and the clean rags were soon folded and placed neatly next to jug and pot. Elektra stood and handed the tray back to the maid. "Good enough?"

The girl gave an astonished gasp. "Good enough? Miss, most ladies would slap me for spotting their . . . er . . . gown."

Her gaze passed over Elektra's ensemble. "But if I may be so bold . . . you don't look very much like a boy. If you wish to pass inspection, you might want to . . ."

The girl mimed putting up her hair. "I'll be right back, miss!"

Elektra opened her mouth to object, but the dark, elfin girl was gone in a flash. She was right about the hair, however. With a twist and a quick repinning, Elektra had her softly waved chignon pulled into a tight, sleek bun.

Then, just as Elektra was beginning to fidget in earnest, the little maid was back, breathlessly waving a brown woolen cap in triumph.

"The boys in this valley wouldn't step out the door wi'out one of these on their heads."

"It's perfect!" Elektra snatched it and plunked it over her hair. The cap said, *Pay no mind to me, I'm just a poor common lad.* Elektra smiled, her real smile. "Thank you!"

The girl blinked. "'Tis nothing, miss. I'd best be on my way now."

Elektra looked at her closely. "Aren't you curious why I'm trying to pass as a boy?"

The girl blinked again. "No, miss. I know why. It's a better life, bein' a boy, isn't it? Safer'n all?"

Elektra sobered slightly. Here she was, a protected woman, surrounded by men like her father and her brothers, who would die to save her. What must life be like for this defenseless little creature? She wasn't big enough to fight off a hedgehog, much less a man with evil on his mind.

On impulse, Elektra dug into Zander's weskit pocket and pressed her last coins into the girl's palm.

"Oh, no, miss! I can't take all this!"

"All this" would buy Elektra no more than a few ribbons and a tin of sweets for Attie. "Take it," she urged the girl. "What is your name?"

"I be Edith, miss."

"Edith, take this. Just save it for . . . for Someday." Elektra didn't know a woman in the world who didn't dream about Someday.

Edith looked down at the coins in her palm. "Aye," she said slowly. "For Someday."

"Now I truly must be on my way. Farewell, Edith!"

Elektra took off down the hall at a full run, for the future of her family was fast getting away!

Edith watched the strange beauty depart until the woman was nothing but an echo of booted feet on the stairs.

To think, a lady like that, getting on her knees to clean up a tray!

Edith had waited on many a toff at the Green Donkey, for it was the only reputable inn on this long stretch of road. Never in her years of service had a lady spoken to her in any fashion other than to command.

And then there was his lordship . . .

Lord Aaron Arbogast was a handsome fellow, sure enough. A big strapping, dark-haired man with the bright blue eyes of a chancer.

That was what Edith's mum called a man like that one. A chancer was a fellow who gambled as easily as he breathed. He gambled with his money, he gambled with his woman, he gambled with his life.

Edith had never met one of the nobility before this week. She wondered if all lords were chancers. Perhaps they were, for they had little to lose by it.

That had nothing to do with her. Edith had always

imagined herself taking up with some stolid farm boy, with whom she might have some farm boy sons, and perhaps a clever daughter to pass on the Knowledge. Unfortunately, she had never encountered that farm boy—at least, she had never encountered one she thought she might like to keep.

His lordship, on the other hand, was in sore need of a firm feminine hand. Edith had only ever really met two ladies, those bright golden-haired creatures who had convened here at the Green Donkey Inn before they had rolled off together onward down the road.

If all ladies were like the two of them, vibrant and indomitable, Edith could just about imagine a lady of that sort taking his lordship in hand.

On the other hand, if ladies were like the ones in stories, all fainting pale in peril, why, his lordship didn't stand a chance of reforming his gambling nature! That would be a pity. Edith saw glimmers of a fine man beneath the gambler. A man, perhaps, who sought the warmth of home fires and the welcoming bed of a wife.

It could be that a chancer was just a man who hadn't found his home yet.

The other maids at the inn had swarmed the man, hoping for his notice, to what end Edith couldn't imagine. A man like that could only want one thing from a common serving girl. She knew that one or two of the other girls didn't mind tumbling the occasional guest and receiving a trinket for their troubles, but Edith couldn't bear the thought.

She might be only a chambermaid, but she had her pride. Indeed, she had little else! But she was hardworking, she could read and write a bit, and she had her mother's wise-woman skills. Her mother had been respected in their village. People had come knocking, begging her healer's skills, offering money or their last pullet. Her mother would take a coin to pay the butcher, then hand back the rest. Healing was her calling, a sacred ability, and not to be sold at high price to the desperate.

But when her mother had passed, lost to a wasting disease that had been far beyond Edith's skills, she couldn't bear to stay in that village. Impulsively she'd set out to journey to London, where she had a cousin or three, according to family legend.

Unfortunately, there hadn't been much coin left to travel on and Edith's adventure had come to a halt at the Green Donkey, where she might be able to put away enough to finish her journey.

So she cleaned up after the guests and kept her head high, for she was an honest and virtuous girl. She didn't advertise her healing skills, for this was a superstitious region, the sort her mother had warned her about. "Them that don't understand our ways like to blame us when crops fail and livestock dies. Be careful. Stay small and quiet, keep the Knowledge to yourself until you're sure it's needed." So Edith's skills were a fact she kept to herself because she'd prefer not to be hunted for a witch next time there was a grain blight, thank you very much.

However, now, here at the Green Donkey, his lordship needed her. The rest of them thought he would soon recover from his chill but Edith knew the signs. She could hear the faint whistle in his lungs, see the fever in his eyes, the tremble in his hands. Pneumonia

awaited his lordship, ready to enfold him like a deadly
lover.

Edith meant to prevent this. She leveled her tray on
one palm and straightened the small pot of her special
unguent. Then she took a deep breath and tapped on
the door of his lordship's chamber.

Lord Aaron Arbogast had seen a bad morning after or
two in his wayward youth. A decade of scrupulously
clean living had not dimmed the memory of a dry mouth,
a pounding head, and eyelids of sand. He held very still
and waited for the swirling nausea that was surely on
the heels of such a hangover. He had drunk—

Nothing. Not a damned thing. Not a drop of brandy,
not a whiff of whiskey.

Furthermore, he was not in a bed, nor even in the
hayloft of the inn. No, he was sitting in a chair, entirely
unable to move. Without opening his eyes or making a
sound, he carefully flexed the muscles in his arms and
legs against his prison. Ropes?

Keeping his breathing calm even in his alarm, he inhaled slowly, trying to sift clues from the scents about
him. Fire smoke, real fire made from wood, not coal.
Candle wax. A draft crossed his face—no, it smelled of
fresh, damp nature. A breeze? Yet he didn't have the
sense that he was out of doors. He smelled moldy furniture . . . and damp plaster . . . and jasmine.

Jasmine? No, that wasn't possible. He was no longer
on the plantation on the isle of Andros. He was in
England, damp, fusty, smoky England. He was home.

"Oh, for pity's sake, open your eyes!"

The melodious feminine tone startled him into doing just that. A single flame seared his vision. He blinked away the blur and focused on the dim form several feet in front of him.

A vision. A creature of shimmering perfection. A golden, nubile beauty.

A goddess.

He blinked. A goddess holding a pistol. Correction, *pointing* a pistol. At him.

Did goddesses carry pistols?

The heavenly—er, heavily armed female who perched daintily on a crate across from him rolled her eyes. "Finally. Really, watching you sitting there sniffing like a hound was fair to bringing on a sneeze." She raised her brows. "So, how close was your guess?"

Aaron reluctantly tore his gaze away from her perfect face—she was a real stunner!—and cast his glance around his surroundings.

Bloody hell! Only years of practice in keeping his impulses in check kept him from exclaiming out loud.

He sat in the middle of a ruin. Toppling walls, leaning doorways, and all. Beneath his feet he could see the muddy, moss-tainted remnant of a colorfully patterned carpet. To his right stood a fine marble fireplace, holding a crackling fire—and a garland of ivy, except that the garland was growing up and across the mantel!

More ivy crept in through the open window—no, not open. Starkly empty of glass or shutters, it was the hole through which he'd felt the night breeze. And there was something wrong with the sound of the crackling fire—the noise faded away instead of resounding through the room.

Aaron looked up—and up—into a black night sky.

The room had no roof at all, but for a few burned rafters over the farthest corner.

"This was the solar, I think," the girl said in wistful tones. "I recall it being quite nice . . . once." She leaned her head back to gaze upward. "My brother Poll calls it 'the lunar' now. It is quite magical when the moon shines full into it. Like something from a dream—"

Aaron began to struggle then. He wanted out. Out of his bonds, out of this creepy hellish ruin, out of the same county as the mad female before him!

Elektra gazed at her captive for a long moment. She wasn't entirely mad, after all. She knew that if she made the next move to capture the king, she was taking an irretrievable step.

Yet this was not hesitation. Not in the slightest. When she thought of her family, she felt not the slightest waver in her conviction that she would do whatever must be done to save them from themselves.

It was only the method that seemed . . . well, tawdry. He was a stranger.

Then again, perhaps it was better this way.

He was a very handsome fellow. His hair was darker than hers, more of a light brown than her own blond. His eyes in the candlelight kept switching from blue to gray. He had a square jaw and quite a lovely set of shoulders, if she was impressed with that sort of thing. She didn't think she'd mind despoiling herself all that much with a man like him. The books her mother had given her—the ones that other girls never even knew existed!—had hinted at the possible joys of the flesh that came from coupling with an appealing man.

Other than that, there was no point to knowing him better. It didn't really matter much if she liked him in the end. Love was for people who could afford the luxury.

And that little voice crying out inside her that she was wrong, wrong, *wrong*—well, that little voice could take a flying leap from the ruined roof of Worthington Manor! She knew what she was doing. She always knew what she was doing.

Declining to waste one more moment on dithering, Elektra rose to her feet and brushed out her skirt—er, oops, her trousers. Bother. She ought to have changed into something a bit more entrancing. Then again, she still had all the required equipment to seduce a man. She'd been born with it.

One deep breath. Then she crossed to where the bound man in the chair still gazed at her in horror. She smiled brightly, to ease his anxiety. Oddly, her dazzling smile didn't seem to relax him at all.

"My lord, I have decided that your search has come to an end."

He drew back. His struggles increased, until the heavy chair creaked against the pull of his muscles. Elektra gazed at him perplexed. What had she said?

Come to an end.

Oh, for heaven's sake. Where had she drawn that silly line from, the dialogue of the villain in some seedy novel? She clasped her hands before her and waited for his alarm to die down a bit. When he again lifted his gaze to hers, she nodded encouragingly, widening her eyes and smiling at him.

"What I meant to say is that you have found me at last."

Now he just gazed at her as if she were drooling and listing slightly to port. Seriously, the fellow was just a bit thick, wasn't he?

Elektra worked her neck slightly to ease her own tension, then showed more teeth. It might be best to speak slowly. Sometimes the upper classes could be a bit inbred. "I—am—your—countess," she enunciated carefully.

He paled, the dusky tan of his skin fading right before her eyes. Really, there was no call for him to take it so hard.

Dreaming of making a brilliant match and kidnapping a man might not seem like one and the same, but Elektra refused to listen to the voice of reason, even when it was emanating from her own mind.

Lord Aaron Arbogast was The One. All the factors matched up. Rich, titled, young, and not from near about. He was looking for a countess. She was looking for an earl.

All she would need was a private moment with the man in order to make him see her point, she was sure.

Around her stood Worthington Manor—at least, what remained of it after all these years. The broken walls supported her like the loving, if somewhat irregular, arms of her family.

This house was the perfect place to have her little tête-à-tête with his lordship. It was isolated enough that no one would hear him calling for help—er, rather, no one would overhear their private conversation.

This is mad.

Yes, but what else was she to do? How else to bring a man—the right man!—to heel?

You've been dealing with your brothers too long.

Elektra suspected that the voice of reason was quite right about that. Unfortunately, it was a laggard voice. It had kept too silent for too long. Now she stood in the very place she meant to save, with her bound, titled victim—er, future husband—in her grasp.

Her nerve began to fail. She ought to turn about now. Or better yet, leave him here, safe in his carriage on the roadside, none the wiser to the identity of his assailants!

Then the clouds passed on for a moment, and the moonlit lines of Worthington House came into view. Graced by a silvery glow, it almost looked as it once had—the lovely, graceful seat of the Worthington family history and stature.

I want to come home. I want us all to be able to come home again.

And I will do whatever it takes to make that happen.

She straightened at that thought. Ah, there it was, flooding back through her veins, no longer faltering in the late hours of the night. Her purpose. The goal that had her riding out behind her brother's saddle, chasing down a carriage in the night, stealing a man from the side of the road like . . . like pilfering a pumpkin from a field! Everything she did, everything she would ever do, had only one aim.

The Worthingtons would be restored.

She had the means. His lordship sat before her. If he didn't wish to listen to reason, she would simply have to take matters into her own hands . . . again.

Elektra took two steps and straddled his lap, settling herself gingerly onto his hard thighs. The trousers were coming in handy once more. She placed her hands on each side of his beard-scratchy jaw and closed her eyes against his appalled gaze.

And kissed him.

Chapter Four

Aaron froze when the madwoman's mouth touched his. Her lips were so damned soft. Her mouth tasted like cherries. Her hands softened on his face when he went still, and her fingertips eased experimentally into the hair behind his ears.

Soft . . . sweet . . . tender . . .

It had been so damned long.

His breath escaped him on a short gust that parted his lips. She parted hers in response. She ran her tongue across her own lips to wet them, and wet his as well. She must have liked the taste of him, because the tip of her tongue came back again and again, slipping just past the boundary of his parted, hungry lips. Sweet, bold little tongue—

Lost in her taste, he sucked that tongue into his mouth and stroked his own over it. Then he dipped his own into her parted mouth, tasting cherries and sweet, hot innocence. She didn't know how to kiss, some distant part of his mind realized. She didn't even realize that open mouths were carnal and wicked and oh, dear God, her mouth was so damned delicious—

He pressed forward, kissing her as hard as he could in his restraints. She responded with a surprised little noise that went straight to his groin, leaching the last bit of sense and blood from his brain in the process. Her fingers slid around to the back of his head, fisting in his hair as she pressed hard into him.

Wild tongues, darting and dueling in the secret hot confines of their kiss. Soft, succulent breasts flattening against his hard chest, small, relentless hands tugging at his hair. God, if only he weren't tied up—

Bound.

Kidnapped.

Cold sense dashed onto the fiery kindling of a decade of abstinence, dousing the flames ignited by her hot, untutored kiss.

Aaron pulled back sharply, whipping his head away, pulling his hair from her grasp, leaving a few strands behind in the process.

Her dazed eyes and flushed features—damn, she was pretty!—hung only inches away. "What's wrong?" Her fair brows drew together. "Is it the way I'm dressed? I know I don't currently look my best, but believe me when I say I clean up fairly well. I shall not embarrass your house or your name."

Aaron fervently hoped he never saw her at her best. He might not survive the event. Then he fought back his instinctive male appreciation to glare at her in dark fury. His countess, she'd called herself. Title by seduction—or worse! What sort of creature was she to arrange her own ruination?

Oh, God. *Ruined.*

Everything he'd worked for over the past decade, ruined. His grandfather would never award him the rest of his inheritance if he believed him capable of defiling a young lady! Not after what had happened before!

Curse his damned fatal luck. How had this come to happen? He'd been riding along, minding his own business, a man with a future and real possibilities at last. Then this unbelievable little maniac simply reached out her dainty hand and, with the flick of one finger, completely destroyed his life!

Well, not if he could bloody well help it! He'd not spoken a word yet in her hearing. Good. She'd best listen carefully now. He gazed into her blinking, green-blue eyes and gave her Hastings's finest sneer.

"Nice try, ducky, but I ain't 'is lordship. Ye've gone and wriggled on the wrong bloke's lap!"

"Ha!" Elektra folded her arms. "Good shot, Lord Aaron, but servants don't ride *inside* the carriage."

He twisted against his bonds. "They do if the master be too bunged up to travel and an urgent message is to be carried on!"

Elektra examined the man before her. The unconscious lord in the rain had been long-limbed and lean. This man was just so formed, although she'd not noticed such a breadth of shoulder in the limp fellow in the yard.

The too-large coat might have misled her, of course.

Yet the man who had been too ill to walk into the inn under his own power should not be now struggling so mightily against his bonds. The ropes creaked, and she worried for the structural integrity of the old chair. Her own knots worried her not at all, for she'd learned how to tie up her brothers years before. It was often the only way to get half an hour of peace.

If only she'd allowed herself a peek at the fellow when he'd been brought indoors! Her worry over appearing unsuitably curious now seemed ludicrous. She'd been too demure to poke her nose from her quarters, but not too ladylike to kidnap a man at the point of a pistol!

Her eyes narrowed. "I saw you being toted out of your carriage myself!"

His handsome face regained the scornful sneer. "Does I seem like I 'ad to be carried out o' my carriage a day ago? I saw you, too, you know, up there in that window, lookin' down on us all—and you saw *me*." His gray—no, blue—eyes bore meaningfully into hers.

Elektra's stomach jumped at the memory of the dark figure of the driver in the rain . . . and the way he'd gazed so boldly at her.

And the way that had made her feel.

She lifted her chin. No, it couldn't be so. Look at him! He was handsome and lean and . . . handsome.

You don't want it to be true. You don't want this man to be a common servant.

You don't want him to be forbidden to you.

That thought shocked her enough to make her wonder if it was not the truth. Never let it be said that inner voices weren't annoyingly blunt.

And usually right.

Oh, shut it!

His suit. She clung to one last hope. It was a good

one, if a bit worn, which could be the garb of a gentleman a bit down on his luck!

Except that Lord Aaron Arbogast was supposed to be wealthy.

A good suit could also be the garb of a good servant, who sometimes received an employer's castoffs. Worthingtons did not toss away perfectly good clothing in such a way, for there was nearly always another Worthington coming up who could wear it—but Elektra knew some people did.

"I tell you, for the last time, you li'l lunatic!—I be not 'is lordship!"

Elektra swallowed hard. Oh, heavens. She could not have gotten it wrong, could she? Did her quarry lay feverish and quaking back in the Green Donkey Inn, his wealthy, titled, eminently eligible brow even now being mopped by some comely housemaid instead of by herself? Had she thrown away her best advantage on the mad, desperate pilfering and imprisonment of a valet?

Her breath left her abruptly.

What have I done?

She sat down again on her crate and dropped her head into her hands, one fist still wrapped about the pistol. *I suppose I am just another mad Worthington after all.*

Inhale. Exhale. She lifted her head to eye the man still bound to the chair. "Well," she said wearily. "This is a pickle, isn't it?"

He stared at her for a moment, then offered her a short, amused snort. "That's puttin' it mildly, I'll agree."

He watched her, no longer fighting his bonds, clearly sensing that she'd begun to believe him.

Elektra stood and set down the pistol. His gaze followed it to the floor. She flapped her hand to release the tension of holding the heavy thing. "Oh, don't worry. I won't set it off."

He shot her a wary glare. "It ain't even loaded, is it?"

Elektra blinked. "Well, of course it's loaded! Goodness, only an idiot would play highwayman with an unloaded pistol!" Shaking her head at the very notion, she bent to tug at her very good knots.

He was silent, so she glanced up at him. Only a foot away, his eyes were locked on her in abject horror. "Ye held a loaded pistol on me all these hours? What if ye'd fallen asleep with that thing pointed my way?"

Elektra gave him her loveliest smile. "I imagine you would have woken me up."

His brows rose. "Aye, with me dyin' scream, ye mad thing!"

"Oh, be still. You've pulled the knots so tight I cannot budge them!"

"Cut 'em, then!"

She frowned. "That's ten yards of very good rope! Besides, it belongs to the Green Donkey. I'd rather not ruin it, thank you." She put her hands on her hips. "Besides, I forgot to bring a knife."

"You—you—!"

It was difficult to tell but she rather thought his features were turning an alarming shade of red . . . or perhaps purple.

*　*　*

Aaron was furious. He had been back in England for all of twenty-four hours and here he was, hip-deep in another scandal!

And in Shropshire, of all bloody places. The quietest corner of the land, bucolic, boring Shropshire—and he'd managed to run smack into the only insane female within fifty miles!

Her single irresponsible action would undo all his years of hard work to convince his grandfather that he wasn't *that* man any longer. No, the last thing he needed was to have his plans thwarted by a headstrong beauty who was willing to shred his reputation along with her own!

For a moment, he contemplated telling her so. He would see how she liked the fact that she'd locked herself into marriage to a destitute blackguard!

Then again, the notion of being a countess, even a destitute, publicly scorned countess, might still appeal to her. She was mad, after all. At last he felt the ropes around his hands part.

His fury boiled over. Without planning to do anything but deliver a sound scolding, he reached up and grabbed her by the shoulders, pulled her face close to his and—

He kissed her. Again. Hard.

Let's see how she likes being kissed against her will—

Well, it appeared she liked it quite a bit, for after a first stiffening protest, her lips parted under his and her arms came about his neck. She relaxed into his lap as if it had been made for her, sinking her body into his.

The soft weight of her arse and the heat of her on his

groin, not to mention the billowy press of her breasts against his chest, made Aaron lose his train of thought. What had he been thinking? Oh, that's right. He'd been thinking that he ought not kill this person, because she was female, and because she was weaker than him, and because killing women was frowned upon in England, and God, she felt good!

No. He would not allow himself to be distracted. Distraction was death.

If anything, this disruption in his schedule ought to make him realize just how important his mission was. He had to get to his grandfather's as soon as possible. To lose his last chance to see himself redeemed in the old man's eyes would be more than he could bear.

And no matter how soft or voluptuous or inviting or tantalizing his captor was, he would not allow himself to think about her as anything but a threat and a nuisance.

Until she kissed him back.

Her mouth was so soft, so warm. As warm and soft as his life had been hard for a decade. He'd allowed himself no softness, no release, no temptations for so long that he was afraid he'd forgotten what it was a man did with a woman pressed to his body. Then his cock surged against her. Oh, yes, that's right. He remembered now.

She wrapped her slim arms more tightly around his neck and kissed him with hard, untutored pressure. Something in his remaining consciousness twanged a warning at him. Part of him would've liked to ignore it, especially the part of him that was now wedged against her rounded hip, growing harder by the minute. And it wasn't as if he could pull away . . . or move away at all. His lower body was still bound. He was trapped, wasn't he? A victim. None of this was his fault.

So he kissed her back, just as hard as she was kissing him.

The kiss evolved, changed, growing into something pure and white-hot between them. It became more than mouth meeting mouth, more than body pressed to body. Something inside him rang out, a bell unsounded ever before. He felt it resonate within him, within her, silvery and strong and mysterious, tangling them deep in their souls.

To hell with his mission. To hell with his grandfather. To hell with anyone or anything that was going to keep him from her, keep him from drinking from this well, from driving himself hard into the sweet liquid softness of this softly panting, willing . . .

. . . Virgin.

He could tell by the way she kissed him. Saucy and strong-willed and convincing as she might be as a kidnapper, this girl was as innocent as a day-old chick.

Damn it.

Obviously becoming aware that he was no longer kissing her, she pressed herself tighter to his body and opened her lips against his, just as he had done a moment ago. She tasted of honey and woman and hot glowing moments of mind-blowing ecstasy that he would remember for the rest of his life . . . except that they had never happened, and never would.

Damn it!

Mustering willpower such as he'd never needed before, he twisted his neck to pull his lips away from hers.

Gasping, he pressed his cheek to the back of the chair and closed his eyes. He would not take the girl. He would not take . . .

He felt her soft lips on his ear warm against his chill flesh. Her warm breath gusted in sensitive places. Dear God, she was without mercy!

"Stop!" He'd intended an authoritative bark. Instead, he practically whimpered it. "Please . . . Stop!" And now he was begging. His day just got better and better.

He felt her weight shift, and the heat of her upper body left his cold and alone. Once he was convinced she had truly pulled back, he dared open his eyes and turn his head to face her once more. She sat sidesaddle on his lap, seeming to find him quite comfortable. Her arms were crossed in front of her delicious bosom, and her perfect brow held a wrinkle of perplexity.

"Well, you started it."

The expression of mild irritation on her face left him breathless with disbelief. She looked as though she'd snagged a nail, while he felt as though he'd been struck by a runaway ale cart.

She showed no sign of revelatory epiphanies. No remnant of silvery perfect completion shone in her eyes.

I must have imagined it. Of course, I imagined it.

He shouldn't have felt so disappointed. This young woman was his worst nightmare on wheels, certain death to his hopes and ambitions. His soul wanted nothing to do with hers.

Too bloody right, it doesn't!

Wildly, he cast about for some change of topic—and some way to get her sweet bottom off his pinned but very eager lap. With a groan he pulled his aching arms between their bodies and rubbed at his raw wrists. "Damn!"

"Let me see." Cool fingers removed his numb ones from the abraded skin. "Oh, look what you've done, you foolish man!"

He gaped up at her. "What I've done?"

She left him—thank you, God!—to stride across the room to a small bucket of water that he recognized as coming from his carriage. After moistening her handkerchief, which had been hidden in her bodice, she came back to bend over him while dabbing the cool cloth to his skin.

He hissed at the sting, and at the returning sensation in his fingers.

"Oh, don't be such an infant. You wouldn't have hurt yourself if you hadn't struggled so! I didn't bind you tightly enough to do you damage."

"Know that for a fact, do ye? You tie men up often, then?"

"Weekly," she assured him absently as she tended him with practiced care. "I have five brothers, which is about four too many on most days." She stood and returned to the bucket, rinsing her handkerchief and wringing it out again over the open windowsill. He wondered why she didn't just spill the water on the ruined floor.

She returned to him and deftly rolled up his sleeves to examine the burns across his biceps he'd given himself in his struggles.

"Brothers." Now that some of his blood supply was returning to his brain, he recalled a dark fellow lunging into the carriage. The struggle had been fierce but brief, for Aaron had been distracted by the sight of the back of his not-quite-hired coward of a driver disappearing from the circle of light cast by the carriage lanterns, fleeing into the dusky blue evening. "Was that one of them, what knocked me out on t'road? Feels like I got meself kicked in the 'ead by an 'orse!"

She drew back to gaze at him warily. "You mustn't blame him for that. I ought not to have involved him at all. He isn't—he isn't completely well, since the war. It was very selfish of me to put him in that situation. I ought to have realized—" She pressed her lips together. "All blame falls on my head, you understand? Swear to me that you'll not pursue charges against him, or—or I won't finish untying you until you do!"

Since Aaron had no intention of ever telling a single soul that he'd been assaulted, kidnapped, and held at pistol point by a girl—even if she'd been assisted by a madman!—well, it wasn't a problem for him to keep quiet about it. He would take this mortifying incident to his grave, although it would probably take him the rest of his life to forget the humiliation. However, something she'd said distracted his attention for the moment. He tilted his head as he watched her. "What 'bout you, then?"

"What about me?"

"Don't ye mean to make me promise not to call the magistrate on ye?"

"I certainly wouldn't blame you if you did," she said absently. "But I'd really rather you didn't. My family needs me far more than I need punishment. After all, I'm hardly likely to repeat this particular offense." She sighed. "I do believe I am an utter failure as a kidnapper."

She'd begun cleaning the graze on his forehead, leaning close to see better in the dimness. He could feel the heat from her skin on his face and neck, but it was the sweet, wild scent of oil of jasmine, grown in the tropics, shipped across the seas, and warmed by living girl that made his throat close tight. She must have stroked it over her wrists and behind her ears after her last bath.

He closed his eyes and pictured the moment, allowing himself to imagine the damp, steamy chamber and hear the slosh of soapy water as she stepped out of the copper tub, her perfect ivory skin gone pink and glowing from the heat of it. The candlelight would shimmer over the swell of her wet hips, highlighting the roundness of her dripping breasts, catching the glint of water droplets as they hung, quivering, from her pink, erect n—

"Ow!"

Chapter Five

Aaron flinched from her ministrations. "What're you cleanin' that with, sand?" He scowled, but he was grateful for the twinge. *Concentrate on the pain. Focus on the fury. Remember what she has done, not what she smells like!*

"Goodness! Men are such babies!"

Aaron felt his annoyance rise higher at her exasperation. Good. "If ye don't mind, miss, I'd like to get me legs back under me as well." Hastings had a way of depicting haughty disdain for the gentry that came in handy indeed. "Since ye don't want me takin' your brother before the magistrate?"

She bit her lip again. "Yes. Of course. It's just a simple matter of . . ."

There was nothing simple about it. In her efforts to conserve rope, she had wound and knotted, wound and knotted, until he was trussed like a pig on a spit.

For the next quarter of an hour, Aaron had nothing better to do than to watch a beautiful girl bend, stretch, tug and wiggle, all while kneeling at his feet. God, she was a beauty. Mad, possibly. Evil, definitely. Yet all the resentment in the world did nothing to deny the fact that she was absolutely delicious.

Ordinarily, he would have been ashamed at his own prurience, but he'd been waylaid, knocked out, and tied up for hours. Any scrap of gentlemanly decency he had left was more than this insane creature deserved.

He particularly enjoyed the bit where she had to lie down with her head beneath his chair and stretch her arms to reach the knots. Her beleaguered shirt-and-weskit combination almost failed to restrain the creamy swell of her breasts as they bounced about in response to her frustrated tugging. Aaron thought he might spy a bit of nipple at any given moment. He never did, more's the pity, but he did greatly enjoy the anticipation.

All in all, it was a very tolerable way to pass the time.

It was when she knelt at his feet and bent over his lap, trying to get at the knots behind his knees, that he had to stop her. Seeing her tousled blond head bent over his groin, bobbing there as she tugged at the ropes, was making him think thoughts a good man shouldn't think—even if those thoughts were about a crazed, kidnapping wench with more beauty than morals!

The fact that he'd hesitated as long as he did, while inhaling the warm scent of jasmine and feeling the weight of her fallen hair draping over his thighs and the warmth of her breath penetrating the fabric of his trousers just over his awakening cock—

Well, no man is perfect, his groin commented. *Let the woman work*.

However, his better instincts won out. He placed both

his hands on her shoulders and pulled her upward. She resisted, obviously absorbed in her task.

"Wait—I've almost done it." She made to reach back down but he held her fast, mercifully high and away from his much-saddened groin, although lifting her had straightened her body to come between his parted knees. If he squeezed his knees together, he would press his thighs perfectly into the dip of her waist.

He manfully resisted the urge. Instead, he scowled at his no-longer-precisely kidnapper. "Who taught you to tie knots, then?"

She shrugged. "My brothers, I suppose."

"Well, they made a muck of it." Aaron would never say "muck" to a lady, but Hastings would. "These knots'll never give."

She smirked slightly. "That is the general idea."

Oh, she was a saucy one. He did not smile. It wasn't easy. Then again, he was still most thoroughly tied up. Instead, he let out a long-suffering sigh. He figured he was entitled to one, since he'd been suffering for a good bit of time. Then he tilted his head toward the gaping window. "Is there any broken glass remaining in that window frame?"

She frowned slightly; then her eye lighted. "No! But there is a bit left in the dining room window!"

She scrambled to her feet, pulling from his grasp with ease. His hands closed on empty air as she strode from the room. She bent to sweep the lantern from the floor as she passed it and left the room, leaving him in utter and sudden darkness.

His stomach lurched slightly at the instant blindness. He wasn't afraid of the dark—but he didn't like being tied up and helpless and blind as well!

His eyes widened, trying to adjust, but this was no moonlit beach in the tropics, where even the slightest star shine reflected in the water and sand. This was a darker, colder, damper world altogether. The night sky above gave nothing away, for there was not a star to be seen through the heavy clouds.

The girl tripped lightly back into the room, swinging the lantern with gusto.

"Agh!" Aaron threw his hands up before his face, but it was too late. The glow of the lantern had seared his night-expanded vision until all he could see was a harsh greenish smear against his closed lids.

"You ought not to look directly at the light," she informed him quite seriously. "It's bad for your eyes."

"Do tell," he muttered. Well, at least he hadn't whimpered. He'd had a very difficult evening at the hands of this—

"What is your name?"

He could feel her hesitation.

"Are you going to call the magistrate on me after all?"

"Probably." Probably not, but he wasn't about to let her off that easy.

He heard her sigh and tried not to imagine the rise and fall of her sweetly curved bosom.

"Even if I cut you loose and get you back to your carriage? After all, you haven't been injured."

"Tell that to my skull. Your brother packs a wallop."

He could practically hear her squirm. He wished he

could see it as well, although his active imagination filled in the blanks quite admirably. It wasn't fair, really, for her to be so very pretty. He would have a much easier time despising her if she were large, hairy, and male.

He told her so.

She laughed. "My brother Orion would say it was a failing of the species or something."

"If you are any example of the current state of British womanhood, the continuation of humankind depends upon it."

Her voice came closer and he realized that she had knelt before his feet again and was now sawing at the ropes, presumably with her scavenged shard of glass. His vision was clearing gradually. His sense of smell had taken no such holiday.

Pretty girls who smelled like this one could likely get away with murder. In fact, their victims probably thanked them for it!

In that moment, the looming clouds above them came to a decision and began a downpour. Not just rain, but a deluge! Ice-cold and so heavy that it felt as if they stood under a waterfall.

Elektra gasped as the cold water instantly began to soak through her clothing. She almost scrambled for the lone bit of shelter near the south wall of the ruin, where a bit of scorched roof remained, until she realized that her prisoner could not flee the downpour. So instead of running away, she found herself rushing back to where he sat, his booted ankles still securely bound to the chair, trying to shield his head from the battering rain with his raised arms.

Elektra bent to pry at the ropes with her fingertips, but the thick hemp had already become soaked and was now swollen into impenetrable knots. The rain beat down so hard she could scarcely breathe, but she had no choice but to stand and lean over him from the front, taking the worst of the rain on her back and shoulders. If she bowed her head over his, the rain ran down over her hair, forming a curtain behind which they both could draw breath.

Then the hail began.

Aaron had been perfectly content to allow the girl to protect his head from the cold rain—until, that is, he saw the walnut-sized hailstones bouncing on the rotted carpet. He looked up at once to find her bent over him with her arms stretched to the back of the chair, sheltering him like a human tent.

Her face was hidden behind her streaming hair, but Aaron heard a single cry of pain when her body shook from a particularly hard impact.

"Get off, you fool! Get to shelter!"

She ignored him, even as her body cringed from more and more blows. Beside him he could see that the hailstones had grown to the size of peaches, some of them harmless and slushy, but some quite hard ones that bounced and rolled away. The impact had to be considerable.

And yet not one had struck him yet.

"Go!"

But she stubbornly remained where she was. Aaron had no choice but to grab her about the waist and force her down to his lap so that he could bow his shoulders over both their bodies. It wasn't a complete shelter for her, but it was better than before. She struggled, but he bent his head to growl in her ear. "Stay!"

Relenting, she curled up in his protection, only disobeying him enough to cup one hand over each of their skulls in meager protection.

The hail passed in moments, as hail does, though it seemed as if they were battered for an hour. Each mushy ice wad that struck them made them gasp. Each frozen lump made them yelp. Their heads stayed tucked together, his arms wrapped about her, hers curled above them. Their breath mingled, and he heard every gasp and whimper she made.

Then, with a few last rolling icy cannonballs the size of hearty pinecones, the hail ceased completely.

They waited for a long moment, unwilling to risk unwinding from their mutually protective posture. Elektra lifted her head first.

"It's done," Aaron whispered. "It's over."

She only nodded. Much of the spirit seemed leached from her by the cold and wet. Slowly, she slid off his lap and knelt beside him. She found the shard of window glass and wrapped it in her sodden handkerchief to protect her hand. Silence grew around them as she sawed at the rope.

Aaron found himself missing the exasperatingly animated girl who'd held him at the point of a pistol and ruined his life. This creature was just an exhausted young woman who needed dry clothes and a warm bed. He actually felt a little guilty that she'd stayed and protected him—as if he'd somehow caused the ropes to wind so inconveniently about himself!

The hemp ropes gave quickly before the wickedly

sharp glass. Aaron was soon free. Taking the lantern in one hand and supporting his captor's elbow with the other, he led her from the ruin back to the front drive where she'd left the carriage and team.

Together they gazed blankly at the vast, long empty drive that connected the main road to the looping curve that passed before the house.

"Horses," Aaron mused wearily, "must dislike hail as much as we do. I don't think we can find them in the dark."

"Oh." She didn't cry, not really. She simply sort of . . . crumpled. That haughty arch to her neck that he'd first noted disappeared. She slumped forlornly with her arms about her drenched body and trembled in silence.

Taking the only route open to them, they slowly walked back into the ruin. The fire that Elektra had built while Aaron was unconscious was now a pile of damp, steaming char. He might have managed to get the last few coals going, if there had been anything dry to burn.

Instead, they searched the place until they had gathered several lengths of draperies, rotted dustcovers, and even a moth-eaten pillow, and made a slightly squishy nest in the most sheltered corner of the ruin.

"You'd best lay close t'me," he told her. "For warmth. You'll catch your death in them wet clothes."

He thought she would make some ladylike protest, but she simply curled against him, tucked into his side, and pulled a musty velvet drapery over them both.

It was a testament to their exhaustion and chill that they soon relaxed into the relative warmth of each other's bodies.

"Y'know, this is all your fault," he said softly.

"It usually is," she replied regretfully.

Aaron blinked against the weariness flooding his body. Shivering was exhausting. Although he'd done nothing for a decade but wish he could return to England, he now felt most nostalgic for the endless sun and balmy summer days of the islands. Half an hour on a sunny Nassau beach would set him up right, he was sure.

Elektra felt herself nodding. She couldn't help but allow her head to rest on the broad wet shoulder next to her cheek. The clammy shirt made her flinch, but soon the heat of his body seeped through the damp fabric and she snuggled deeper.

"Still . . . you ought not to ride in your master's carriage," she informed him sleepily. "People ought not to be blamed for getting the wrong idea."

She felt his shoulder move under her cheek and realized that he was laughing at her. Well, laughing was usually better than shouting . . . . or at least, it would be if her pride were not involved. This time, however, she had no pride. She'd mucked it but good and there was no getting around that. Mr. Hastings had every right to laugh at her.

Besides, he was big and warm and she was very tired and very cold.

I smell jasmine.

Even with the deluge, somewhere on her skin remained a slight scent of rain-washed jasmine.

She shivered against him. Almost against his will, he put his arms about her and pulled her closer to his body. He at least had a bigger body to stay warm. She was a slight little thing despite her curves.

No. No English ladies! Even the best of them assumed that he would do the protecting, that he would fix all the ruin they had wrought, that he would take the consequences for their errors . . .

She'd stood over him like the sheltering wings of an angel.

Angel. Devil. What an odd girl.

She pressed closer to him in her chilled sleep and he reminded himself, Woman. Grown woman, capable of making ridiculous amounts of trouble for him if she ever discovered the truth of his identity.

He had even begun to feel responsible for her. True, he was here alone with her against his will. True, he'd arrived unconscious and bound. True, he hadn't asked for this and wished he'd never laid eyes on her.

Yet surely she had people who missed her. Surely all her brothers weren't as mad as the silent, vicious bloke who'd taken him down so fast and so hard that he was a bit embarrassed to think on it. Humiliated, really. Of course, he'd been taken by surprise . . . and he'd been unarmed.

But he was too weary to swing back to anger now. If he remembered how angry he was, he would have to set her aside and stalk away and she was very soft and the poor thing was so cold and he was so weary . . . .

Henry Hastings, former unrepentant gambler and convicted felon, now semi-reluctant valet and parolee, wasn't the sort of man to believe in heaven, at least not for the likes of him.

Hell, on the other hand, was a concept a man like him ought to keep conversant with. His own hell would likely involve alternating waves of fire and ice, of sweating and shivering, of noises that rang through his aching head like great brass gongs—yes, he could believe in that sort of hell quite easily.

A place he seemed to be right at that moment. He tried to thrash his way free of some torturously constricting trap.

"Shh, milord. Don't fret now. You'll only tire yourself."

He stilled. At last a sound that did not grate his ears raw. A voice like that, rich with a lilt he almost recognized, soft and light, was a balm across his exposed nerves. But the voice fell silent and although Hastings strained heroically, he could not summon it again.

His bonds were fair to smothering him. He kicked madly, trying to free his trapped legs.

"It's all right, milord."

Who? Who was "milord"? Was it him? He tried to remember, almost had the thought pinned down, then lost the thread as his blood abruptly switched from boiling to freezing.

So cold. He tried to worm his way deeper into his bonds, seeking warmth, desperate to stop the shivers that racked his body. A tender touch upon his brow stopped him. Fingers, warm and gentle, stroking soothing smoothing—

The fingers moved to his chest, caressing his bare skin. Bare? When had his bonds been released? He could escape now. He could flee this hell.

He did not move, lulled to stillness by the sweet, circular strokes of those small, gentle fingers. He could stay in hell a bit longer for that touch, although now hell included a strange, green odor like rotted vegetables, or a pond gone stagnant—with perhaps a goat carcass submerged for extra flavor.

The smell was quite possibly the worst he'd ever known, and he'd been in a tropical prison for a year, so he knew a right stench when it hit him in the face. It was a testament to the power of that tender touch that he did not rise up and flee the awful aroma. Instead, he ignored the rude assault to his raw nasal passages and focused his full attention on the fingertips sweeping sweetly across his pectoral muscles.

A small hand. A lady's? No, he could feel the slight roughness of her fingers on his oversensitive skin. A woman who worked for a living, then. A nurse?

A nurse would be good. This gave him the distant understanding that he was not actually in hell, that he was ill. This led him to recall that he'd been out in the rain—bloody cold English rain, when his body had known nothing but island temperatures for nearly twenty years. If he listened now, he could still hear that icy rain slashing hard against a nearby window.

A fever, yes. He had a fever, and he was in England.

He just couldn't remember why.

His nurse continued her ministrations, rubbing something deeply nasty onto his chest. It seemed to warm him and ease the wheezing passage of air into his lungs. Hastings felt soothing sleep pulling him down, freed at last from his nightmares of hell. A fever, a cold English rain, and a nurse with an angel's gentle voice and a disturbingly erotic touch.

As he drifted off to sleep, he deeply and profoundly hoped that the angel wouldn't spot his towering erection.

Chapter Six

Elektra opened her eyes upon a sea of mud-stained linen. She blinked. No, it was only a relatively wide expanse of shirt compared with the size of her hand, which had slipped into the neck of it, her fingers pressed to warm bare skin.

My goodness.

It was morning. She blinked up into a pink-and-gold dawn sky above the roofless room. She lay in a warm, if slightly damp, nest made of fusty cushions and draperies. Even now, a decade after the fire, she could still detect the smell of smoke on them. The man who was not Lord Aaron—what was his name? Oh, yes, Hastings. Mr. Hastings held her close, his arms about her, his hand gently tucked in the crook of her waist, his torso rolled toward her as if to curl protectively around her.

At some point in the chill and the dark, she seemed to have curled snugly into Mr. Hastings's large, warm body. Now she pressed fully against him, with her head upon his shoulder and her knee drawn up to cover his . . . er, well.

Mr. Hastings was a very affectionate sleeper.

Or perhaps he was simply trying to stay warm.

The poor man had given her the driest, most sheltered bit of the protected space. She'd benefited greatly from that consideration. She ought to have caught her death last night, and instead she felt fine.

With the greatest restraint, she lifted her fingertips one by one, relieved when the wide chest beneath them didn't sir. Then slowly, she slid her hand out of the placket of his shirt. Then she carefully removed her thigh from its, ahem, grip about his, heavens-was-that-his—?

Forcing her gaze aside, she eased herself away from his sleeping form. She couldn't bear the thought of him opening his eyes to find her wrapped intimately in his arms . . . well, that would be highly embarrassing! She allowed herself to think that the flash of heat in her face was based in that hypothetical moment of discovery and not in the way his hands tightened about her when she carefully tried to roll away.

Pity, for she'd been most comfortable. She was very nearly warm as well, which had seemed like an impossibility the night before.

Oh, blast!

She had spent the night in the arms of a strange man.

That was the plan, was it not?

Well, one hesitated to label that impulsive abduction and attempted self-ruination with any description so dignified as *plan*. More temporary insanity than good old-fashioned plotting. Hardly worth a Worthington's time, really.

Not to mention it had been a dismal failure.

A quick glance down assured her that she was most clearly untouched. Even her filthy shirt and crumpled weskit were not askew in the slightest. So, despite the intimacy and helplessness of her pose, this Mr. Worthington had not taken the slightest advantage.

Well, of course he hadn't.

A servant who accosted a lady wasn't long for this world. Most didn't even make it to the magistrate, but merely ended up the victim of some tragic and entirely fatal accident while everyone involved had excellent alibis.

That was the way the world worked, and Elektra was in favor of it, in general.

However, if her brothers ever discovered that she'd spent the night so intimately with a manservant, even factoring in the necessity of survival, the fellow wouldn't last a day. Nor would her reputation survive if anyone outside the family ever knew.

Elektra wasn't at all sentimental about her virtue. The sooner she married and disposed of the endless boring restrictions of purity, the better. Wives had ever so much more freedom than did maidens. Married women could shop and travel alone. They could dance at balls without first having to have their partners vetted by bossy matrons. Heavens, Elektra longed simply to be free to stroll by herself in the park in the middle of the afternoon!

However, until the day she took some not-too-old, not-too-hideous, not-too-stupid man's ring upon her hand, her reputation remained a vital weapon in her armory. She could never land a duke or an earl if she didn't have VIRGIN stamped upon her like an indisputable brand.

She sat up, her thoughts already churning the problem through the Worthington mental processes, the ones that allowed that anything was permissible if one followed a single simple rule.

Don't get caught.

Now, there was only one person who knew what she'd done. Lysander didn't count. He barely spoke to her, much less anyone outside Worthington House.

It all hinged upon this man. Mr. Hastings had nothing to gain by carrying tales of her actions, unless he liked to live dangerously.

Nothing of import had happened anyway.

Just two things. Just two kisses that nearly made you forget everything you have based your life upon for the last decade.

Elektra felt fully able to excuse her enjoyment of the first kiss. After all, she had thought she was kissing her future husband! How joyful to discover that he riveted her sensual attention so thoroughly!

That happiness had been unfortunately short-lived. The discovery that her captive was only an ordinary manservant had been most disappointing.

So why did you kiss him again?

He kissed me!

And you kissed him back. A lot.

She had indeed. In fact, she was a little stunned to realize that in both kisses, er, cases, it had been Mr. Hastings who had the presence of mind to call a halt to matters.

I must be losing my looks.

Then again, maybe she wasn't. Elektra's gaze slid sideways to where Mr. Hastings lay sleeping still. There remained a definite *shape* beneath his trousers.

Elektra turned her gaze virtuously away, but she allowed herself a smirk. She still had everything required to turn a man's head. Which meant that Mr. Hastings was an exceptionally well-behaved fellow.

How alarming! The last thing Elektra needed was a man who felt compelled to Do the Suitable Thing. No, she needed Mr. Hastings to be the sort of bloke who looked assiduously after his own skin—that was the only way she could be sure that he would never breathe a word of what had happened last night.

Restless, she rose to her feet and began pacing the squelching carpet. She had to make a plan. She needed to brush the cobwebs from her mind and *think*.

The sun flashed in her eyes and she went still in a warming shaft of sunlight coming through a broken window. For a moment, the past dozen years slipped away and she could see the room the way it was.

The high arched windows filled the room with light that gleamed from polished furnishings and made the exotic patterned carpet glow with jewel colors. Two little fair-haired girls ran giggling through the room, chasing across the fine rug, dashing around the spacious chamber, until a laughing dark-haired boy sprang from behind the luxurious settee to startle them, screeching with gleeful terror, back down the hall.

Little Calliope and Elektra and Lysander, from a time when the world was full of magic and promise. It was more than another time. It was another world, another Worthington family . . . none of which still existed.

No one knew how the fire started. Elektra had long suspected one of Orion's experiments, or perhaps it had been the twins brewing up something foul in one of the fireplaces. Whatever the cause, the result was a house that was naught but walls and broken slate, still filled with the possessions that had been too ruined to take away, too broken even for vagrants to steal.

It can be saved. Someday, Attie will run through these halls that she was robbed of. Someday these cracked walls will fill up again with a whole, perfect family, just as it used to be.

Elektra know how to get it back for Attie. For them all. If she made the match of the decade, they could have it all back.

As she stood there, her hand stole to the ribbon that hung from her neck. Lifting it, she pulled out the key.

The beautifully scrolled iron key from the front door—the key that no longer worked on a door that no longer locked. The door itself had long been carted away to fuel someone's fire.

Still she kept the key. She carried it always. Someday that door would be repaired and when it was, she would have the key to open it.

Aaron felt sunlight on his face and for the first time in a thousand years, some tiny fragment of him was warm.

No, that wasn't quite right. There was a heated portion of his anatomy that had not given him this sort of problem in years.

Out of a male instinct as old as man, he reached for a bit of coverlet to pull over his lap even while still nearly asleep.

The cover was unpleasantly damp in his hand. This shocked him enough to open his eyes.

Good God, what a beauty.

Miss Elektra Worthington, detestable madwoman and scofflaw extraordinaire, stood before the window in a shaft of golden light, her face uplifted and her hands clasped before her bosom. Her eyes were closed.

She took his breath away. Even filthy and rumpled, with her tangled braid come half undone—and dressed like a boy for pity's sake!—there was no hiding the vulnerable yet powerful arch of her neck, or the achingly perfect parallel lines of her cheekbones and jaw that he could happily gaze upon for the rest of his life.

Unfortunately, the rest of his life was not available. After the first shock of her perfection wore off, he considered that this girl was no better than he had once been, spoiled and thoughtless, ruining people's lives as a game. A game he had no intention of playing.

Aaron cast through possible opening lines and settled upon mockery. Hastings was very good at mockery.

"Prayin' for mercy?" he drawled. "Be ye askin' the good Lord for forgiveness for kidnapping a poor workin' man and puttin' him in an icy damp hole all night long?"

"I'm asking God to strike you dead," she responded tartly, without so much as opening her eyes. "I've put in a request for a nice bolt of lightning, since it would leave less messy cleanup, but fire, flood, or famine will do in a pinch."

She turned her head, opening her eyes to glare at him. If he was not mistaken, she was as grateful to caustically mask the awkwardness of their night together as he was.

Her green-blue eyes were uncanny in the golden light of day, large and wide-set in her ivory face. She was a bit too thin, he noticed. It only encouraged the impression that she was some sort of fairy creature hiding in this strange unearthly ruin.

He looked around him, realizing at last the full and hideous extent of the devastation. The room had apparently been some sort of drawing room once. Odd bits of charred or broken furniture still stood, placed purposely about the space in some mad mockery of graciousness.

Though the corners still dripped from last night's weather, the sun poured through the gaping holes that were once lovely arched windows, as if determined to illuminate every moss-tinged element of the shattered gentility of the past.

It was a horror that struck Aaron like a cold fist to his gut. This had once been a pretty place, even somewhat grand place.

Like Arbodean.

Now look at the state of it! Like his worst nightmare come to merciless light, the story it told of a gracious home, ruined by fate—and then, because it could not be restored, left to rot away under a coating of rubble and green mold.

This might be his own future, staring him down. Arbodean was vast and elegant—and expensive. He was the last of his line; there could be no denying him the title and the estate, no matter his disgrace.

The fortune, on the other hand, belonged to his grandfather, the current Earl of Arbodean, alone. Without that inheritance, Aaron could never maintain the gracious estate of his ancestors.

Worthington Manor was an apt illustration of that worst of possible scenarios—and precisely what he would end up with if his grandfather ever learned of his night with Miss Elektra Worthington!

How had this happened? How could he prevent such a thing from happening to Arbodean?

"This place is—Was there a battle? Was it cannonfire?" Or an earthquake, with a touch of pestilence and a dash of volcanic eruption?

"No," she replied absently. She dropped something down the front of her man's shirt and then dusted her hands. "Just an ordinary fire. Five brothers, you know."

"You say that a lot. Brothers ain't exactly an act of God, like a hurricane or an earthquake."

"You haven't met my brothers."

"No, and I don't intend to, me. One was enough, thank ye."

She turned to him fully then, folding her arms across the front of her ludicrous weskit. Aaron just knew that for the rest of his life he was going to have fancies about girls in weskits. Damn it.

"About that . . ." She regarded him carefully. "You and I both know that nothing happened last night."

"Hmm." Aaron stood, though he pretended to be gathering up an armful of the bedding . . . for some inexplicable reason. "I suppose other than a bit o' crime, nothing did happen."

"Exactly." She nodded vigorously. "But some people will misunderstand."

"You mean a magistrate? I think the magistrate'll understand crime just fine, he will."

"No, I mean my bothers. And my father, although he would likely just Shakespeare you unto death." She shrugged uncomfortably. "My brothers on the other hand . . . well, how fast can you run?"

Aaron blinked. "If'n I leave now, I can be in Scotland by afternoon."

She didn't smile. "Excellent. Then we're agreed?"

Aaron normally wouldn't agree to anything that wasn't in writing, for he'd been the recipient of one too many "understandings," thank you very much.

However, he found himself nodding mindlessly while thinking that her hair was less golden than it was the color of evening sunlight on snow . . .

"Wait. What did ye say?"

"I said that we were going to agree to put all this"— she waved a hand to the nest of mildewed velvet— "behind us. There is no profit for either of us in ever mentioning it again."

Aaron couldn't believe his good luck. His silly Hastings ruse had worked again. He was free! Free to get away from this mad girl and this ruin, this brutal reminder of what happened to an estate when there were not the funds to care for it properly.

"Indeed. We are agreed!"

He stuck out his hand. In an instant, he realized that he had let his façade slip, so he drew his hand back and spit on it. "Well? It's a deal, ain't it?"

She rolled her eyes. "Boys." Then, astonishingly, she thrust her own hand into his and shook it firmly. "Deal."

She might be criminally insane, but she wasn't a snob; he had to give her that. He couldn't recall ever meeting a lady who would shake on a deal sealed in spit—or kidnap a man, or kiss a stranger—

No. Don't think about that. You just got your lap back.

It was nearly three miles back to the Green Donkey. They set out across what had once been a vast front lawn but was now a vast, brushy meadow. Still, it was a grand day, fresh-washed and shining, and they both had very important matters to attend to. With committing this error with Lord Aaron Arbogast's lackey, Elektra had decided to cross his lordship off The List. Mr. Hastings was a loyal servant to his lordship. Over time, he might somehow let slip what had happened. His lordship would not respond well to knowing that his wife had slept entwined with his manservant . . . after kissing him a little.

A lot.

Men were odd about that sort of thing.

Therefore, Elektra wanted to get back to London as soon as possible. The Season was carrying on without her. New matches were being made every day. If she didn't hurry, all the best bachelors would be taken!

Then Mr. Hastings halted suddenly. Lifting one hand, he stopped her in the middle of the meadow. He lifted his head and turned his handsome face into the sun. "Someone's a-comin'."

Rendered rather grumpy by her inability to ignore his good looks, Elektra glanced askance at Mr. Hastings. Then she also caught the faint rattle of wheels and jingle of harness from far down the lane. Together they walked around the corner of the ruin to where there had once been a gracious circle of white graveled drive. Someone was indeed coming. A pretty lily-white pony clopped down the lane, head high as it pranced along, pulling a quaint little pony cart picked out in enameled maroon and gleaming brass.

It was a fine lady's vehicle and indeed there was a fine lady driving it with her own gloved hands. Elektra's astonishment grew, for who in the world would come to the deserted ruin of a long-abandoned manor— *today?*

Elektra and her former prisoner watched as the tidy little pony cart drew up in the long circular drive. There wasn't much to see of the driver but a gown of smartly striped blue-and-white muslin and a dainty confection of a pin-straw bonnet that made fashion-conscious Elektra grit her teeth in envy.

Belatedly, Mr. Hastings stepped forward to hand the young lady down. As the figure turned fully toward them, Elektra saw a pair of wide eyes tinted the exact guileless blue of summer sky and a truly impressive bosom artfully packaged in the very latest, very finest style of the great Lementeur.

"Hello, cousin." The achingly stylish stranger greeted Elektra calmly, seeming entirely unsurprised to find her muddy and wrinkled, dressed like a boy, standing before a ruin with a strange man.

Elektra's day soured further, though she'd thought it impossible.

It seemed that the Just Wonderful Miss Bliss Worthington had arrived at last.

Chapter Seven

Miss Bliss Worthington picked her way daintily along the drive until she stood before Elektra.

"I had hoped you would be waiting for me when I arrived at the Green Donkey," Bliss stated calmly. "I was so looking forward to a bit of breakfast."

Elektra, whose belly suddenly began clamoring, stared at her alleged cousin. "Where have you been?" And, in the privacy of her own mind, *If you'd arrived on time I never would have gotten myself into this pickle!*

Bliss's serene expression did not alter. "I didn't leave my home in Little Downbrook until this morning, actually."

"This morning?" Elektra stared at Bliss. "But we've been waiting for you at that inn for days!"

"Well, I could hardly drive in the rain, so I stayed home, warm and dry. Dreadful weather yesterday, wasn't it?"

Warm and dry. Elektra could still feel her feet squishing in her clammy boots. "Couldn't you have sent a message or something?"

Bliss blinked slowly, her placid gaze unchanged. "I thought it obvious enough. Why send anyone else out in the rain if I wasn't willing to go?"

She folded her gloved hands before her. Elektra couldn't take her eyes from those perfect white lamb-skin gloves. Not a smudge!

I am filthy and dank and dressed like Zander. I just failed this particular femininity bout.

One point for Bliss.

"At any rate, no one was there to meet me. I asked for you and Lysander at the inn and they told me that you both left suddenly on one horse but that your things were still in your rooms. One of the grooms mentioned that he thought he saw Lysander race past alone late last evening."

"Oh, God." Elektra covered her face with her hands. "Lysander, you idiot."

"Why?" Mr. Hastings asked. "What's he done?"

Elektra felt a bit faint. "Why, he's gone back to London for reinforcements, of course." Hopefully, he'd been delayed by the same bad weather.

Bliss went on. "I considered the matter and recalled that Worthington Manor was close by. It seemed possible that you and Zander were making a pilgrimage to our old home."

Elektra dropped her hands to blink at Bliss. "'Our old home'?"

Bliss tilted her head. Elektra despaired at the perfectly cunning way in which that drool-inducing bonnet accented the mannerism, making it utterly adorable.

"Oh, yes. I lived here, with you and your family, until the fire. You and I were the very best of chums. Everyone called us 'the other twins.' I'm surprised you don't re-call."

Two fair-haired little girls, running through the sun-lit rooms.

Elektra had remembered the other child as her sister, Calliope. But Callie was years older than Elektra. She wouldn't have played like a small child. And Attie was born just after the flames devoured the house. Elektra remembered her mother standing just over there on the drive, gravid and pale, leaning upon her husband's arm with her features lighted by the burning manor.

So the little girl who had run with her through the gracious house, hiding from Lysander, laughing and shrieking and living the perfect childhood along with Elektra . . .

Had been Bliss.

"Oh, hell."

"Oh, my." Bliss shook her head. "Language, cousin." She gave Elektra a righteous tsk-tsk.

Two points for Bliss.

Childhood chum or no, Elektra thought she could very easily do some unladylike violence to the Just Wonderful Miss Bliss Worthington.

But her cousin must realize that Elektra's situation, rising from a ruin after spending the night with Mr. Hastings, knowing that Lysander was long gone, was a bit on the untoward side! "Bliss, are you not going to ask why I am out here at Worthington Manor alone?"

"You are not alone. Mr. Hastings is with you. As am I."

"I know. Yes." Was the girl simpleminded? "I mean to say . . . surely you are thinking it is an unusual situation for a young lady to be in."

"Is it?" Bliss looked to her left, then to her right. It was all Elektra could do not to follow that childlike gaze.

"I'm sure I wouldn't know. I fear I do not leave Little Downbrook often," Bliss went on. "I certainly don't find it odd for you to be here at the manor. It is yours, after all."

Elektra regarded her new/old cousin warily. "So you won't speak about . . ."

Bliss blinked her summer-sky eyes. "Speak about what, cousin?"

Hmm. Elektra was determined not to like Bliss. She had no intention of forgiving the girl who was stealing her Season! Still, Bliss was, according to all sources, indeed a Worthington. And she did resemble Dade, a bit, especially about the nose and chin.

"That's settled, then."

Bliss tilted her head fetchingly. "When was it ever not?"

"Indeed," Elektra agreed grimly. It would be worth putting up with Bliss if she could put this whole kidnapping and tying-up and kissing thing behind her. She turned back to Mr. Hastings, who had busied himself picking straw out of the pony's perfect fetlocks.

"She's a pretty little thing, ain't she?" He grinned at Elektra.

Although Elektra was reasonably certain that the man was referring to the pony and not Bliss, she felt a twinge of something she refused to define. He was far too handsome, and far too raffish. She ought to be immune to handsome, having grown up surrounded by handsome to the fifth power. And anyway, so what if he did think Bliss was pretty? Most men would, would they not?

"That is not in question, Mr. Hastings. Now that my cousin has joined our party, we are quite adequately chaperoned. We may make our way back to the Green Donkey without fear. Your carriage is likely awaiting you there, for the horses would well remember the nearest shelter, don't you think?"

He looked down at the pony's mane, fingering the strands that were, at the moment, better groomed than Elektra's own.

"Aye, and I ought to check on 'is lordship, and all. Tell 'im I got delayed by the weather."

"Yes," Elektra nodded. "That pesky weather. Why, your horses took off on you and I was separated from my beloved brother! Two entirely unrelated events, one might say. How lucky we were that Bliss found us both! Heavens, what a wicked storm!"

His gaze met hers for a single blazing instant and she deeply regretted her light use of the word *wicked*. Heat swirled through her belly and a bit lower as well. She hid her disturbance with a brisk nod and turned back to Bliss.

Oh, she could tell that that kiss was going to haunt her for the rest of her days!

Which one? The first kiss or the second kiss? The one where you thought you had to, or the one where you simply wanted *to?*

Aaron watched Miss Elektra Worthington saunter back to her cousin as if he and she had indeed merely been discussing the weather. Other than a slight widening of her green-blue eyes, she'd showed no sign of feeling the jolt of memory that he had felt.

Yet he knew she had. He'd felt it resonate through her, as if they were roped together, somewhere in the vicinity of their bellies, and something had tugged hard on that rope. He'd wanted to step closer to her, to reach out his hand to touch her, to lean close enough . . .

Close enough to smell jasmine.

Yes, it was a very good idea for them to part ways. Being attracted to a selfish, social-climbing-unto-madness woman was the last thing he needed!

You did spend the night alone with her, a lady, a maiden.

True, he was bound and held at gunpoint, but should the truth ever come out, her life would be entirely ruined. Could he truly allow her to go on without making things right?

To *be* honorable, or to *appear* honorable?

Aaron closed his eyes and let the pony ruffle his shirt with her warm breath. Everything had been so simple yesterday.

I wish it were yesterday.

In the end, it was decided that since Elektra had no option but to head back to the inn in her boy's attire, she should continue in that role. With mischief glinting in her eyes, she stuffed her hair into that silly cap and clambered onto the back of the cart, looking for all the world like a boy nicking a ride.

I am forever going to be having fancies about girls in caps, aren't I?

Oh, yes.

Aaron brushed off his third-best suit as best he could

and took the reins. Miss Bliss Worthington sat beside him, looking as fresh as spring itself in her striped gown and sporting a fetching parasol that matched her bonnet.

"Although you really ought to have the parasol, cousin," she told Elektra gravely. "You already have three freckles on your nose."

Aaron saw Elektra flinch, but thought better of reassuring her that he found them quite attractive. Hastings wouldn't bother. Sometimes it was a bloody relief not to be a gentleman!

When they arrived at the Green Donkey Inn, a mere half an hour later at the pony's brisk trot, Elektra hopped off and made for the back of the building.

"Ask for the maid Edith," she'd ordered Bliss. "Tell her to meet me back there and help me sneak back to my room."

Aaron lost track of the ladies at that moment, for standing next to the stables he spied the mud-splashed wreck that used to be his very nearly impressive carriage.

Oh, hell.

He could have sworn it had once had four wheels, not three. And he certainly would have noticed previously if there had been a door missing. The other one was still there, although with the broken cant of the carriage, it hung dismally from one hinge as though it were considering putting an end to it all.

He knew the feeling. How was he to go on now? He'd put everything he had into that carriage, in order to arrive at Arbodean in style. Now he'd be lucky to arrive at all! As Aaron stood there, his jaw dropped in shock and dismay, he was joined by the cheeky young groom.

"Aye, it's a rum'un, ain't it?" The boy scratched his bare head, and Aaron dimly realized where he'd seen Miss Elektra's cap before. "Them horses come flyin' back into the yard after midnight, draggin' that old thing on its side, neighing like the devil himself was after them! It were a sight, I tell you."

Aaron swallowed hard. "I'll wager it were." He turned to the groom in sudden concern. "Are the horses all right?"

The boy made a face. "Filthy nags are just fine, sorry to say. Kicked and bit all the while we was cleanin' 'em up. All your master's horses are right bastards, you know. Like that great hammer-headed brute y'left behind. That'un's got a mean streak as wide as this valley!"

I still have a horse.

Relief swept Aaron. The "gentleman's mount" had been for show, but now all Aaron cared about was getting on his way to Arbodean—and getting away from Miss Elektra Worthington before her army of brothers came looking for him.

That's why you're running away? Fear of the brothers? Or fear of the sister?

"Can't it be both?" Aaron murmured.

"What's that?"

Aaron turned to the young groom. "I'll be needing to saddle that hammer-head now."

The groom shrugged. "Go ahead. No business of mine." He stuck a straw in his mouth and strolled away.

Right. He was not his lordship today. Today he was Hastings, who saddled his own damn horse. Either way, both Hastings and Lord Aaron needed to get away from this place as fast as they could!

* * *

It hadn't taken Elektra long to realize that she and Bliss could not stay alone at the inn without Lysander. There was also some urgency to make their way back to London before all the Worthington men worked themselves into some sort of Knights of the Overturned Table chest-beating frenzy and set out for Shropshire to rupture a few spleens.

So as soon as she'd stripped off her muddy kidnapping togs and Edith had efficiently buttoned her back into actual girl clothes, she fled back out into the inn, stopping to pull on her damp walking boots at the top of the stairs.

With no thought to decorum, she ran full-tilt down the stairs while twisting her hair into a self-contained bun at the back of her neck. Oh, she must hurry before—

As she burst through the front door of the inn, she saw Mr. Hastings in the yard with one foot in the stirrup getting back on the journey that had been so rudely interrupted.

Oh, no! He was getting away!

"Hastings! Wait!"

He didn't seem to hear her, although the young fellow holding the reins turned to stare at her pell-mell rush across the cobbles of the yard.

"Mr. Hastings! Please, wait!"

He lifted his head then. When he turned to look behind him, she saw a rather familiar desperate glaze of male apprehension in his eyes. Her brothers had that look sometimes. Elektra decided to be charming.

She slowed her progress and pasted a prim little smile on her lips.

Suddenly Elektra couldn't meet Mr. Hastings's gaze. She'd managed to distract herself on the journey back to the inn by concentrating on the massive inconvenience that was Bliss Worthington.

Bliss had better clothes, a better bosom, bluer eyes, and from all appearances a far greater financial incentive for her suitors. How was she, Elektra, supposed to stand side by side with Bliss and not be outshone?

Of course, Elektra knew her doting parents had no idea what they'd done to her. They probably thought she needed a friend, a bosom companion upon the road of Society.

This welcome indignation had done much to soothe Elektra's mortification over Mr. Hastings and his kisses. Handsome or not, Mr. Hastings lacked a few natural-born advantages that Elektra desperately needed. Enormous wealth and impeccable standing, no handsome face required.

Now, however, Elektra had no choice but to look at that handsome face directly. "I fear I must ask one more favor of you, sir."

His expression was wary. He cast a longing look over the horse's saddle at the open road before him. "What's that, miss?"

"I must beg your indulgence for a few more days. Miss Bliss Worthington and I must make our way back to London at once—and we cannot do this alone."

His eyes widened, and she saw him swallow. "I— It's—" His gaze darted back and forth from her to the road he'd been mere seconds from gaining. "But—"

Urgency made Elektra's patience slip ever so slightly

awry. "Well, you cannot very well leave two ladies alone! It would—it would be—*irresponsible*!"

Well, perhaps that was going a bit far, as evidenced by his sudden flush of fury. "Irresponsible? Me, the irresponsible one?" He released the saddle and turned fully upon her. "You and your criminal brother think you can do anything you like—with no thought for the consequences! You don't care who y'hurt!"

Stung, Elektra lifted her chin. "I am not a criminal! I am a Worthington!"

"What's the difference, eh?"

She gaped at him, her face flushed with fury.

Aaron couldn't hold it back any longer. He was bloody tired from his night in the ruin—and he was still reeling from the jolt of seeing Miss Elektra Worthington all washed up, in a fetching little frock that made a man want to fall on his knees and beg. "Because from where I stand, the two o' you are on a fast road to Newgate Prison, with time for a quick stop at Bedlam!"

"I explained all of that!" She folded her arms over her chest. "There's no need to get snippy."

"You forget, don't you? The man you thought to trap with your little plan is my own master! His lordship doesn't deserve that fate, wedded to you. No man does! You're a selfish little horror, with no more thought for others than a house cat!"

She glared at him. "What could you possibly know about me?"

He sneered. "I know y'think nothing of kidnappin' and assaultin' some poor man into marriage! If a man did that, he'd go to prison and rightly so!"

She set her jaw at a mulish angle. "I had my reasons."

"Shallow, silly reasons! Lookin' above your station, that's what!" He eyed her with disdain. "What makes you think a man would be thankful to wed such a hellish female as yourself anyway? Sure, you're as lovely as a perfect morning—but then you have to go and open your bloomin' mouth."

"You think—" She closed her mouth and stared at him strangely.

"What?" Wait a moment. What had he said? Oh, hell. He'd told her he thought her beautiful. Damn. Still, it was bound to come out sooner or later. It could hardly come as a surprise to her. She owned a mirror, after all.

She was still frowning at him. "That was . . . poetic, Mr. Hastings. Especially for a—"

Oddly, he bristled in defense of the real Hastings. "You think a man needs toff parents to have a soul? I haven't any parents at all and I can appreciate a song or a poem as well as the next man."

"Or a perfect morning." A tiny smile curved the corners of her lovely mouth.

"Aye! I—" Damn it, she'd done it again. He gritted his teeth. He would not feed her vanity further. "A statement of fact ain't a poem, miss. Birds fly, fish swim, you're a right looker, the end."

Still that smile teased at her lips. "Mr. Hastings, I do believe you like me a little."

He threw up his hands and gazed at the sky. The perfect morning mocked him, even as the hellcat let out a soft gurgle of laughter that ran up his spine and made his scalp tingle.

"You're me worst nightmare come to life. I no more like you than I like a bad cold! You both take three days to get shut of!"

Her smile gentled further. "Mr. Hastings, now you claim to be infected by me."

"That—you—I—" His throat closed in fury and no small amount of alarm. Could she be right? Could her wry humor and her quick wit—and yes, her lovely face!—be getting under his skin?

Elektra felt a giggle start to rise at the look of pure horror in the poor man's eyes. She ought not to tease him so. It just made what she needed all the harder to ask for.

She would not beg. Not him. Not ever.

Unless, of course, it would get her away from the scene of her crime, away from the memory of her failure, away from the ruins of Worthington Manor and all the significance of that pile of rubble that so symbolized her family's fall from status.

"Fine! I'll beg, if that will satisfy you!"

He seemed only more alarmed by that, and held up both hands in self-defense. "No, really, miss!"

Speak softly, before he runs away! "I'm sorry. You are perfectly correct. It was all such an awful, terrible idea. I regret it deeply." That part was no lie, to be sure. "Mr. Hastings," she begged with all the sweetness she could muster, "will you please, please accompany Miss Bliss Worthington and myself on the road back to London?"

She even clasped her hands before her. She batted her eyelashes. She *begged*. Her brothers would be agog.

Mr. Hastings only twitched, as if he could not decide whether to stay or run for his life. She watched him carefully, noting the moment when he realized that there was no possible way he could honorably leave two ladies to travel on their own.

He let out a long breath, then made a deep and gentlemanly bow to both her and Bliss. "It would be an honor, Miss Worthington, Miss Worthington."

Elektra blinked at the graciousness of his acceptance. For a moment, he almost could have passed as the real Lord Aaron Arbogast. Then he ruined that brief impression by stepping closer to her and whispering in her ear.

"Ye know ye're ruinin' my life, ye demented li'l criminal!"

Oh, excellent! Now she no longer had to pretend to be sweet! Elektra raised her chin and bared her teeth in his face. "Thank you, dear sir! Your assistance is greatly appreciated!"

She turned away from him and swept a graceful hand toward the waiting Bliss. "Come along, cousin!" she trilled. "Let us go refresh ourselves at the inn. Mr. Hastings has graciously agreed to manage everything." She turned to shoot him a smile of pure rage over her shoulder. She knew her fury translated, for she saw his eyes narrow and his lips thin in response.

Satisfied that she'd scored evenly, if not gained a length ahead, Elektra showed more teeth. "Absolutely *everything*!"

Chapter Eight

Aaron stared at the retreating back of the most infuri-
ating female ever born to the human race. What had
he just done?

I think you are on your way to London.

Was he that much of an idiot, that a pair of fluttering
green-blue eyes and a pair of dainty hands clasped
before a truly delicious bosom could make him throw
away everything he'd worked so hard for over the last
decade?

He passed a hand over his face, trying to pull himself together. In the darkness behind his lids, he once
again saw that delicious bosom in that rain-soaked shirt,
felt the touch of those dainty hands in his hair, saw those
eyelids flutter closed when she pressed her soft, warm
lips to his—

He wasn't the first man to be an idiot for a pretty
woman. Maybe not even the first man to be an idiot for
a pretty criminal!

He was, however, quite sure that he was the first man to throw away a hundred thousand pounds and the regard of his last remaining family just to be the beast of burden for a pretty criminal!

Although if all criminals looked like Miss Elektra Worthington, there might be a few more fools like him about.

Fine. He'd agreed to do this unimaginably distressing thing—namely, toss his mission aside and trot back down the road to the one place he ought to avoid like the plague!—but he would drop in on Hastings first and fill him in on the new plan . . . if one could call following Miss Anarchy Worthington around like a lapdog a plan.

If Aaron's manservant thought there was anything odd about his employer scrambling into his room through the open window, he didn't comment. Aaron had to grin. Trusty Hastings!

Hastings listened to Aaron's latest adventure with nary a guffaw, but that might have been due to his sore throat. He offered Aaron a cup of his broth, which Aaron politely declined. Hastings shrugged and took a slurping sip. "My Edith is a right good cook!" he exclaimed hoarsely. "Ah!"

Aaron narrowed his eyes. "Hastings, you are not here to flirt with the maidservants."

Hastings smirked. "Says the man who spent the night with that fair-haired minx! How long had it been for you, eh? Years?"

Aaron went very still. "Hastings, you have earned my

everlasting gratitude. However, if I ever hear another such slur upon Miss Elektra Worthington, I will kill you before you manage to inhale once more."

Hastings drew back, something oddly like respect in his shadowed gaze. "Aye, then," he muttered. "If ye feel so strongly about it."

Aaron held his gaze. "I do." There was no reason for his hot and sudden rage. He fought it back with difficulty.

Hastings, usually irrepressible on the topic of carnal prospects, changed the subject. "Are ye goin' on to the estate now?"

Aaron wished he could reply in the affirmative, but he couldn't. He wished he could run for his life and leave the young ladies here to await their family!

When would that be? A day? A week? The two young ladies in question—one simply mad, the other decidedly contrarian—had already proved that they could not be trusted to the care and feeding of a pebble, much less take proper heed of their own safety. Aaron shuddered to think what mischief the two of them could concoct in a matter of hours, much less possibly days!

Stay here with them until help arrives.

Help in the form of the demented soldier and assistant highwayman brother, who ought not to have let his sister out of his sight in the first place? Thank you, no. Aaron didn't need help like that.

He'd be better off taking them back to London by himself.

Oh, hell. Aaron ran one hand through his hair.

London.

Hellfire and damnation.

London on the way to his destination had been visited as swiftly and silently as possible. They'd scarcely left the docks. Hastings had purchased the carriage and team while Aaron had watched from the background. The fine clothing had been had from a secondhand stall in the market, again with Hastings as the front man.

Aaron had always known that he would have to face the city again someday, but he had hoped it would not happen until he was rightfully the Earl of Arbodean—and even then, he wouldn't have minded giving matters a few more years to die down.

Then, of course, his plans were struck by the cannonball that was Miss Elektra Worthington!

Hastings choked on his broth when he heard. "London? Are ye mad? If anyone recognizes ye—"

Aaron shrugged helplessly. "There's no other choice. Besides, I'm just an irascible manservant named Hastings, remember? Beneath anyone's notice, right? Isn't that how you slide past close scrutiny?"

Hastings smirked. "So ye have been payin' attention to me lessons. What about yer grandpapa, then?"

Aaron thought it through for a moment. Casting his gaze about the room, he saw a small stack of foolscap and a bottle of ink that had been provided for "his lordship." Swiftly, he inked a quill and in his finest handwriting delivered a nicely worded apology for his "indisposition" and tardiness, along with the inn's address.

He did not seal it. "Let the innkeeper see it before he posts it for you."

He also wrote out the address of Worthington House in London. "Here is where you'll find me if you need to. I don't expect to be more than a few days away."

With a very Hastings-like tip of his hat, he climbed back through the window.

He thought his urgent schedule might encounter some argument from the young ladies, but he discovered they had already returned to the pony cart.

"Of course." Miss Bliss blinked uncommonly blue eyes at him. "I should like to begin my Season as soon as possible. If I am any later," she told him earnestly, "the best matches will already be made."

"I had already decided so." Miss Elektra scarcely bothered to look at him. "You'll ride alongside, of course. Bliss's silly little pony can't pull three." She turned away, muttering something about "men, always needing to state the obvious!"

Once Aaron had given in to the winds of fate, it was surprising how quickly the three of them were once more upon the road. Miss Bliss set a brisk pace with her pony. Bonnet ribbons flying in the breeze, the two ladies looked very much alike from Aaron's position behind and properly to one side. Cousins indeed.

Except there was a lissomeness to Miss Elektra Worthington's figure—although most would probably find Miss Bliss Worthington's charms more impressive. And Miss Bliss had a sweetly modulated voice—yet Miss Elektra seemed rather more interesting to listen to.

They were both very pretty young ladies. *Are you trying to choose between them? Because here's an option— choose flight! Forget this gentlemanly gesture and ride this ill-tempered nag north as fast as it can gallop!*

Except that it wasn't a gesture. Somehow, somewhere along his journey to prove to his grandfather that he was a worthy man, he'd stopped thinking about how things looked and begun to care about how they truly were.

And in his heart, he could not turn his back on two vulnerable women. He could not ride away without knowing she—they—were safely in their family's embrace once more.

Having a conscience was bloody damned annoying.

Aaron's mount, a bay gelding of particularly stupid and lazy nature that Hastings had immediately dubbed Lard-Arse—which had unfortunately stuck, since Aaron honestly couldn't think of any moniker more fitting—had taken a liking to Miss Bliss Worthington's perfect little pony mare. The mare, well aware that she was a pedigreed beauty and that Lard-Arse was an inferior oaf with suspicious intentions, had loathed him on sight.

Aaron had no differing opinion to offer in defense of Lard-Arse, so he tried to keep the gelding an inoffensive distance from Bliss's dainty pony.

However, with pounding head and indecisive stomach not improving from the ride and Lard-Arse's jolting trot, Aaron became distracted in his mission of hauling the stupid beast's head in a more suitable direction and let the reins slacken.

Before he could catch the idiot, Lard-Arse had lowered his brick-shaped head to the level of the pony mare's silken tail and offered her an unseemly compliment.

The mare, who up till now had posed as a creature of extraordinarily good nature and training, bestowed upon Lard-Arse three lightning kicks directly in his lewd and unbearable nose, screeched abuse upon his lack-witted head, and took off down the dusty road as if demon-possessed.

"Bianca! Bianca, stop!" Bliss stood up in the seat and sawed at the dainty ribbon reins with admirable skill and some unexpected muscle, while Elektra leaned her full weight on the decoratively cast brake while clinging to her cousin's skirts with her other hand.

Unfortunately, the cart and ladies were quite light for a sturdy pony's strength, and Bianca pulled them along, rocketing wildly from one side of the lane to the other.

Aaron and Lard-Arse were so surprised by Bianca's insane flight that they stopped short with unfortunately identical expressions of witless astonishment on their faces.

Aaron came to first, and leaning forward, lashed Lard-Arse with the reins, digging his boot heels into the horse's sides. "Hah!"

Lard-Arse took off like a shot. He might not be smart, or well mannered, or particularly reliable, but his pretty pony darling was disappearing over yon hillside—and he had longer legs and he meant to use them.

There was no screaming, Aaron would recall at a later point.

Not a girlish squeal. Not a feminine screech. The two young women held their tongues and held on tight. Bliss didn't look to be sawing on the reins, either—a beginning driver's last resort, and one not inclined to soothe an irate equine.

Though small, ponies, like this sturdy Welsh pony, were bred for backbreaking work that would kill a proper horse. This one had speed and the endurance of generations of mining beasts. The pony would simply have to run her fit of temper out.

Aaron encouraged more speed from the gelding anyway, for although the pony would not mean to run into danger, she was hardly the best judge of that at the moment.

And sure enough, danger loomed. The road dipped once over that last hill, and without the drag of the cart, the pony gained speed. The decreased elevation of the road could mean a simple valley between hills, but that valley could hold—

Yes. Aaron's gut flipped sideways as he spotted the river ahead. He'd recalled it correctly. At the base of this particular stretch of road he'd had a bad moment driving his ill-fated carriage over it. Swollen yet further by the recent rains, it rushed with white curls of foam mere inches below the humble log bridge that spanned it. The bridge was hardly wider than the wheels of an average carriage, so in normal circumstances the dainty pony cart should have no issue crossing—

The speeding wheels hit the planks of the bridge with a sound like rolling thunder. Bliss stood in the driver's seat, fighting to keep the pony centered on the narrow span. It wasn't a wide river, and the bridge was no longer than six or seven yards. Aaron raised himself in the stirrups, holding his breath even as Lard-Arse gained on the cart, unable to tear his gaze away from the prettily lacquered wheels of the cart, so damned close to the rough edge of the bridge.

Then a thick branch hit the side of the bridge, carried on the strength of the storm-swollen current. The pony shied, just a bit, but it was enough. The left wheel flew over empty space and the cart flipped hard into the downstream side of the roiling water.

"No!" Aaron didn't bother to dismount. He pulled his feet from the stirrups and dived from the saddle directly into the water.

He came up quickly to find himself bobbing along in the current alongside the cart. It had flipped fully until now it swept sideways before him, pulling a frantically swimming pony along with it. Aaron grabbed the side bar and pulled himself higher, casting his gaze frantically around him. In the cart, Bliss's fetching bonnet swirled lazily in the circling water that sloshed inside.

There! A fair head rising from the froth! The sun shone from the soaked blond strands, and Aaron breathed a sigh of relief when he saw Elektra strike out for the bank with a strong swimmer's stroke. But where was Bliss?

The river narrowed here, between high banks, and rushed fast and deep. Up ahead, Aaron spotted a hand flailing from the rapids. Then a dainty booted foot. Bliss was being tossed hem-over-teakettle by the rushing water, unskilled or unable to free herself from the pull of the current!

Aaron clambered over the bucking cart and dived forward into the river. Swimming hard, he reached the last place where he'd spotted the struggling Bliss. The current was fierce and unstable. It was all he could do to remain upright, yet he tried to kick himself higher, the better to see ahead. Where was she?

"There!" came a cry like a bird over the roar of the river. "She's there!"

Aaron looked up at the bank to see Elektra running

alongside, slipping in the muddy grass, pulling herself around saplings, running hard like a boy. She was pointing ahead, her gaze locked on something in front of them both. Aaron struck out, as powerfully as he could, trusting her to direct him.

"Left!" he heard, and pulled hard to the left.

"Faster!" He put his face into the water and pulled mighty strokes from his aching arms and thrashing legs.

"Just there! Just ahead!"

Aaron reached out and felt the drag of waterlogged fabric in his fingers. He twisted it hard into his fist, knowing that he had little time left, and followed it up with his other hand, letting the current pull him and his limp burden along as it would. If he could just reach her head, get her face above the water—

He pulled a dripping blond head from the current and raised it to his shoulder, holding Bliss close as he swept the dripping hair from her face. "Breathe!" he ordered, and she did.

Never had he heard so sweet a sound.

This girl would not die.

He continued to hold Bliss up with one arm about her waist while stroking the other through the water, slowly pulling them to the bank where Elektra still ran, following them in the current's grasp.

Then Elektra's strong hands were pulling at her cousin's shoulders and Aaron dragged himself onto the bank on his knees. The current still dragged at his sodden boots and he had the random, exhausted thought that he hadn't been truly dry in days.

"She's breathing! She's alive!"

Quickly Elektra worked over her cousin. Aaron stayed

on the ground next to her, but it was all he could do to draw breath while she turned Bliss on her side to cough up river water while Elektra pounded her on the back. When her cousin was breathing evenly at last, and her blue eyes opened, Aaron watched Elektra sit back on her heels next to him.

Reaction seemed to hit her at last. Her breath caught once, then twice. Then she turned right into his arms.

Her chilled body quivered in his hands. He thought of a bird he'd found once as a boy. The poor creature had flown into one of the great paned windows of the manor, tricked by the diamond clarity of the spotless glass. It had sat, shaken and shocked into stillness in his cupped palms. He'd thought it most horribly wounded after having taken such a blow, until it suddenly spread its wings and beat its way into the air before he could close the tent of his fingers around it.

That was much the way Elektra suddenly shook off his tender hold, pulling back, then pushing herself onto her feet, putting her safely out of his reach.

Did she think I meant to put her in a cage?

The only sign of distress she displayed now was a swift brush of her fingertips across her eyelids . . . or possibly it was only a brisk brushing of her fallen hair away from her face.

"Well. That was rather unpleasant. Tell me, Mr. Hastings, whyever did you bring that unruly beast?"

So that was how she wished it to be. Fine. He could play along. "Oy!" he protested, every bit the put-upon commoner. "You mean, when you begged me t'come along?"

She pursed her lips and rolled her eyes. "Men!" Then

she shook out her heavy wet skirts like a woman momentarily brushing against a rubbish bin, turned on her heel, and sauntered away with her head high.

Aaron watched her go, seeing through her ill-tempered pose at last, seeing the pallor of her skin, and having felt the hummingbird pulse of her fear against his own chest. *I think she may just be the bravest person I have ever seen.*

Miss Elektra Worthington—fashion plate, Society beauty . . . warrior.

Who would ever have thought it?

Chapter Nine

Miss Bliss Worthington was also revealed to be possessed of unexpected resilience. Once she regained her breath, she sturdily put her feet beneath her and climbed the riverbank herself.

"I'm perfectly well now, thank you, cousin." She tied her rescued bonnet snugly beneath her chin once more. "Goodness, it was only a bit of water."

They were all soaked, down to their squishy shoes. To Elektra's surprise, Bliss was not at all upset about her gown. "Well, it was quite new," Bliss confessed. "I hadn't truly grown fond of it yet."

It spoke to something rather impressive about this mysterious cousin of hers, that she was upset neither by her own near-drowning nor by loss of material things. Elektra admired her for it.

Blast it.

They gathered up the exhausted pony along with the surprisingly undamaged gig.

"Good Shropshire craftsmanship," Bliss declared stoutly.

Lard-Arse hadn't wandered very far. The great long-legged monster had deserted them all in their time of need, of course, and only the temptation of the sweet green grass of the riverbank had kept him in the vicinity.

Or maybe it was the dainty pony mare, who still sneered at the big brute, but now allowed him to walk within a respectable distance.

They picked their way back along the grassy flat at the top of the riverbank, intent on reaching the road once more. Aaron found himself putting shoulder to the cart to help the weary pony roll the conveyance through the muddiest bits.

If he were Lord Aaron today, he might do such a thing, but then the grateful ladies would gaze upon him admiringly and make much of his strength and heroic willingness to exert himself. "Hastings," however, was lucky to receive a brisk thanks from Elektra and a serene blink from Bliss. To be sure, in less democratic company he might have been berated for his lack of speed!

Aaron leaned his hands on his knees after one particularly sticky patch of mud and breathed hard. Perhaps Hastings did not have the easier road after all.

At last they came into sight of the road, with the bridge visible across a grassy meadow, an area presumably washed clean of trees and brush by floods past. It was a pretty place, the width of a city block, brilliantly in bloom with green, pink, yellow, and the bluest of blue.

"I did not see this on the way here," Elektra exclaimed.

"It is the rain, cousin," country girl Bliss explained pedantically. "It tends to bring on the blossoms."

Elektra did not snap at her cousin for stating the obvious, as Aaron half expected. Instead she simply gazed across the lovely, peaceful meadow with a look of delight upon her face. "Indeed it does," she breathed.

They all stood in reverent silence for a moment, willing—what with the recent brush with danger and all—to waste time in simple appreciation. A sweet-smelling breeze swept the meadow, setting the grass to rippling and causing the blue flowers to—

Fly?

The air about them began to fill with hundreds—no, thousands!—of brilliant blue butterflies.

"Oh, heavens!" Elektra lifted her hands lightly, as if she longed to take off with them.

Bliss gazed on with obvious pleasure, even as Aaron laughed aloud at the sheer, mad, random beauty of it. On impulse, he ran straight into the cloud, stirring the tall grass with his outstretched hands, releasing more of the lovely creatures to the air.

Bliss laughed with him, and reached for Elektra's hand. "Come, cousin!"

Elektra ran through the magical floating wings of blue with Bliss. It was a moment of relief and laughter at the insane splendor, running hand in hand with Bliss through the meadow, just as she had, long ago, when she was a dreamy, playful little girl, racing down the halls of the manor.

A new lightness filled her chest—or perhaps it was an old feeling, one from years past. For the first time in many years, Elektra wondered if perhaps that girl had not disappeared completely, after all.

Mr. Hastings shot her a boyish grin of delight and Elektra smiled back without reservation, without consideration of place. They had all survived, thanks to him. Imagine, a man who was there when she needed him! Impulsively, she reached for his hand and they whirled Bliss about in a celebratory circle until they all collapsed in the tall grass, laughing up at a gray sky filled with blue.

Aaron looked up into the glowingly joyous disheveled features of Elektra—his nemesis, his nightmare, the queen of his deepest personal hell—and thought that he'd never seen anything so beautiful in his life.

I am in so much trouble.

"Oh, hold still, you evil creature!"

Aaron looked up from where he struggled to secure the pony with the soaked and swollen leather cart harness to see Elektra trying to coax a bit of reasonable behavior from Lard-Arse.

Personally, Aaron didn't know whether to cook the beast for dinner for his role in causing the accident, or make him a flowered laurel for his speed and bravery. Either way, Lard-Arse had no intention of allowing any more of this nonsense of following commands. Elektra was trying to assist Aaron by cleaning the mud from his wet saddle, but although she didn't seem to feel any fear of the rangy gelding, she couldn't keep him from walking away from her as he tried to mow the entire riverbank by himself. Even with a bit in his mouth, he pulled huge ranks of damp grass out by the roots and gulped them down, roots and all, as if he'd not been fed for days.

Aaron felt a bit guilty about that.

"Cousin?" Bliss watched them both. "I find that I have lost my reticule in the river."

"Pity." Elektra frowned absently, distracted by the gelding's behavior. "Was it very dear?"

Bliss shook her head. "Not particularly, for it was new as well. However, I have no more coin for our journey."

Elektra looked up at that. "Oh, drat."

Bliss gave a gentle tsk. "Language, cousin."

Elektra ran a hand through her fallen hair, which had been left to dry in the warm breeze. "I have nothing to hand myself. Lysander left without seeing to the innkeeper, and it took all I had to persuade the man to release our things."

They both turned to look at Aaron.

He stepped back. "What?"

"We are out of money."

"That is impossible."

She gazed at him. "It is entirely possible because it is true."

"But Miss Bliss is an heiress and you are—" He halted because even though she stood before him as fashionably gowned as a slightly damp duchess and as lovely as a siren, he hadn't the slightest idea what she was.

"And I am . . . what?"

There was no mistaking the dangerous spark in her eye. Even the most obtuse man—and he was definitely in the running—would shut up now.

"You are . . . Miss Bliss is an heiress!"

"Yes. Heiress. Definition: one who will inherit.

Meaning she isn't presently trotting around with her bonnet padded with banknotes."

"It would ruin the set, anyway," Bliss interjected placidly. "It is maddening enough to arrange all this hair."

Elektra nodded. "Men have no idea what we do to look attractive, do they?"

Bliss sighed in agreement. "Remaining at the peak of fashion is a constant career."

Aaron gazed at Bliss in confusion. "Hair? Weren't we talking about money?"

Bliss blinked slowly. "Not for ages. Now we are speaking of bonnets."

Elektra folded her arms and cocked a brow at him in irritation. "Do try to keep up, Mr. Hastings!"

He glared back at her. "Oy! What did I do?"

"Honestly, men! You find it completely impossible to stay on topic!"

"Er . . ." He cast back through his boggled mind for clues. "Bonnets?"

Her jaw worked. "Money! Of which we are out!"

She was pretty when she was angry, which meant that she was usually pretty. He wondered what she looked like when she was happy. As he dug into every one of his pockets in turn, he wondered if she even knew. He came up with a farthing, two cinnamon candies in a paper twist, and his signet ring, which he had carried for a decade and yet never worn. His cousin had thrust it into his hand as she had bid him a deceptively dry-eyed farewell. Her manner had said *Don't come back* but her gift had said *Don't forget who you are.* He had carried the ring and done his best to be a man worthy of wearing it.

Of course, the maddening Elektra pounced on the ring at once. "Aha!"

Sourly, Aaron bent to retrieve his last farthing that she had so dismissively knocked from his hand. "Aha, what?"

"We can use this!"

Bliss came closer. "Oh, yes. That will do nicely."

Aaron looked on in growing alarm. "Oy!" he exclaimed, because that was what Hastings would say. "That's mine! Hands off!"

Elektra only glanced at him. "Don't be silly. It can't be, not really."

He took a step toward her, his fury hot and sudden. "Hand it back at once!"

She held it behind her with a teasing smirk. "Oh, please spare us the offended-gentleman routine. This is obviously your master's ring!" She tilted her head. "Did you steal it from his ill and dying hand?"

Instead of horror, she only exhibited a casual curiosity. What manner of female was she? Aaron was even more surprised to see Miss Bliss standing next to the insane Elektra with an identical expression of mild curiosity.

"Oh, is your master dying? That would be awfully inconvenient."

Elektra turned to her cousin, brow furrowed. "Would it? Why?"

Bliss nodded confidently. "Oh, yes. If Mr. Hastings is not respectably employed by a gentleman, then his accompaniment on our journey would be entirely inappropriate. It would certainly incite comment."

Elektra touched her lips for a moment, smiling.

Aaron on the other hand was not. "I ain't givin' you his lordship's ring!"

Elektra's smile drooped and she blinked at him with huge, sad eyes. "If you think that's best, Mr. Hastings. I'm sure that Bliss and I will not suffer too terribly sleeping out of doors tonight. Although . . . my clothes are still damp . . ."

Aaron closed his eyes, but that sweet, achingly sad face lingered behind his lids. *She's a liar and a kidnapper!*

She's a woman who will spend the night on the cold, hard ground!

Aaron nodded stiffly, his eyes still closed tight. "Take it, then!" *I am a fool.*

He opened his eyes in time to see Elektra smile and clap her hands happily.

"I shall have the innkeeper take it as security. If your master wants it back so much, he can send funds to buy it back!" She smiled brightly. "It's called pawn. Isn't that a clever invention?"

How did a lady of standing know anything about pawnbrokers?

"There's no need to worry, Mr. Hastings," Bliss told him placidly.

"Indeed." Elektra lifted a knowing brow. "I shall do the bargaining!"

The two women exchanged arch glances and Aaron was struck by a sudden and powerful family resemblance.

But that was because he now knew what sheer madness looked like on a woman.

Chapter Ten

Of course, Bliss and Elektra were correct. When they arrived at a small but well-appointed inn that evening, the two vixens swept into the place, all fluttering eyelashes and porcelain distress. Had the two of them been sporting those bosoms all this time? Before they had been admirable bosoms, but now they were positively *stuffed*!

Aaron found himself not only properly housed and fed, but gifted with a couple of pints of rather nice ale while the innkeeper's gobsmacked son questioned him about his "mistresses."

Aaron, not one to pass up a shot at a real breakfast, loaded up the poor bloke's fancies with hints at evil relatives, vengeful lords in pursuit, and even—after his second pint—a tale of near-ruination by a dastardly earl using a servant's disguise to gain access to the innocent and lovely ladies' trust.

"Cor!" breathed the young lout, who bore the unfortunately imaginative name of Siegfried. "It's like a player's tale, it is!"

Aaron nodded. "All true, every word of it." He gazed wistfully at the bottom of his pint, but Siegfried was too far gone to notice.

Fresh out of fiction, Aaron meandered his way to his comfortable room in a relaxed haze. He couldn't recall the last time he'd had an evening out with no responsibilities but to toss back half a gallon of bitter ale and fend off the appreciative glances of Siegfried's roundly nubile sister, Gilder.

Hastings really had the life.

At the top of the stairs, Aaron blinked slowly twice, recalling that he'd taken a left somewhere while toting luggage earlier that evening. He was as likely to be right as he was wrong, so he turned on his heel and marched smartly, if a bit unevenly, to the end of the hall, put his hand on the latch, and pushed.

Miss Elektra Worthington had an amazing figure.

Aaron stood frozen in shock and sudden, crippling arousal at the sight of Elektra, hair rippling free and golden down her back, wearing nothing but a brief chemise that appeared to be made entirely of morning mist and good intentions, those good intentions rendered powerless by the light of the candle set upon the dressing table behind her.

Aaron's ale-muddled brain tried to send him a vitally important message—*Virgin! Lady! Warning! Warning!*—that his pounding heart was trying to drown out with an opposing viewpoint—*Luscious! Hungry! Want! Want!*

He was so far past hungry. He was starving. He was an empty shell of a man, lost and aching and only the sweet, wet, silken grasp of her femininity could save him—

He must have taken one tortured step forward, a single footfall, like stepping on a fallen branch in the forest and startling the delicate doe just as he was almost close enough to—

"Mr. Hastings!"

Now it was her wide, furious gaze that had him riveted in place.

Oh, hell. Oh, damn.

"What are you doing here?" she hissed.

What was he doing here? What was he doing standing one step inside the forbidden fortress of a lady's bedchamber, after all his years of treading the straight and narrow, of careful strides into an upright and virtuous life?

His first brilliant defense came out something like, "Erk!"

Then his brain doused his body with an icy shower of dismay and he found he could manage human speech once more.

What would Hastings say? Aaron willingly let his insouciant manservant take over this dangerous moment.

"Miss Elektra? What're ye doin' in me room?" He narrowed his eyes and folded his arms in disapproval. "I'll have ye know, I ain't that sort o' bloke!"

Hastings, now and then, was something of a genius.

Elektra stopped in her tracks and gaped at him in utter confusion. Unfortunately, she had the presence of mind to gather up her dressing gown and press it over the front of her skimpy chemise. Well, a man couldn't have everything. For the moment, he would have to be satisfied that, for a single instant, he could see her actually wondering if she had perhaps taken the wrong room!

It was a cheap victory, but he would treasure the look on her face for years to come.

Then, as her inner recounting obviously informed her, she realized that he was indeed standing in her room while she remained in dishabille.

"Get out!" she whispered furiously. Coming toward him like a goddess caught in a compromising moment, she looked magnificent and ridiculous and utterly charming.

I really shouldn't drink. I think it makes me ever so slightly bonkers.

Only a man with no sense of self-preservation or common sense would allow himself to be attracted to the lividly insane tangle that was Elektra Worthington.

Or any man, really, or at least one bearing a pulse . . . although that mouth could probably persuade a dead man to give life another go . . .

That mouth was raking him over the coals at the moment, castigating him thoroughly in a furious-wet-cat hiss.

"Why are ye whispering?" he asked in a normal tone. "Isn't anyone to 'ear ye but yer own cousin down the 'all. The whole inn is fast asleep." Except for Siegfried, who still stood dreamily wiping the same section of the waxed countertop downstairs, casting himself in the role of rescuing adventurer in a tale of double damsels in distress.

For a moment, Aaron considered the danger of Siegfried discovering his trespass into the sacred Chamber of the Virgin, and rather thought the stocky younger man could probably do painful amounts of damage to Aaron's manly pride. He hadn't been in a fistfight for a decade, after all. That was a long time to go without punching something.

The scent of jasmine swept through his senses, and he closed his eyes against the wrench in his gut. A decade was a very, very long time to go without a lot of things . . .

Elektra. You'd be worth a fight to the death, you would.

"Well, the death part is accurate enough, I assure you."

Aaron's eyes popped open as his belly turned to ice. "Did I say that out loud?"

She had her dressing gown on now, neatly tied in front and covering her from throat to toes. It didn't matter. She was still naked underneath.

Nonsense like this tended to emerge when he breathed the same air as Elektra Worthington. The intensity of her effect on him was such that he'd likely get tongue-tied looking at her shadow on the ground.

She tilted her head. "Have I ever mentioned that I have five brothers?"

Aaron passed a hand over his face. Teasing aside, he ought not to be in this room with her, especially not in a state of lack of self-control. He'd been a bad sort of man once—a selfish, impulsive lout with more vigor than brains—and although he'd never crossed that particular line, he'd not veered far from it, either.

"'M sorry, miss. I took a wrong turn down the 'all . . ." Backing up two steps, he put his hand back on the bloody dangerous latch that had led him so far astray. "Ye might ought to lock this."

She frowned at him. "Mr. Hastings, have you been drinking?"

He let out a sigh. "Indeed I 'ave, miss. Sorry to disturb ye."

He moved to close the door.

"Wait." She held up one hand and stepped forward.

Didn't she know that she ought to move away from the wild beast in the night? Didn't she have a single shred of common sense in her wild, deadly swift mind?

Apparently not, for she not only approached him but licked her lips uncertainly.

Don't do that. Really, really don't do that.

Unfortunately, this time he didn't speak it aloud. She continued to come closer, until he could see the color of her shadowed eyes.

"Mr. Hastings, this door does not lock properly . . . and . . . that big fellow down in the dining room kept *looking* at me!"

She was asking him for protection. Him? He stood before her sporting an erection that only the dimness of the room could hide, with her scent in his nostrils and her voice in his ears and—

"Don't laugh." She put one small warm hand over his on the latch.

He yanked his hand away as if she'd burned him.

She fluttered her fingertips in apology and went on. "If I asked one of my brothers for this, they would guffaw. I'm the fearsome one. I'm the one who isn't afraid of anything." She blinked and looked away. "Do you know I've never been anywhere without my family around me? I've never been alone, not for one single minute." She looked back at him then, her eyes large and liquid.

"Except in the manor ruins," he reminded her, his voice grating in his throat. When she'd kissed him as if her life depended upon it. When he'd driven his tongue hard into her sweet, hot mouth as she'd squirmed on his rigid lap.

She frowned slightly. "Yes. Of course. I had quite forgotten." Then she smiled. "That doesn't count, of course. You were there."

Aaron's lust gave a last despairing wail and fell beneath the wheels of his honor.

"I'll look out for ye, miss," he managed in a choked whisper. "No need to worry."

Now, firmly and steadily, he reached for the door latch and pulled the door shut with a decided click.

Then he put his back to it and slid down it until his arse settled on the hard floor of the hall, where it would remain until dawn, needlessly protecting the Misses Worthington from the utterly harmless Siegfried . . . simply because she had asked him to.

No wonder they hadn't needed more money.

Aaron closed his eyes and leaned his now-pounding head back against the hard wooden door, careful not to make an alarming thud with his skull.

The bloody stable would have been more comfortable.

Back at the Green Donkey Inn, Hastings—the real Hastings, whose illness had been one part exhaustion, one part lousy head cold, and two parts duplicity to

make the damned sod slow down!—had thought himself settled into the luxury of the inn quite nicely, with
a soft bed, a staff of pretty girls at his beck and call, hot
soup and brandy as needed, and no more midnight rides
through the damned rain.

It was all a bloke could ask for.

Until he took a turn for the worse. Now his body
throbbed, chills convulsed him, and his lungs felt as if
they were filled with wet clay. The soft bed might as
well have been filled with jagged, broken rocks for all
the comfort he felt. The pretty girls were a blur of bustling bosoms (as seen from the level of the pillow) and
cold hands. He couldn't stomach the brandy; the hot
soup was the only thing he could keep down, and even
then it was a near thing.

He felt quite comfortable blaming bloody Lord Aaron
Arbogast for every miserable moment, and did so loudly
and at length. This alarmed him in his saner moments,
for he feared he'd given away the plot and would be
turned out forthwith, but it seemed that the inn staff took
the nobility speaking of themselves in the third person
as nothing odd in particular.

Luckily, he never slipped in his posh accents, not once.
Then again, he could run a scam drunk or sleeping—and
occasionally both!

So the staff took his madness in stride, except for
one, the dark-haired girl with the luminescent skin and
the deep, black eyes of a sorceress of old. This was no
misty English beauty.

Edith.

She came from far Cornwall, she told him. He had
laughed at that, her thinking Cornwall was far.

He wasn't laughing now. He was shivering and his tongue felt thick and dry in his mouth and he cursed bloody Lord Aaron to hell and back.

"Hush, now. Hush," soothed sweet Edith of the soft warm hands and the only voice that didn't rasp his tender ears. "You mustn't say such hateful things to yourself. It isn't proper. You're a fine man, a lord even. Be proud of yourself and your accomplishments."

This made Hastings want to giggle like a madman, but he thought it might frighten any sane person from his vicinity and he truly, deeply wanted Edith to stay and spoon hot soup to his lips and stroke his forehead when she thought he was asleep or too incoherent to know, like right now.

He stopped ranting, because she asked him to. He lay still and breathed as deeply as he could, because she asked him to. Unfortunately, this had the effect of her gathering up her tray and preparing to leave him to his rest.

That wouldn't do. If he had to stay here and not curse and rave and toss, then he wanted his Edith by his side.

He must have said it out loud, for she blushed and tried to slip her delicate hand from his grip. He'd taken her hand? When had he done that?

Oh, well. Now that he had it, he thought it a fine acquisition and didn't plan to return it anytime soon.

"If you leave," he wheezed, barely remembering to keep Lord Aaron's well-born tones, "I shall go back to raving at the heavens. Only if you stay with me can I rest."

She drew back at that and gazed at him warily. It seemed he was not the first man to request her continued presence in an inn room. Seeing her suspicion, he released her hand at once. He would never be the man to put that look in sweet Edith's eyes again. Never.

"I apologize. I meant nothing untoward." It was a good thing Lord Aaron was such a prig. Hastings had a thousand such phrases at hand! "I only meant that I do not feel well at all, but that I do feel somewhat less horrid when you are nearby, Miss Edith."

Stay. Stay and stroke my brow and feed me soup and let me pretend for just a moment that I am a different sort of man.

I am a scoundrel. She is an angel.

He wasn't a fool. He'd been all over the world. He knew such things never amounted to much.

So why did he have the unshakable feeling that this quietly pretty Cornish maid would haunt his dreams for the rest of his life?

"Stay," he wheezed. "Please . . . stay."

She stayed.

Chapter Eleven

Up at just past dawn, with her bag packed and her inn-room tidied, Elektra tucked a last strand of hair away into the smooth knot she'd created and brushed her hands down her skirts.

She would be home later this morning! As maddening as her family could be at times, she adored them all and worried for them when she couldn't monitor their doings. Had Lysander had another nightmare? Was Mama using the teapot to store her turpentine? Was anyone making sure Attie didn't go about armed?

She shook off her worries. There was naught she could do from here, and she'd be home very soon. Ready, she checked herself in the mirror.

Her traveling dress was getting wrinkled and a bit dusty, though she'd sponged it most carefully last night in that long painful delay of sleep. She had done every little thing she could think of to avoid blowing out her candle!

She felt a bit silly about it in the light of day. Goodness, she stayed in a perfectly respectable inn, frequented by respectable people. There had been no reason to think the faulty lock on her door was anything but a simple malfunction. She ought to have pushed a chair before the door and closed her eyes in peace!

She simply hadn't been able. Every creak of the structure was the footfall of a vandal! Every sigh of the wind was a faraway scream!

It seemed she was only practical and pragmatic when surrounded by dreamers. Take her from the bosom of her imaginative family and she became as inventive as the rest of them.

If Mr. Hastings hadn't stumbled into her room, she might have stood there brushing her hair endlessly into the night, keeping the candle lighted and the heavy pewter candlestick at hand. He'd been quite gallant, really, in a drunken sort of way. A bit distracted by something, but he'd seemed sincere in his desire to help.

She buttoned her spencer with a wry twist to her lips. He'd likely tiptoed off to bed a few minutes after that promise, but he had at least enabled her to ease her fears long enough to fall asleep.

When she placed her hand on the faulty latch, the thing gave at once, leaping from her hand. The door flew open as if pushed from the other side.

Mr. Hastings fell into her room and landed on his back on the floor at her feet. His eyelids parted slightly, and he winced.

Elektra could only stare down at him. "You stayed? All night?"

He groaned and wrinkled his entire face in an expression that said *That was the worst night's sleep of my life*, then gazed blearily up at her.

"I said I would, didn't I?"

"Y—yes, you did." Elektra bit her lip, rather fiercely moved by his grumpy steadfastness. Her experience with asking male persons for irrational favors had led her to believe they would flight off at the slightest excuse, dismissing her needs with a laugh or, worse, mockery. Oh, she knew her brothers would die for her—but God forbid she ever ask them to protect her from imaginary nightmares!

Lifting her skirts slightly, she lowered herself to a demure squat to gaze into Mr. Hastings's sleep-smudged features. He looked absolutely awful. Dark circles ringed his eyes, his thick sandy hair stood straight up on one side, and there was a reddened patch on his face where the carved pattern on the door had pressed a design into his skin.

Elektra gave him her very best smile—the one that almost no one got to see, the one she saved for her dear Iris and Attie. "Mr. Hastings, you are not an ordinary man."

"No, miss," he agreed hazily. He seemed a bit gobsmacked.

Poor fellow. Still smiling, warmed by his consideration and charmed by his lopsided hair, she rose to her feet. "Shall I order breakfast for you, sir? I should like to resume our journey directly afterward. Eggs and bacon?"

He turned a little green and shook his head. "No, miss. No thank ye. I'll see to the horses, straightaway."

Elektra took pity on him and pretended that she knew nothing about men and liquor and hangovers, although she'd hauled one or both of the twins off to their beds during their younger, wilder days, then poured hot black coffee and raw eggs down their throats the next morning.

She smiled brightly at Mr. Hastings. "Excellent! I shall gather up Miss Bliss and we shall join you out front very soon."

He moaned something and wiggled his fingers good-bye at her, then dropped flat on the floor once more. Elektra stepped neatly over him and ventured down the stairs, where she knew Bliss would already be. Bliss, she had no doubt, was one of those people who was always precisely where she was supposed to be.

All night.

He'd watched over her all night long. She'd been far away from her home and family, all those brothers and father, too—and yet she felt so safe.

Just as she had in the ruins.

Aaron lay on the floor, knowing he looked ridiculous sprawled half in, half out of the room. That seemed to be a recurring problem with him. When his soul wanted out—as it had when Miss Worthington had requested his help to go home—his honor kept him in. When his soul wanted in—as it had when she'd stood so close to him dressed in naught but fine-spun linen and golden hair—his honor kept him out.

Now, when all he wanted to do was to find his room— which he'd never even seen!—and sleep the morning away, she wanted him to help her on her way.

Had any other woman in recorded history ever turned a man so inside out?

Helen of Troy.

Lady Macbeth.

Guinevere.

He'd have done it all over again, just for another glimpse of that smile. *I am an idiot for that smile.* He thought about the innkeeper, and poor lovelorn Siegfried, and every other fellow caught in the beam of that smile. *I must remember that I am nothing special to her.*

He rolled—or rather, flopped—over onto his face, feeling the stretch of cramped muscles but also the welcome sensation of his numbed arse joining the party.

I am not Alexander, or Macbeth, or Arthur.

They had all lived their lives. He blinked at the carpet, which was much too close, and pushed himself up on his hands and knees. At this rate, he was definitely destined to die young.

I just might be Achilles. He most definitely had a weakness.

He made it all the way to the stables without his numbed legs giving way beneath him. He even managed to saddle his horse himself, although he gratefully accepted the groom's help with Bianca and the pony cart.

Therefore, he was impressively ready for action, despite the pounding in his head and the storm-at-sea feeling in his belly, when the ladies emerged from the inn, looking as fresh and rested as a good breakfast and a good night's sleep can make one look.

Aaron tried not to snarl as Miss Elektra thanked him prettily for his prompt attention to details.

In fact, she was astonishingly good-natured toward him for at least an hour after their departure. At first he'd welcomed the respite from her sharp tongue. Then he began to worry. Sweetness and courtesy were not natural states for her. She must be feeling the strain by now.

He became convinced that danger was nigh. She could blow at any time.

In a house in a once respectable, now genteelly shabby neighborhood in London . . .

Time for breakfast. Lysander Worthington sat up in his bed, where he'd been lying fully clothed. As usual, sleep had eluded him, so he'd stared at the cracks in the stained plaster ceiling all the long hours of the night.

He'd had a long hard ride home yesterday from Shropshire, all night and all day, slowed by pounding storms and hock-deep mud. His mount was the second-best horse in the family, but even a fairly decent-quality creature could not slog home any faster than that.

He ought to be weary, he supposed. He sat on his bed and waited, trying to feel weariness. He felt nothing much at all.

He rose to his feet and reminded himself to join his family downstairs.

Most of the time, using his own gray-washed memories, Zander tried to be a good brother and a good son. The only problem was, it would have helped if he could actually be a good person first.

He didn't feel like a human person. Not a real, warm, flesh-and-blood, feeling, thinking, reasoning being of the human persuasion. He'd been one before and he remembered that once, he'd been just like everyone else, a real man.

Now he was more like a reflection of one in a smoke-darkened mirror, or a crisp shadow on a sunny morning—the outline upon the ground complete, but with nothing but black inside.

Everything looked fine on the outside. Even he could see that in his looking glass. He breathed, he walked, he ate, sometimes, and on rare occasions he even slept. His oldest brother took him to a tailor, so his prewar clothing looked as if it belonged to him, the postwar Zander.

Yet there was no denying that something was wrong. He was broken, damaged, probably forever. He felt as though, if someone cut him open, they would find cables and pulleys instead of blood and muscle. He felt as dry and dark inside as a long-neglected attic room—empty but for the leftover possessions of past existence, worn and covered in dust.

How could he even begin to fill that empty room? How did one refurbish a vacant heart?

The stairs led down. He went down.

In the sunny, shabby breakfast room, he found his eldest brother, Daedalus, along with his younger brothers Castor and Orion, bolting down breakfast and discussing the journey ahead. Ah yes, Elektra's rescue.

Pausing, Lysander tried to recollect the atypical urgency that had led him home at a gallop to report his sister's actions to the family. It had seemed very important at the time, so he'd pushed himself and his horse with single-minded purpose.

He remembered everything that had happened, of

course. It was the emotional content of the events that had drained away too quickly, like water on sand.

He did not speak or make a sound, but abruptly all eyes turned to gaze at him standing in the doorway of the room. From his vague and dreamy parents to his intensely vibrant youngest sister, Atalanta, those eyes asked him a question. Even his new sister-in-law, Miranda, gazed at him as if looking for something in him.

Don't bother, he wanted to say to them. *You won't find anything. I am an unoccupied husk, wearing tailored clothes.* Of course, he said nothing. He never did. Nonetheless, they all seemed to believe he was better, because he hardly ever shouted out in the night anymore.

He couldn't remember feeling that nightmare horror. He couldn't even remember why he'd cried out, except for a nauseating sensation of falling that sometimes still interrupted his infrequent sleep.

He missed Elektra's presence. Her determined focus and brisk assertiveness always made him feel as though she made up for any lack in him. Add in her irritable, silent compassion and he knew that with her, he need not pretend to be a person, or brother, or son. When he was with his bossiest sibling, he simply did as he was told, relieved from the strain of thinking for himself. He was ill equipped for that, what with his dusty-attic mind.

Unfortunately, it seemed that Elektra was not as sensible as he'd believed her to be. Now he'd helped her do something that Daedalus and the others—well, mostly Dade—thought was odd or unsafe or appalling in some way.

Zander knew that what he and Elektra had done was wrong. He just wished he could remember why it was wrong.

Miranda looked the most worried. Well, she was somewhat new to the family and therefore still fairly normal. Cas looked unhappy about leaving his pretty wife behind in her condition but otherwise not so worried about Elektra herself. Orion looked as though he were considering the radial symmetry of sea urchins or some such thing. Zander knew that Orion's perpetual distraction was nothing like his own broken speechlessness. Orion had a whole mind, a very fine one—one much too busy with important thoughts to be fully engaged in silly matters such as paltry runaway sisters.

Little Attie gazed up at Zander with narrowed green eyes. At thirteen years of age, Atalanta was a spindly creature made up mostly of freckles and iron will. Out of all of the family, Zander rather thought Attie understood him the best. Attie was broken, too, in her way. She had no concept of the rules of right or wrong that applied to the world outside these walls—or if she did, she frankly chose to ignore them.

Zander knew the rules as well. There was nothing wrong with that part of his memory. He just couldn't remember why they were supposed to be so important.

Dade shoved a last bite into his mouth and stood, still chewing. "Come on, you lot," he said to his brothers. "The mounts I've rented should be here by now." Daedalus had a horse of his own, a fine spirited black named Icarus, of course.

Zander's horse, a brown gelding that he'd acquired, didn't strictly belong to him in the usual sense of ownership, but no one else had seemed to want it so he'd untied it from the post in front of the military hospital on the day he decided to depart from it and ridden it home.

The stolid brown beast had no name at all. It breathed, it ate, it trotted on his wordless command. It was enough for Zander.

He hadn't eaten, though no one seemed to notice anything different about that. His horse had been fed. That was likely good enough for Zander's purpose. Though the both of them had just ridden into London the afternoon before, the sun was barely up before they joined the others and rode out again. The horse seemed rested enough, so Lysander didn't complain.

Complaining required talking—and it also required giving a damn.

Zander had mostly forgotten how to do either one.

Mrs. Philpott scuttled into the breakfast room. "They're here, missus! They're home!"

The city grew around them as they neared the center. Low buildings turned to high ones, scarce houses became attached rows. The noise of a thousand souls and their doings began to hammer at their ears, causing them to raise their own in response.

The city. Aaron had intended to avoid London entirely. So, of course, the dangerous Misses Worthington needed to be returned to London. He slouched down on Lard-Arse, pulled Hastings's battered hat low over his face, and hoped for the best. This had been the location of the worst of his youthful offenses. The throbbing heart of Society—and worse. A restless and bored young man, with a long and powerless heir-hood before him, could find plenty of mischief with which to occupy his senses.

He had, indeed he had. Now that past weighed upon him like a millstone strapped to his back.

See her home, then be on your way.

Still, he couldn't keep his mind off the puzzle that was Elektra Worthington.

Aaron had learned through very difficult years of trial and error never to judge by appearances, first in his error-filled youth, then later as he'd tried so hard to rebuild his character and regain his honor.

Along the way he had come to understand that heroic-looking fellows could be the greatest cowards, and sweet, demure ladies could vindictively destroy one's life with a single word. In the end, he'd learned to keep to himself but for a few worthy companions, carefully chosen not for their rank or wealth, but for their fine deeds. Even rascally, gutter-born Hastings had shown Aaron moments of outstanding valor and a hidden streak of gentlemanly decency—at least, on rare occasions.

Actions told the truth, as outward show did not, and there was surely no certainty to be found in anyone's idle words!

So what did he know of Miss Elektra Worthington? From beneath the brim of his hat, he studied her straight back as she sat beside her cousin driving the pony cart. Her bonnet hid her golden hair and her astonishing face from him, making his task a bit easier, although every swaying motion of the cart draped her gown across her tiny waist and rounded hips—thank goodness the low seat-back hid her bottom from his view!

With determination, Aaron cleared his mind. Yes, she was most pleasing to the eye. So was a fine sunset or a well-formed horse. Setting aside that delicate beauty and mouthwatering figure, looking past her fine gown and polished manner, what did he see? What had she shown him through her actions?

Determination shone from her, he decided. Her goals might be superficial and social-climbing, but there was nothing short of pure Sheffield steel composing that poised, erect spine. He recalled the way she'd urged him not to make her brother share in her punishment. Her family needed her, she'd claimed. That remained to be seen, but he sensed that her kin loyalty was strong, though she claimed to be weary of drowning in brothers. She obviously possessed an intelligent mind, though woefully lacked in good judgment—for had she not impulsively kidnapped a man?

Then the way she'd pulled herself from the river and immediately turned to her cousin's rescue. Courage, she clearly had in bucketloads. Dangerous amounts, actually, in one so sadly misdirected.

Brave, clever, strong-minded, and loyal. What a pity she was also utterly selfish and shallow, not to mention entirely mad!

Aaron did not really notice when his mind went back to admiring the sweet, female curve of hip and waist. When he tapped his heels to his mount to come alongside the cart so that he could catch a glimpse of joggling buxom bounty as well, his consciousness simply refused to acknowledge the action. He was simply riding along, minding his own matters, was he not? Nothing wrong with that.

What might have alarmed him more than recognition of his harmless voyeurism, had he only realized it, was that he paid no attention whatsoever to the jiggles and joggles of the equally comely and far more sane and sensible Miss Bliss Worthington!

"We're here! At last!"

Chapter Twelve

Elektra hesitated just outside her front door. Home. The exterior did not stand out from the others on this block. Fine houses, gone a bit less fine over time, yet still mostly respectable. The interior, however . . .

As if she'd run through the house at full speed, flashing through her mind came the vision of what lay in each room . . . room after room of cluttered creative madness and random odds and bits of whatever someone had picked up and put down with no discernible rhyme or reason. Piles of books lay everywhere, even infesting the front entry hall, here and there, in the corners and on the lower shelf of the side table, creeping in like unwanted dogs vying for a bit of human attention. On the wall above that table hung a mirror, gone dotted and grainy with time and damp and hanging very obviously askew because that best covered the gaping hole in the plaster caused from someone leaving a Chinese rocket where six-year-old Attie could reach it. The resulting fire hadn't been much ado, but the crack

in the wall ran vertically above the mirror like a sap-
ling, branching out when it reached the ceiling.

Just like the manor, Worthington House in London
was a ruin. Still standing, but battle-scarred and tattered
by the endless, eternal, explosive Worthington search for
amusement.

Searing self-consciousness flooded her belly.

How we must look to him! Her throat was tight. On
the outside, however, Elektra knew she had not so much
as flinched. Her chin remained high, for though she
cringed inwardly she would not show it for an instant.
Worthingtons might not be able to lay claim to much,
but they did have their pride.

Belatedly, she also wondered what Bliss would think
of it all. Of course, Bliss was allegedly a Worthington,
so perhaps she would think nothing of it at all.

Then the door opened and the Worthingtons flowed
out. Amid the babble, they were all three swept back in,
pulled by the tide of family ties.

Aaron had never seen the like of Worthington House in
his life. At first it seemed cluttered. Upon closer observation, it seemed *insanely* cluttered.

There were books, upon stacks of which stood works
of art from thirty different cultures, strange bits of machinery, books, a few taxidermy animals whose moth-
eaten fur had seen better decades . . . and then there
were some more books.

The only thing missing was possibly a little more
clutter.

He turned to his companions in astonishment. Bliss

smiled serenely at him, then stepped confidently into the hall. "Greetings, cousins."

Elektra brushed past him to embrace the woman standing to greet them. Aaron had not even spotted her in the chaos, but he could now see clearly see that she had once been a great beauty herself. Elektra swept the silver-haired woman into her arms and kissed her on the forehead.

"Oh, Mama," she said with a laugh.

The woman definitely resembled Elektra—an older, shorter, rounder version of Elektra with hair of the finest silver instead of the finest gold.

Miss Elektra Worthington would age beautifully. Some lucky man was going to have a real beauty to look at for the rest of his natural life. Perhaps it would make up for living with a madwoman.

Bliss floated forward serenely and held her hands out to the older woman who must be Mrs. Worthington.

"Auntie Iris," Bliss smiled and bent to give her aunt a kiss.

The entry hall began to fill up. There were a bewildering number of Worthingtons. There were tall ones, and short ones, and dark ones, and light ones. There were young ones and old ones, and strange, ethereal elfin ones.

A stout, grizzled man stepped forward to take Bliss's hand. He bowed deeply and formally, as if to royalty. "*And with her breath she did perfume the air: Sacred and sweet was all I saw in her.*" He straightened, then grinned and smacked a kiss upon the back of her hand. "Hello, Bunny!"

Mrs. Worthington looked on benignly. "*The Taming*

of the Shrew, Act One, Scene One," she informed Aaron in a confidential tone. "Isn't he marvelous?"

Aaron was careful not to betray any sign of his classical education. "Them's pretty words, right enough, missus."

Then Mr. Worthington turned to his missing daughter. With a big smile, he took her by the shoulders. "*O, she doth teach the torches to burn bright!*" Then he pulled her close for a bear hug.

Mrs. Worthington sighed in delight. "*Romeo and Juliet*, Act One, Scene Five!"

Aaron nearly choked. Fiery Elektra was no sweet Juliet!

In the meantime, more and more Worthingtons were popping up. One by one they dashed into the room, from the hallway, down the stairs, one even coming in the front door—magically appearing as if on command. Elektra was beaming, and exasperated, at the chaos and the noise and the shouted questions and the way her little sister was dangling on her skirts as if she were half her size.

Aaron could not take his eyes from her shining face. He'd seen her by lamplight and daylight, prim as a schoolteacher and muddy as a farmer.

Now, at home, laughing aloud, surrounded by the madness of her silly crazy family, she was truly alight.

"You are a tall piece of handsome."

Aaron looked down at the stately but odd Mrs. Worthington. She gazed at Aaron coyly and whacked him on the arm with the fringe of the trailing shawl she wore. Without taking her eyes from him, she waved a beckoning hand over her shoulder.

A tall, dark bloke approached. He attended his mother's call without objection, but with a look of distant tolerance that said he'd rather be somewhere else.

"Orion," Mrs. Worthington stated. "He will pen great works in science. Mr. Hastings brought your sister and cousin home."

The fellow shook Aaron's hand, then slipped away as another young man approached, this one accompanied by a lovely lady who seemed to be expecting. "Hullo, I'm Cas, this is Miranda. Thanks for hauling Ellie back." He rolled his eyes. "You wouldn't believe what we thought she'd gotten up to!"

His pretty wife smiled at Aaron even while planting an elbow in her husband's midriff. "You are most welcome, Mr. Hastings."

Aaron figured he was in for more introductions, although it seemed that no one meant to introduce him to a certain familiar-looking fellow who kept to the background. That would be Lysander, of the thudding fist and poor judgment. Aaron shot the man a narrow glance, but Elektra had mentioned that her brother spoke little. It seemed that his Hastings façade would hold up well enough in this household.

"This is our youngest." Mrs. Worthington waved a long, lacy handkerchief, and a little girl stepped forward.

Aaron gazed down at the scrawny creature that stood before him. She had amber hair that coiled in tight ringlets like her father's where it wasn't braided into strange random locks. He was pretty sure there were feathers woven into the braids, and he only hoped they were not still attached to the birds. She was oddly garbed in a too-large dress, a too-small cape, and giant horseman's boots as well, not to mention the arresting impression of freckles covering her nose, the chip in her front tooth, huge green eyes, and a set of cheekbones that would someday rival the greatest beauty in the land.

"I am Atalanta," the strange being stated flatly. "I'm dreadfully brilliant, but socially backward."

It was the final touch of madness. Through a giddy sense of unreality rising within him, Aaron didn't smile . . . barely. He bowed. "Hastings, miss. I'm roguishly likable, but vastly underestimated." He was talking about the real Hastings . . . wasn't he?

The odd child smiled darkly. "So am I. The underestimated part. I find it comes in very handily, don't you?"

Aaron gave her roguish Hastings smile. "To be sure, miss."

The child turned to the tall fellow who had been introduced by the unlikely name of Daedalus. "I like him, Dade."

Dade—thank heaven for nicknames!—only gazed sourly at Aaron. "That's what worries me."

I truly ought to get out of here.

"Mr. Hastings has some post, missus." A stout, graying woman who looked to be a housekeeper by her voluminous apron handed Mrs. Worthington a letter.

"Already? Aren't you clever, Mr. Hastings!" Mrs. Worthington handed Aaron the letter without a glance at it, although Dade craned his neck slightly to see. Suspicious fellow—but since he was currently lying through his teeth, Aaron couldn't justifiably take offense.

Enfolded within a scrawled and essentially unreadable note on the Green Donkey's paper from Hastings was a sheet of rich vellum. Signed by Aaron's cousin, Serena, who watched over the Earl of Arbodean's sickbed. Aaron stepped away from the crowd for a moment to open Serena's letter.

The earl's health has improved. He is sitting up and taking food again. It is such a relief to hear him speak again! The physician is cautiously hopeful, but warns that Grandpapa is still fragile. Any upset could set him back. I reluctantly must suggest that you postpone your visit, just for a few days. Please, Aaron. For me?

In eternal gratitude,

Serena.

Aaron folded the letter thoughtfully. A few days? After the great urgency of the past weeks journeying home, he felt oddly as if he'd stepped down a stair that wasn't there.

Having gotten the young ladies safely to London, Aaron knew he would be justified in leaving them there and being on his merry way. After all, none of this was his affair. However, his curiosity outweighed that drive toward his grandfather's estate—not to mention his niggling sense of responsibility toward Miss Elektra Worthington's honor.

He looked around him. This house was chaos and madness and everything he hated—everything he never wanted to experience again.

And yet he couldn't leave. Until he had made sure that Elektra suffered no ill effects from her strange moment of complete madness, he was obligated to stay and watch over her.

At least for as long as he was able. If he got word that his grandfather was growing worse again, he would have to journey up north once more. However, a few days ought to be long enough to assure himself of her clear reputation, that no trace of scandal followed Elektra. If, say, a week went by without Society being alerted to her stumble, it was likely that it would never come to light. There would be new and fascinating scandals for the gossips to chew upon, and then Aaron would feel much better about leaving the outrageous female to her own devices.

Elektra found a room had been made ready for Bliss not far from her own. It had been very nearly cleared out, although the stacks of items in the hallway before it had simply grown. Bliss's trunks—and trunks and trunks!—fit against one wall. It was hardly the gracious reception that Elektra would have liked for guests, but it was the best that Worthington House had to offer. At least, Bliss's things had not ended up in Elektra's precious sanctuary!

Quickly, Elektra set Lysander and Orion to shuffling things about in the farthest small room on the floor below. Orion had been using it to store past projects, but Elektra ordered him to throw half on the trash heap and to put the other half in his study down the hall! She was surprised that her brothers followed her wishes with so little protest.

I scared them. They were afraid for me.

It was a gratifying thought. She knew this agreeable

compliance would not last, but it touched her nonetheless. They were all a bunch of sweet lummoxes sometimes!

It did not take long for her to gain the use of the small room for Mr. Hastings.

"You wish me to stay?" He blinked at her. "In the house?"

She rolled her eyes. "Well, you can hardly stay in the mews!"

Bliss joined in her plea. "Of course you must stay, Mr. Hastings! Your poor horse is so tired and we must feed and entertain you in reward for your kindness."

Aaron gazed at the two young ladies helplessly. He'd meant to keep an eye on Elektra—but not under the same roof! Not sleeping on the floor below hers, knowing how she dressed as she slept—

Knowing that that door wouldn't be locked, either!

Oh, his kindness just kept paying him off, that was for certain!

"I—" Green-blue eyes and sky-blue eyes fluttered beseechingly at him. He was no Greek hero to resist that siren call. He was just a man with a brand-new careful set of ethics and the need to look after those who asked it of him. "That's mighty kind of you, miss." He bowed his head in defeat. "I am grateful."

I am doomed.

From the look in Daedalus's eyes when he learned of the plan, he was indeed not long for this world. Seized by a sudden fey death wish, probably due to the imaginary Hastings infecting his mind, Aaron grinned mischievously at the sour eldest Worthington brother.

Poor bloke is as helpless as I am against the com-bined beauty of "the other twins." Let him sulk!

Dade glowered more darkly. Avoidance seemed to be the best course. So it was that Aaron spent half an hour seeing to Lard-Arse and Bianca in the family sta-bles behind the house—which consisted of a few rick-ety stalls remaining in a space that had been overtaken by a great cluttered workshop filled with bits and bobs and strange machinery.

"It belongs to the twins."

Aaron turned to see the strange Atalanta shadowing him. She leaned against the stable door and twined her fingers through her mad braids.

"Poll went away, so when I want to see him, I squint at Cas and pretend."

Aaron blinked. "Does that work?" If he looked at Bliss and squinted, it wouldn't make up for not seeing Elektra.

She gazed at him silently for a long moment. Then, "No. It doesn't work at all."

Then Lard-Arse stepped on Aaron's foot—on pur-pose, by God!—and when he stopped hopping about and diligently not-cursing, the girl was gone.

Dinner was surely to come soon, and Aaron still looked and smelled as if he'd taken a swim in a river and then slept on an inn floor. Good manners compelled him to try to do something about it, so he decided to try to find that room Miss Elektra Worthington had directed him to.

There were a great many doors in the hallway where Aaron's room was located. He'd tried to pay attention to the path and landmarks through the stacks of books and strange assemblages of gears and pulleys and one strangely plaited sculpture made from strips of copper plating that reminded Aaron queasily of a man-eating plant.

At last he made it to the room halfway down the hall on the left that he could have sworn was his cluttered but comfortable room.

He opened the door and stepped inside with a backward glance to be sure he'd lost that eerie child's pursuit.

His first clue that he'd chosen badly was the harsh squawk of something large and most definitely not native to the British lowlands.

He swung about to get a mad jumbled impression of a room filled with skeletons and rigidly stuffed creatures. What concerned him the most was the whirling dervish of white wings and red, burning eyes that dived at him with vicious three-inch dagger talons extended—

The door was just behind him, thankfully, and his hand found the latch on the first try, thankfully, and he managed to shut the door on the demonic winged beast—

Unfortunately, that was where his luck ended.

Stumbling backward, he tripped over the pile of books on his right. The falling volumes drove him spinning off to his left to avoid the heavy wooden blows upon his skull—and he rolled directly into another, higher arrangement that teetered over his head—

Aaron shouted out in alarm, hoping for succor before he was buried in books and dust and mad, disturbing sculptures that had no place in a family home—

He flung both arms over his head and went helplessly down before the onslaught.

At last it was over. Only the sound of more books falling, on and on down the hallway, like a string of slithering dominoes, until the very last pile of books thumped into the very last doorway and the thrumming, twanging sound of fraught metal finally stilled.

Unbelievably, he found himself still alive.

Aaron breathed in a slow lungful of dust and bitter, molding paper. A great weight of books and machinery pressed him hard into the floor, and something sharp was poking him rather disrespectfully close to his groin, but he could not reach his own crotch, for his arms were pressure-locked about his own head.

So he did what any brave, self-respecting bloke might do in such a situation.

He inhaled and began to yell for help.

Chapter Thirteen

When no one came to Aaron's aid as he lay stifling beneath the weight of several centuries of literature, he began to curse. When still no one came, he began to beg.

Finally he heard movement, almost more as a vibration through the rubble than as sound. Someone was coming.

Unfortunately that someone stopped in the book-crossing progress directly over his chest ribs, and he felt the last of his breath wheeze out of him as the books above him settled more firmly about and on top of his body.

"Ugh."

It was all he could manage.

He heard some shifting activity above him, and then he began to see daylight through his crossed arms. Small glints of daylight began to seep through the jumble of books.

Finally, the last book above his face was removed,

and he found himself gazing gratefully up at the dusty smeared elfin features of the Devil's Spawn.

She glared at him. "Well, now you've done it, haven't you?"

"Ger . . . off!"

She scrunched her strange little face at him. "You get off. This is my house and these are my books and you ruined everything!"

"Ger . . . o . . . off!" His wheeze was fainter than ever, but he saw Attie's little face lift away from the gap and then her weight lifted from his chest. He took a better but still-hampered breath, so grateful to feel his ribs expand that he might have cried if he hadn't heard the voice of Elektra's eldest brother, Dade.

"What a bloody mess! Attie, what did you do?"

"It wasn't me! It was that nasty Hastings man! The blighter ruined my book cave!"

Aaron heard Dade sigh. "Attie, you never take responsibility for anything. You are as bad as the twins. And don't say 'blighter.' It isn't appropriate."

"I didn't say it about you," Attie muttered resentfully. "I said it about Pasty Hastings."

As much as Aaron would have liked to see the brat get a good dressing-down from her brother, he would rather live to see the sun set, so he sent up a last desperate shout for help. He couldn't be blamed for the quavering tone of it, to be sure. It was the weight of all the bloody books!

Dade's look of surprise was almost worth it—at least until the eldest Worthington let a speculative look cross his regular features.

The bastard wasn't really considering leaving him to die, was he?

"Mr. Hastings? Oh, heavens! Are you all right?" Aaron heard the voice he most wanted to hear at that moment—a thought so ironic that he didn't allow himself to think it later, that he looked to the mad Elektra for rescue!—which thankfully seemed to remind Dade that it was better to be a Good Samaritan than to leave a man to die by literature. Either that, or he was leery of explaining matters to the magistrate—or, worse, his sister.

Aaron felt in no position to be picky about his savior's motives!

Dade let out a sigh of resignation. And turned his head to speak to his youngest sibling. "Attie, will you fetch Zander and Rion, please? This is going to take more hands."

In the end, it took all the Worthingtons, some more helpful than others, like Archie and Iris who stood watching the entire proceedings like eager spectators at a sporting event, side by side with a serenely interested Bliss and a pregnant Miranda. A bucket brigade of sorts was formed, the brothers and Elektra digging their way to him despite the primate antics of spindly little Atalanta.

As Aaron was helped from his word-filled quicksand, he cynically wondered if someone ought to be roasting chestnuts.

"Put him in his room!" That was Elektra.

"We'll never get him out again" came a protest, which sounded like Cas, the brother who was a twin.

"We're just as likely to lose him in Orion's study!"

The room with the attack bird? "Not Orion's study!" Aaron gasped.

"See?"

He was half carried, half dragged down the hall over the hundreds—thousands?—of spilled volumes, then dumped on a narrow bed. A cloud of dust rose from the covers, but it was a real bed, with a mattress.

At last. He hadn't lain in a real bed since he installed himself in the tiny cabin of the ship from the isles.

Aaron felt cool hands on his forehead. He opened his eyes to see concern in Elektra's green-blue gaze. Several strands of her hair hung down, long enough to trail over his half-open shirt and stream cool fire onto the skin of his bare chest.

Near-death by literature might be worth it if a bloke can be nursed back to health by a goddess.

She smiled, and it was the sweetest curl of her lips that he'd yet seen. "Mr. Hastings, has it occurred to you that you might be considered ever so slightly accident-prone?"

Her voice was soft. Her fingers were soft, and if he was not mistaken they lingered just a little as they left his hair.

Her fingers tangled in his hair as she kissed him . . .

The flash of memory sent heat through his bloodstream. "Miss, you're the only accident a man needs."

Her lips took on a wry tilt. "To ruin your life, you mean?" She straightened. Her hands fell away from him. He saw that she sat with one hip on the dusty mattress—entirely improper for a lady with a man.

God, she doesn't think of me like one of those damned brothers, does she?

He reached out and caught that retreating hand. Nothing seemed to matter to him but to know that she saw him as a man, not a brother, not a servant.

She went quite still, but she did not pull her hand away. "Mr. Hastings—"

"That is not my name."

She blinked. "Henry, isn't it?"

God, yes, right. He was Henry Hastings, and she was death to his dreams! Except that he couldn't drum up the same sense of horror as he had a few days past.

Her hand curled into his. "Henry?" Her touch was light and cool, like the touch of silk. Soothing . . . and he was so damned tired. So many nights on the tossing ship, in haylofts, tied to chairs . . .

No, don't miss this—she's being so sweet—

But I'm horizontal—in a real bed—and there's no hope—

Elektra sat back. Her hand slipped from his lax grasp. "Henry?"

He was fast asleep, poor man. She gazed down at his relaxed features for a long moment. He was a secretive fellow, despite his seemingly outgoing manner. She hadn't realized until this moment how his expression always retained a shadow of wary alertness—as if he thought something was about to leap from the shadows at any time. Now, however, he looked—well, one hesitated to use such a word about a rascal like Mr. Hastings, but it was the best she could think of—heroic. A champion.

A man upon whom damsels in distress called when shining armor was required.

Elektra knew that her brothers had made themselves scarce, as they usually did when there was a mess to clean up, but she cast a glance toward the door, just in case Attie lurked there.

Attie was ever lurking, poor little mistrustful one.

Then, in the single moment she found herself alone with only her own wishes to see to, she leaned closer and lightly ran her fingertips through the thick, golden-brown hair at his temples. Warm. Silky.

Just as she remembered, every night when she blew out her candle and allowed the memory of that wondrous kiss to fill her thoughts. She had almost convinced herself that the entire impact of that moment had been her imagination, overexcited by her fear and exhilaration at her own daring deed.

But if she'd imagined the whole thing . . .

Why did it feel so wonderful to touch him again at last?

A distant male voice, raised in some sort of debate, penetrated the quiet of the room. Elektra sat up, then stood and briskly rubbed her palms together.

There was a mess in the hall. She could shout the roof down before her brothers would take care of it. She decided that a hard task like that would be just the thing.

Just the thing to make her forget the feeling of her fingers deep in his hair . . . and his hot mouth . . .

Books. Hundreds of books. Lying all over the hallway.

She turned away and did not look back at the sleeping man in the bed. Not even once.

Well, perhaps once.

* * *

There were, in the end, over two and a half *thousand* books in the hallway.

Truly? Elektra counted the careful stacks of fifteen again. They lined the longest wall of the attic, standing two stacks deep. It was true. They stood neatly squared, spines out, all turned the same way, titles readable. Now, one could, if one wished—and she most heartily did not!—systematically catalog the collection with some semblance of order.

The other oddments—where had that awful sculpture come from?—were shoved unceremoniously into random elderly wardrobes and dressers with recalcitrant drawers, or packed tightly into crumbling trunks.

Elektra sneezed for what had to be the fiftieth time. She dusted her filthy hands. "Enough."

Strangely, once begun, it hadn't been as overwhelming a task as she had imagined. And she'd actually had a bit of help!

After the first wary observation, Attie had apparently decided that this was not some plot to tempt her to lower her defenses and had, in fact, lowered them somewhat.

When Elektra had asked her little sister to carry a single stack of books into the attic, Attie cheerfully— well, willingly—moved books for over an hour before she happened to open one and lose herself in it, plunked down cross-legged in the hallway so that Elektra had to walk carefully around her for the rest of the job.

Her sister looked so intent upon her find that Elektra had not the heart to shift her. Instead she finished the job alone and silently, letting Attie read undisturbed until the job was done, still turning pages, a small figure in the oddly bare hallway.

Now Elektra, truly physically weary, smiled as she descended the attic stairs. What would Attie say when she looked up from her book and registered her surroundings? Would she for a moment wonder if she was in the same house?

I did this. I made this house—I made us—*a little bit better.* And then, a dangerous notion—*I didn't even have to marry a rich stranger to do it.*

Madness. An afternoon of tidying wouldn't fix what was broken in Worthington House. Only a flawless match would bring it all back.

After all, wasn't that what she'd been born for?

From the shadowed doorway of his room, Aaron watched Elektra descend into the hallway from a small door set into the paneling, likely an attic.

She looked a right mess, from the dusty smudges on her face to the smeared skirts of her wrinkled gown. Yet it was the soft glow of affection in her absentminded smile as she looked down the hall toward Attie, and the way her weary hand trailed on the railing . . . as light a touch as her tentative fingertips in his hair on that long-ago night alone in the ruin.

Had it only been a few days?

She was always stunning and vibrant, even when she driving him mad with her single-mindedness. Now, with her expression soft and kindly and her proud erect posture sagging a bit with weariness, she looked like an angel after a hard day's work granting miracles.

Only when she passed him and descended the stairs,

leaving his sight, did he take in the changes she'd wrought.

And stopped short in surprise.

The hallway was entirely clear of books and clutter. For the first time he could see the gracious width of it and the elegant linenfold carved into the now gleaming wainscoting. Not only that, but the sconces gleamed and the shabby jewel-toned runner fairly glowed in the light of the newly brightened lamps.

In the center of the hall, halfway down, sat a small, hunched figure. Bony knees jutted awkwardly through her crumpled skirts, and her unusually braided hair hung askew. Little oddity Attie was the only thing out of place in the long, generously proportioned hallway.

Aaron walked closer, laughing inside as he observed that her skinny little bottom covered the only patch of unswept carpet in the long stretch.

Attie finally blinked at the toes of his boots penetrating her field of vision and then lifted her chin to squint up at him. "I cleaned the hall for you. Say thank you."

Aaron thought that Attie made a very fine doorstop. Still, it was obvious that her efforts on his behalf had been unusual enough for her.

"Thanks then, Miss Atalanta. I appreciates it, I do."

She shrugged and looked back down at her book.

"Did you know that the African elephant and the Indian elephant have completely different ears?"

Aaron smiled. "Yes. I did know that."

"Have you ever met an elephant?"

"I have."

"They seem such odd creatures. Those long noses . . .

what do you suppose they do with them while they sleep? I think they must roll over on them. I rolled over on my braid once and couldn't move for an hour. I was stuck like a turtle on his back. Zander had to push me out of bed. I had to yell simply forever. Now I tie my braids to the headboard. It's ever so much safer."

Aaron smiled down at the littlest Worthington. "Elephants are not the oddest creatures I've met in my travels."

He raised his gaze to look down the spacious hallway again. Something warm glowed deep in his belly He wasn't an idiot. Obviously Elektra had done it for his benefit, and he didn't think she was looking for praise. She had done it so that he needn't fear for his life stumbling over books in the dark. She done it for Attie, to show her that there was another way to live—one that did not necessarily include clutter and obstacles and madness.

He had been so wrong. She was not shallow, or selfishly ambitious. It was her family she climbed for, that she scratched and clawed and fought for.

That she'd kidnapped and kissed a stranger for.

What would it be like, he wondered, as a man who had been run from his home by his own family, to have that sort of loyalty and determination directed his way?

Dinner at Worthington House. Aaron thought that everyone should experience it at least once. It would save so much time in lengthy description.

The food was not fine, first of all. It was well cooked, and it was filling, and there was some attempt to enliven the plainness with fresh herbs from the garden—

which he'd seen, and which he wouldn't brave without a machete and local guide!—but there was no hiding the pedestrian nature of the meal.

Most of the Worthingtons partook heartily. The food disappeared from the platters quickly, and no one but Aaron seemed to notice that two of the elegant but badly chipped and crackled plates were scarcely sullied by contact with food.

One belonged to the silent Lysander. Oh, he put on a decent show. Aaron saw him chewing and swallowing a few times, but for the rest of the dinner he merely moved items from one side of his plate to the other, cutting them smaller and smaller with each go. Clearly, he'd had a great deal of practice at this particular subterfuge.

The other plate belonged to Elektra. This surprised Aaron, for he'd seen her tuck into the meat and potatoes at the inn on the road home. Neither Elektra nor Bliss had let a shred of that meal go to waste.

Now, however, Elektra took no meat at all, and only a little of the vegetables and gravy and a single small chunk of bread.

Vanity was his first thought. Then he caught himself in that uncharitable assessment as he saw her push another bit of roast onto Attie's plate, urging her little sister to put down her book and finish her meal.

She is too thin to pass her food to another.

There was something going on here, something that had nothing to do with vanity or fitting into a ballgown.

Whatever it was, it was not his concern. He would soon be on his way. The secrets in this house might drown a fellow if he hung about too long.

Chapter Fourteen

After dinner together, Aaron had supposed the Worthington family might gather in the drawing room for cards or some such. Instead, Cas escorted his wife to their chamber to rest, then took himself off to the workshop in the stable.

Iris and Archie decided on a stroll about the moonlit garden, now that the rains had passed. Orion disappeared into his hellhole of a study, and Dade shut the door on his as well. Lysander simply disappeared, there one moment, silently gone the next.

Bliss excused herself, pleading the need to see to Bianca. Aaron rather thought Bliss didn't trust Lard-Arse. On second thought, perhaps she was wise not to.

Aaron looked at the shattered mess of the dining table where Attie sat alone, her plate pushed back, her book open on the table, with scarcely enough light in the stubs of candles in the tarnished pair of candelabras to see the words on the pages.

Elektra bustled through the room with Mrs. Philpott,

stacking plates and platters. Aaron blinked. Miss Elektra Worthington did the washing up?

Ten minutes later he found himself elbow-deep in hot water and potato peels, laughing at Mrs. Philpott's stories of the Worthingtons as children and cherishing the wearily grateful look Elektra had given him when he'd ordered her from the kitchen. He dared Attie to help him by implying that the water was much too hot for a child. She now stood next to him, enveloped in one of Philpott's aprons, listening wide-eyed as Aaron repaid the housekeeper with tales of the Bahamas and the other strange lands he'd seen.

It was fun, actually. As Lord Aaron, he would have scandalized the poor woman with his offer of immersing his noble hands into her soapsuds. Hastings, on the other hand, got a piece of toweling tied about his waist, a series of stories—although he didn't believe the one about the flaming bird for a minute!—and a cup of strange-tasting tea pushed into his hand.

He'd taken a single deep sip when Attie had leaned close and whispered in his ear. "I wouldn't. I really, really wouldn't."

He could hardly spit it out, so he swallowed manfully, smiled and thanked the woman, then left her to sip her own cup in her rocker by the fire. He dragged Attie into the larder.

"What's in the tea?"

Attie gave him an arch look that reminded him of Elektra in a mood. Oh, hell. "What did I drink, Miss Attie?"

She folded her arms. "Have you ever heard of Dr. Philpott's Cure-All? It's available all over England."

Aaron shook his head. It felt a bit disconnected from his neck. "I've been far away, haven't I? What is it?"

Attie wrinkled her freckled nose. "I think you're about to find out. Don't worry. You'll be fine as long as you don't go riding or use sharp implements." She held out her finger to show him a half-inch glossy scar on the tip. "I tried to touch the flames. Watch out for the flames." She took her finger back and gazed at it with critical consideration. "It didn't scar very much. It felt much worse than this at the time."

Aaron watched the little girl turn and walk down the hall away from him. Her light footfalls seemed to echo oddly in his mind. He turned back to the kitchen, determined to get a straight answer from Mrs. Philpott, but she only smiled dreamily as she rocked and rocked in her chair, her gaze locked on the fire in the hearth. On the little table next to her was a cup with dark leaves floating in the dregs.

Aaron turned away, carefully not looking at the flames.

This time it was easy to find his way to his room. All he had to do was to wander down the only open, uncluttered space in the house. Aaron dreamily spread out his arms and let his fingertips just brush each wall. If he weren't so weary, he would run down it, just because he could.

His room was the end. Just as he approached the door, it opened and Elektra emerged.

She was in my room.

I wish she would stay in my room. Aaron smiled at his insane but lovely Elektra.

Turning at his approach, she blinked at him in startlement. "Mr. Hastings! I was just—" She waved a hand at the closed door to his room. "Candles! And—and a fresh pitcher for your washbasin—" She stopped speaking and swallowed. Hard. He saw her throat contract. Such a pretty throat.

"Thanks for that, miss." He spread his arms again. "And thanks for this as well." He gestured at the lovely pile of nothing in the hallway. "You didn't need to do that for me."

Elektra didn't smile, because then Mr. Hastings would have known that she thought he was adorable when he was trying to be nice. So she only nodded somberly. "Yes, I hadn't realized it had become such a danger. Better you than Attie, I suppose."

He blinked at that, but could hardly disagree. "Aye, that wouldn't 'ave done at all."

She tilted her head. "So you see, it is you who should be thanked, for revealing a dangerous situation to us before a *Worthington* could be harmed." It was all she could do not to laugh when he twitched slightly.

Best to leave while they weren't yet arguing. Giving him a quick sisterly pat on the arm, she began to move past him.

When his big warm hand covered her own, she halted in her tracks. His palm tenderly flattened her hand on his bicep.

"Ye can let a bloke say thanks, Miss Elektra," he murmured almost in her ear.

The deep affectionate timbre of his voice resonated through her, vibrating down deep in her belly and making her heart stutter.

He moved a step closer to her until one half of his chest overlapped one half of her bosom, separated by mere inches. "Ye can say *yer welcome*, or even *'twas nothing*."

She parted her lips to give a breezy answer, but there was something wrong with her breathing and her mouth was just a bit dry—

His warm palm slid slowly down her bare forearm, his long fingers wrapping around and warming her skin. It was a touch both innocent and intensely exciting. Elektra had read a great deal on human reproduction at her mother's encouragement, but never had the words *stimulate* and *arouse* been so plainly defined.

It was clear that more research was in order.

She turned her palm upward, laying the back of her hand upon his sleeve to allow his work-roughened palm access to the sensitive skin inside her elbow. He took the hint quite neatly, but then, she'd never thought Mr. Hastings to be a stupid man.

The heat from his palm warmed the pale blue tracing of veins there, flowing directly into her blood and coursing through her, a hot, sweet injection of desire, the perfect medicine for a chilled, lonely heart. She closed her eyes against the rich infusion and it felt like falling, or perhaps flying . . .

His palm slid away and she nearly whimpered at the loss, until his warm fingertips began to stroke their way north along her upper arm, as if following that throbbing vein directly to her pounding heart.

Oh, yes. Yes, please.

Touch me. Feel me. See me.

Know me.

Here, alone in this crowded house, surrounded by everyone she loved to the point of hurting, her heart ached at the way this rough, outspoken man truly saw *her*.

His breathing had deepened as well. She could feel the heat of his exhalations on her bare cheek and throat. She tilted her head slightly to allow the warm sensations to flow over her throat and collarbone. This seemed to affect the tenor of that breath. She felt a faint moan emanate from him, or perhaps it was a growl. Then he bent to press his warm lips to a point perfectly between neck and shoulder.

Elektra couldn't remember when she'd dug her fingers into his sleeve, or when she'd reached for him with her other hand. All she knew was that his hair was hot silk sliding between her fingers as she pressed his mouth to her neck, to her shoulder, to her throat—

"No." She'd meant it to be a shout. It came out a whisper. A plea. She swallowed and tried again. "No." This time she managed a small step back.

He lifted his head. His gray eyes focused on hers. "I see the flames in your eyes," he whispered. "Attie warned me not to look into the flames."

Elektra froze. "Mr. Hastings? Did you drink the tea, Mr. Hastings?"

He blinked. She peered into his eyes and saw the size of his pupils. Her breath left her in a sigh that was half laugh and half sob. A man in the throes of Philpott's tea would likely kiss his own horse!

Thank goodness she'd stopped him!

I wish I hadn't stopped him.

The moment hung in the air. She breathed slowly and carefully.

Then she swallowed hard. "Off to bed with you, Mr. Hastings. Sleep well." She turned and walked toward the stairs. A strange ache bloomed in her belly at the loss of his warmth and shelter.

Although the hallway was level, she felt as if she climbed a steep mountain, such was the pull he exerted upon her.

Just keep climbing.

Left alone in the dim hallway outside his room, Aaron blinked in an effort to focus his oddly distorted vision. *No*, she'd said. *Sleep well*, she'd said.

Yes. She was right. He was . . . not himself at the moment. Even at his worst, he'd never been a man who would kiss a virgin in a darkened hall late at night. No, that wouldn't do at all.

She was a lady. She'd been most proper to stop him.

Or maybe she just didn't care for him at all. And what kind of well-bred girl toyed with a servant?

He shook his head, confused. Wait . . . was he angry because she didn't kiss him or because she almost did?

I have lost my mind in this madhouse. I have become just another inmate.

Elektra made it to her own room and closed the door softly before she allowed the trembling take her over.

Off to bed with you, Mr. Hastings.

Her own bed mocked her, for she knew she would not sleep well tonight.

You have no right to turn to him. You have no freedom to break convention and choose a man like that. To let him think anything else would be cruel beyond measure!

There were women who did. Not simply the ones taking a commoner as a secret lover, which according to Philpott's gossip happened every other Tuesday, but the other sort—the women who turned their backs on their worlds, who chose to be shunned by society, who gave it all up for the love of a man with rough working-man's hands and muscles not rendered by fencing practice.

Mr. Hastings would make a fine husband for any woman, she had no doubt. He was strong and chivalrous, in his irregular way, and he fulfilled his smallest promises as if they were holy vows.

If she became one of those women, she need not fear the loss of her family's regard. The Worthingtons might be irresponsible to the point of madness, but they only wished her to be happy, not titled or wealthy.

And what of Attie? If you allowed yourself to be as mad and irresponsible as the rest of them, what sort of options would that leave Attie?

A family already notorious, thrust into true scandal by her eldest sister wedding a strange, albeit wealthy, hermit. Her twin brothers recently involved in a scandal with a wicked widow—only Miranda wasn't wicked. Only a bit unwise, although that had come out all right in the end if one didn't count the loss of Miranda's large inheritance and the estrangement of Poll, who was everyone's favorite of the twins—

No. It all hinged upon her, Elektra. The family teetered on the edge of financial and social ruin, yes, but it had not passed the point of no return, not yet. She could bring them back, lift them up, return them to their past unity and happiness!

Or she could plunge them into an inescapable abyss of ruin. Her ill-considered choice could tip that crucial balance. Orion, Lysander, Poll—what decent woman would have them then?

Despite her doubts, her long journey and subsequent adventures, not to mention countless trips up and down the attic stairs, caught up with her in a tide of weariness that left the room spinning when she closed her eyes.

As she fell into the blackness of an exhausted slumber, she heard those words again.

I see the flames in your eyes.

His voice. There had been something different about his voice . . .

Elektra spent the early hours of the morning restoring her bedchamber to order after her adventures in Shropshire.

Adventure. Shropshire.

One didn't connect those two thoughts every day.

She didn't smile. Her mad mistake and subsequent acquaintance with Henry Hastings aside, that journey had cost her a prime opportunity to reach her original goal.

A goal only reinforced by last evening's lapse of judgment.

His touch. His heat. His mouth on her skin.

She put it firmly from her mind. No more of that nonsense.

When she had sorted out her dressing table, which she had left in a mess during packing—livid because some stranger cousin was on her way to parasitically attach herself to Elektra's Season!—she found a thick envelope addressed particularly to her.

An invitation. It must have arrived while she was gone. Philpott wasn't one to recall events of even a few hours past, so it was no wonder she hadn't mentioned it. Elektra slid her ivory opener beneath the wax seal, admittedly without any trace of excitement, to discover an announcement.

> *Lord Neville, Duke of Camberton, entreats your presence once more at his birthday revel, which has been regrettably delayed by inclement weather for those traveling from far parts to attend. The event has been rescheduled for Wednesday Night. His Grace begs your forgiveness for the inconvenience..*

Today was Wednesday. She had not missed it, after all. There still remained time to fix matters. For Attie's sake. For everyone's sake, including that of Mr. Hastings, who deserved better than to get himself into some impossible situation, fixing his attention upon her.

I am not free to suit myself.

If you were, are you quite sure a valet would suit you?

Yes. No.

Yes. She shook her head sharply. *I don't know—and there's no point to wondering, because I have no choice.*

Elektra lifted a book from her night table. From between the pages, she slid free a sheet of foolscap and unfolded it.

Lord Aaron Arbogast, heir to the Earl of Arbodean.
Underlined three times. The List.

She had missed her opportunity with Lord Aaron, of course. That entire debacle was best not thought on too long. Slowly her gaze moved to the next name, which had once been the first name.

Lord Neville, Duke of Camberton.

How could she have lost her focus so completely?

Of course, Bliss's arrival had interrupted all of Elektra's carefully laid plans to entrap . . . er, interest the duke. However, now that she thought about it, Bliss might very well serve a higher purpose indeed.

Elektra put all thought of Mr. Hastings from her mind and strode purposefully from her bedchamber. Bliss had taken over the larger room that had once been Callie's, two doors down on the left.

The door stood open and Elektra saw Bliss, who was of course an early riser, sorting hatboxes onto a teetering pile already atop the wardrobe, humming contentedly.

Without preamble, Elektra narrowed her eyes and pounced.

"I don't suppose you brought something suitable for the Duke of Camberton's ball?"

Bliss turned to her with a serene expression. In her hands she held two perfectly perfect bonnets, each more cunning than the other. "Why, cousin—"

Elektra closed her eyes. "Sorry. Silly question."

Chapter Fifteen

Aaron rolled over in his sleep and there was room. He stretched his legs out long, and there was room. The simple luxury of sleeping with a straight spine made him want to laugh out loud in purest gratitude.

A real bed. A true night's sleep. He stretched again, luxuriating in the length and breadth of an actual bed.

Oddly, he had no recollection of going to sleep.

He opened his eyes to gaze about the small chamber, still dusty and cluttered as it had been yesterday afternoon when he'd woken from his book-avalanche-induced nap to see Elektra and the cleared hallway . . .

Elektra in the hallway.

Oh, God. He sat up straight in bed. That had been a dream, hadn't it? It had a sort of smeary fog to it, like a dream . . .

Except he could still taste the silken skin of her neck.

He swung his feet to the floor and noted dully that

he had lain down fully clothed, right down to his once fine but now much-battered boots.

The damned tea.

He didn't know what was in that abominable brew, but a single sip had hit him like a brick to the skull. He recalled the floating, unreal quality to his vision . . . and the incredible sensitivity of his other senses.

He could still smell jasmine.

So, it was real. He had accosted the daughter of his host in a darkened hall. The gentleman's code of honor demanded that he confess at once and fling himself upon the mercy of Archimedes Worthington. That wouldn't be so bad. Archie was a good sort, if a vague and dreamy patriarch.

It was Daedalus who would muck it all up. Matters would definitely come to blows—if not swords or pistols! Aaron rubbed his face, recalling Elektra's ancient pistol, the family heirloom. It threw a huge lead ball with great force but poor accuracy.

If he fired it, he might be able to intentionally miss Dade. Or he might kill him.

Hell, by the look of the thing, he'd be lucky not to take out two or three witnesses!

Or you could just marry the girl.

Aaron swallowed hard.

Marry her?

Wed Elektra.

Wake up to tropical-sea eyes and sunlight hair every morning of his life, until time transmuted the gold to silver . . .

Yes. Oh, yes please!

It would cost him. God, would it cost him. A quick, scandalous match with the First Family of the Peculiar would erode the last thread of possibility of reclaiming his inheritance from the highly conservative earl. Aaron tried to imagine introducing rumpled, Shakespeare-spouting Archie and dreamy, paint-spattered Iris to his haughty, patrician grandfather. *Your new relations, my lord.*

Oh, hell. *Attie.* Would she curtsy with a scowl, spreading the skirts of her too-large dress, dipping her jumbled tassel of braids to the floor? Would his grandfather freeze like a block of ice, as Aaron had seen him do from time to time—too highborn to overlook such oddity, too well mannered to show his disdain?

Protective anger surged through him, directed toward anyone who would pour scorn upon Attie's tangled little head. Or would it be much worse than that?

Grandpapa is still fragile. Any upset could set him back.

Well, this ought to do it. Aaron fought the slightly hysterical need to laugh.

In his incompetent hands, Arbodean might very well crumble into ivy-twined rubble, as Worthington Manor had. Perhaps, if he worked very hard for the rest of his life and had just a tiny bit of good fortune—no flood, flame, or pestilence, for example—it was possible that it would not happen.

At least, not in his lifetime. Perhaps that was the best any man could hope for.

Once he'd risen and made himself as presentable as possible, thankful indeed for the washbasin Elektra had so thoughtfully provided, Aaron set out to throw himself upon the mercy of Mr. Archimedes Worthington, patron saint of madwomen and hooligans.

Oddly, he found himself whistling.

Aaron opened his door and turned down the hall toward the stairs.

He stopped at the sight of a rolling ball of skirts coming down the hall in his direction.

It was a lumpy sort of ball, the kind with bony knees and pointy elbows and the odd red-amber braid trailing behind upon the elderly carpet.

Attie's somersaulting path led her nearly to Aaron's feet. This left her sprawled on her back at his feet, gazing up at him. He blinked down at her in silence. He'd already come to understand that, as with a cat, it was best to let Attie begin each encounter on her own terms.

She considered him for a long moment. Then she wrinkled her nose. "You sleep quite late for a servant."

Heaven save him from an observant child.

"Had a rough day, didn't I? You stepped on me, you know."

Attie scowled fiercely at him. It was quite an intimidating glower, or it would have been if not for the ridiculous angle.

"It's rude of you to remind a lady of a mistake."

Time for a subject change. "Where is everyone?"

"You mean, where is Ellie?"

Aaron didn't deny it. Those otherworldly green eyes saw far too much as it was. He didn't care to try her perceptiveness further.

Attie rolled her eyes dramatically and flopped back on

the carpet in abandoned boredom. "She and Bliss are getting ready for a ball tonight. Ellie is scouting out some duke she's had her eye on, I suppose. *I* was not invited."

A ball. With a duke.

"A duke beats an earl."

Attie smirked. "My sister will be the most beautiful duchess in England." Then her odd little pointy face fell. "Does that mean she'll have to go live in some old stinky castle? I wouldn't go, if I were her. Castles have bats. And . . . and . . ."

"Ghosts?" Aaron offered helpfully, though for the life of him he didn't know why. Of course, Elektra would be flinging herself back into the breaches, eternally ready to sacrifice herself for her family's return to glory.

You won't give her glory. You have a title and a doomed estate—and enough notoriety to drown even Attie's chances of that golden future.

Aaron swallowed. Perhaps, before he made his confession and forced Elektra's hand, he ought to consider her wishes.

If he cost her this chance, she would never forgive him. A lifetime with a happy Elektra was a tantalizing vision. A lifetime with a furious, betrayed Elektra?

Aaron shuddered. Then he noticed Attie's gaze sharpening on his face. Subject change. "Are you trainin' for the circus, then?" *I hear they can always use more monkeys.*

Her expression soured as if she had heard his thought. "I believe there is a slope of at least five degrees from this end of the hallway descending toward the stairs."

"Hm." Aaron tilted his head severely to squint down

the hall carpet. "I don't agree. It looks entirely level to me."

Her green eyes took on an evil tint. "Opinion is worth nothing. Where is your evidence?"

That was how Aaron came to be somersaulting up and down the hall just when Elektra mounted the stairs with her brothers Orion and Dade.

Aaron froze in the middle of a roll, which only had the unfortunate effect of toppling him sideways—quite possibly the only way he could have looked any more ridiculous at that moment.

Daedalus Worthington had obviously spent some time perfecting his expression of exasperation, for he was very good at it. He turned on the spot and walked away, returning down the stairs whence he had come.

Elektra's mouth quirked in amusement even as her brows rose in disapproval at Aaron's antics. Orion merely gazed at him as if he were a not-particularly-interesting insect.

Yet Aaron couldn't help grinning as he rose to his feet, dusting off the seat of his trousers and running his other hand through his tousled hair.

"It's the 'allway—" he began, but Orion turned to Attie.

"I perceive an altitude variation of four degrees," he stated to his youngest sibling, just as if debating with someone of his own scholarly stature.

Attie shook her head. "Five, at the very least."

Aaron, who had indeed observed that it was slightly more difficult to tumble up the hall than down, nodded sagely, but had nothing more specific to offer to the discussion, which quickly became heated when Attie dared her elder brother to produce his own evidence.

Elektra stepped forward and tucked one hand through Aaron's arm. "Mr. Hastings, why don't we step aside and let them thrash it out. It could take hours, or even days. I daresay we'll find them rolling down every hallway in the house for the next week, plotting out the altitudinal variations of the scullery versus the kitchen hearth."

Aaron laughed and willingly allowed himself to be led away. "I was afraid to tell 'em that I only noticed a three-degree drop!"

Elektra flashed him a smile of such mischief and laughter that Aaron found himself descending the stairs quite short of breath, dizzied not by the height but by the new, playful Elektra.

Would he never plumb the depths of this unexpected creature?

Er, perhaps he ought to rephrase that thought, even in the privacy of his own mind!

"I have a favor to beg of you, Mr. Hastings."

Aaron inclined his head. "Anythin' for you, miss."

"I must visit my dressmaker and I cannot seem to dislodge any of my brothers from their activities to escort me. Would you mind terribly?"

Since he rather thought he'd be willing to face a dragon or three to see that smile again, he nodded mutely. His reward came at once. There it was, like a wash of light on a diamond.

She left him at the bottom of the stairs, begging his patience while she fetched her wrap.

As Aaron blinked away the visual afterimage of that

fey grin, he wondered how many times Elektra had been left to fend for herself by her brothers.

Elektra found she actually didn't mind having Mr. Hastings's company on her errand. When he wasn't waxing judgmental, he could be an interesting and amusing companion. The fact that he was handsome—and broadshouldered, and rather deliciously tall, and that she continued to have startling memories of his hot, exciting mouth on hers—well, that had nothing to do with it.

He was a convenient escort, one who did not seem impatient as her brothers so often did, and she was able to go about London without waiting for Orion to finish his dissection of something with too many legs, or for Lysander to snap out of his brooding, or for Dade to find the time out of his busy, busy day.

They had nothing to fear. They were men. They could simply stand up and walk from the house on a whim. They needn't change their clothes or consider the propriety—and danger, for this was London!—of going about alone.

And she didn't wish to take Iris, who would dawdle endlessly and flirt with every male above the age of— well, her mother had a way with men of any age, frankly. They seemed to find her either adorably helpless or adorably dotty or in the case of Elektra's father, Archimedes Worthington, simply adorable.

Elektra had never quite managed to carry off *adorable*. She always seemed to garner adjectives such as *striking* or *stunning* or other such faintly violent words— not that she read any such thing into the world's opinion of her. What should she care?

If something wasn't going to help her achieve her goals for the Worthington name, she refused to waste a single second of her life upon it.

Still . . .

"Mr. Hastings, if you were to define me in one word, what would it be?"

"Complicated," he replied absently. Then he seemed to truly hear the question and, subsequently, his answer. His expression took on a sudden pallor and she could have sworn he flinched a bit.

"I'm sorry, miss. That weren't very gentlemanly of me. I mean to say . . . er . . . multifaceted. Yes, that's the very word, it is. Multifaceted, like . . . a diamond!"

She narrowed her eyes. "You think I'm hard."

He blinked and seemed inclined to move away a step, although he staunchly stayed by her side, just with a slightly larger space between them.

"Not the hard part—I mean, you see, the shiny part."

"So you think I'm gaudy? Obvious?" Now she was just having fun with his visible terror. Men were so easy. "Sharp?"

He must have had enough at that point, for he stopped cold in the middle of the walkway and turned to her.

"You aren't any harder than a soldier in a war and ye aren't any more obvious than a diplomat fighting for peace. Ye may think you're foolin' the world with this, this . . ." He waved his hands about her. "This façade, this foolish, shallow, social-climbing veneer—"

Elektra's belly went cold at his words. Could it be that this man, this irreverent, poorly trained servant, could see what she'd ensured that no one else in the world could perceive?

Her chin went up and she was about to cut him dead, but then he said the single thing she'd never, ever heard from anyone's lips in her life.

"But, well, I think it's just plain magnificent the way you look after that house of bedlam and everyone in it!"

He nodded as if he'd finally said something he'd been dying to get off his chest, then he bowed and gestured her onward, following at the discreet distance of the perfect manservant. She had no choice but to breathlessly turn and continue her errand, as if the world had not just upended itself and the sky turned green and the trees blue!

How could this be?

If anyone had told her a month ago that she would meet a man who truly understood her, she would have laughed bitterly and assured them that they were soon for the madhouse. No one but her dressmaker grasped her real reasons for the devastating wardrobe, for the haughty demeanor, for the practiced perfection of her face and form.

When one had a purebred horse for sale, one groomed it within an inch of its life. When one had a pretty daughter and an empty bank account, one—if one were not Iris or Archie Worthington—dressed her up for market and displayed her to her best advantage.

To everyone's best advantage.

How terrible to discover the single man in the world—who was not a dressmaker!—who understood her, and then to have that man be as far away from her socially as a draft horse was to the aforementioned thoroughbred filly.

Torn between joy at such a discovery—Mr. Hastings!—and rage at its impossibility—Mr. Hastings!—Elektra found herself quite without words for the rest of their short journey to Bond Street.

The shop of Lementeur—if one wished to designate such a fountain of beauty and style as a mere "shop"!—was completely discreet. There were impressively carved doors, inscribed with the trademark looping *L* that graced the dress boxes and hatboxes and glove boxes that made every woman in London swoon. These opened with soundless polish as if pushed by magical simultaneous hands, and Elektra strolled into one of her favorite places on earth—although not for the reasons that most people would think.

This shop was the workplace and home of a man she thought of as a benevolent uncle, or perhaps benevolent wizard, or sometimes as simply one of the two—perhaps now three!—people in the world who understood her.

A perfectly beautiful young man stepped forward and bowed deeply. "Miss Worthington."

Elektra dipped a gracious nod. "Cabot." She looked about the shop, which was really just the public face of a much more complex operation within. "Is Himself about?"

Cabot didn't smile at her irreverence, but merely nodded. "Of course. He would never miss an appointment with you, Miss Worthington."

Mr. Hastings was staring about at the surroundings with the appalled face of a man who was more comfortable waist-deep in danger and adventure than standing

in a forest of lace and silk and well, she had forgotten
about that particular display of unmentionables . . .

Elektra Worthington was laughing at him. Aaron
knew it, even as he knew that the tall, lean fellow was
hiding great amusement behind those cool gray eyes as
he escorted Elektra away.

Aaron also knew that he was completely out of his
depth at this moment. Although he'd once walked Bond
Street with its tailors and dressmakers and drapers, it
had been a very long time since he had done more than
purchase the barest necessities.

Then again, to Miss Worthington and probably many
women in Society, the creations of this Lementeur fellow were considered necessities!

Chapter Sixteen

Elektra had always felt comfortable with Cabot. They had a lot in common, after all. They were both attractive, both cynical, and both pursued by men.

The greatest difference between them, other than the obvious dispersal of parts, was that despite his world-weary demeanor and his impenetrable severity, Cabot still believed in love.

One only had to watch his cool gray eyes follow his small, mischievous master to see the complete devotion burning within him.

One had to wonder why Mr. Button couldn't see it, not one little bit.

There was a time a few months ago when Elektra could have sworn that something happened between the famed Lementeur and his protégé. Cabot had seemed . . . happy? . . . well, perhaps hopeful.

Now there was a haze of sadness in those misty evening eyes that made Elektra's heart ache for him. For them both, actually. She didn't understand why Button didn't simply fall in love, when love was just waiting there to catch him!

She would kill for just that chance—

Except that her heart wasn't anything anyone would actually want. Not like the kindhearted Button, or the faithful Cabot.

Or even the chivalrous Mr. Hastings, who could have ruined her with a word, yet kept his silence with no expectation of reward.

Whereas she herself had lost count of her own lies and deceptions and manipulations. Her own family thought her shallow and vain. The world thought of her in pointed praise that never actually included words like *sweet* or *good*.

I am not good, I am . . . indomitable.

How about "just plain magnificent"?

An afterthought, surely. A stretch of the imagination when she'd teased him for calling her "complicated."

It didn't matter what Mr. Hastings thought, anyway. It only mattered what Lord Neville thought.

Cabot walked Elektra deeper into the sacred halls of fashion. "And your master plan? It goes well?"

Elektra indulged in an unladylike shrug. Cabot never judged. "I am hoping to permanently fix the attentions of the Duke of Camberton tonight."

"You sound deeply thrilled at the prospect."

Elektra had to smile. No one did irony like Cabot. "I know. I cannot help it. Things have changed. Nothing . . . nothing is the same since I returned from Shropshire."

Cabot never smirked, but his lips twitched. "I hear Shropshire can do that. Catastrophic levels of peace and quiet. It's disturbing to one's equilibrium." Then, as he opened the door to the grand showroom, where many ladies, duchesses, and the occasional princess had their gowns revealed to them with appropriate pomp and circumstance, he turned to her. "Nothing in London has changed in the last week. If there is a difference, you might want to look within, rather than without."

She bowed her head. "I shall ponder your words, O wise one."

"Mockery, for my pains. Very well. In you go. And please remind him that he needs to eat sometimes."

When Elektra entered the "gallery"—which was what Lementeur called his showroom—she found a short, slight, pointy-featured fellow dressed in utmost perfection, with not a hair out of place, standing in the center of the room regarding the ceiling most intently.

Elektra did what everyone does when they see someone staring at something. She followed his gaze upward, where she saw a brand-new fresco worked into the plaster of the domed ceiling.

It was a beautifully rendered blue sky with fluffy clouds fringed with heavenly golden light. Peeking around the edges of some of the clouds was a trio of cherubs wearing nothing but mischievous grins, quivers filled with golden arrows, and some strategically placed cloud-wisps.

The artist had done more than supply the grand room with a grand ceiling, like icing roses on a wedding cake. He had also managed to imbue the three cupids with expressions of twinkling mischief and relentless cheer that reminded Elektra rather forcibly of the establishment's owner.

"I don't know what it is," the small man said. "There's just something about those cherubs." He scowled comically, though he might not have realized it. "I don't trust them."

"Well, then, I suppose you should keep your eye on them." Elektra came to stand next to him and tilted her head back to gain his perspective. "Truly a nefarious bunch," she agreed.

"Hmph." He lowered his gaze and fixed it upon her, beaming as if she were a gift wrapped in green silk and peppermint sticks. "What can I do for you, my child, my flower, my darling muse?"

Elektra might have been a little more flattered if she hadn't seen Bliss's swoon-worthy wardrobe not an hour past. Still, her dearest Uncle Button loved her to tiny little pieces, she knew. "It is the Duke of Camberton's revel tonight. I wished to consult with you over my gown."

"I'd heard he rescheduled." The small man's eyes crinkled in glee. "High on The List, is Lord Neville?"

Elektra managed a smile, though she couldn't seem to capture her former . . . intensity regarding the hunt. "I wonder . . . there's a particular color of blue."

She told him of the meadow full of butterflies. As she described the rush of wings, she found herself longing to be back there, even doused and filthy as she'd been. It was such a single shining moment, there among the magical fluttering blue butterflies . . . running through the tall grass with Mr. Hastings, handsome and laughing in the sunlight, feeling invincible after their brush with danger, feeling . . . happy.

"Ah!" Button listened rapturously. "I know the precise color!" Then his face fell. "I cannot possibly have something new ready for you tonight, my pet."

Elektra swallowed and shook her head. "No, of course not. It was only a silly thought." She lifted her chin and forced her thoughts back to practicalities. "What does the Bond Street rumor mill have to say about His Grace's wardrobe this evening?"

Button tapped his fingertips together as he tilted his head back to gaze at the frescoed ceiling. "He favors purples in his own dress. His tailor just finished a new fancy-dress weskit for him yesterday that is the precise color of wine grapes."

Elektra nodded. "So, the violet silk, do you think?"

Button frowned, as if the ceiling had done something rather naughty. "You wore that to the Whittingtons' reception three weeks ago."

"Well, it was very well received." Elektra had no illusions about being able to afford something new. As it was, everything truly fine that she owned had been a gift from this man. An investment, he'd called it. She would land a brilliant match and become the fashion plate of Society, wearing only Lementeur, of course. He would rake in the boodle and become richer than Prince George.

Elektra had accepted the "investment" at the time because she had no choice. She would not beggar her friends in her quest . . . unless of course, she had to.

Lementeur waved a hand impatiently at the cherubs above him. Naughty cherubs. "It won't do. Send the dress 'round and I'll kerfuffle it. No one will be the wiser."

Elektra folded her arms and gazed at her dearest

friend. "Mr. Button, you'll not skip your dinner just to 'kerfuffle' a gown for me."

Button finally tore his disapproving gaze from the ceiling to smile at her. "Of course not, my darling!" He gave her wrist a little pat. "I'll have Cabot do it."

When Elektra left Aaron to cool his heels in the foyer, he toyed with the idea of being annoyed at being treated like a servant. Then he reminded himself that even the Prince Regent himself didn't get to follow a lady into her dressing room—at least, he ought not to!

So he folded his hands behind his back and picked out a focal point—a bright yellow drape of silk across the room. It reminded him of Bahamian sunlight, or the inside of a ripe lemon, or the flame of a torch stuck down into the sand—

"Who are you?"

That Cabot fellow was one stealthy bastard! Somehow he'd managed to reenter the room and make his way within arm's reach of Aaron without him knowing it.

Now the man stood there, gazing at Aaron as if he was still deciding whether to let him in or throw him out. The master's guard dog, apparently. Aaron would have liked to dismiss the fellow as a mincing tailor who'd never lifted anything heavier than needle and thread, but this Cabot fellow moved like a man who had seen his share of violence and come out on the winning side, or at least come out to fight another day.

"Dark edges," Aaron said aloud.

"I beg your pardon?"

Aaron turned to face Cabot fully and looked him up

and down. "You 'ave dark edges, you do. Like the light don't go all the way 'round. You cleaned yourself up, but shadows don't wash off. My money's on you in a back-alley brawl, any day."

Cabot's eerie gray eyes narrowed slightly. "And your own shadows, my lord? Having any luck cleaning them away?"

Aaron drew back. "What's this 'my lord' business, eh? I'm a workin' man!"

Something that might have passed as a smile to someone more innocent crossed Cabot's face as he offered a short bow of apology. "My mistake . . . Mr. Hastings."

Then he straightened and shot Aaron a look that sent a chill up Aaron's neck. "You'll be moving on soon, then? Away from Worthington House?"

Away from Elektra, he meant. Aaron admired the bloke's loyalty even as he mentally threw up his hands at the way everyone assumed he was after something he had no right to. He was *protecting* Elektra—from *herself*!

So he folded his arms and gave Cabot an equally—he hoped, although his own gray eyes weren't particularly eerie—chilling look. "If the rest o' you would stop 'elpin' 'er sell 'erself off like a prize cow, I might could move on a bit sooner."

Cabot didn't blink. "She knows what she's doing."

Aaron rolled his eyes. "She's madder than a cat with a Chinese rocket tied to its tail! She's bound to—"

"She's bound to save her house and name. She sees it as the answer, the only way to bring her family back. It is a worthy cause. Can you not see the point of her sacrifice?"

Aaron looked away. "Aye. 'Tis a shame, is all. She's . . . she's . . ." He threw out his hands.

Cabot tilted his head. "I have known her for some time now. If she were a man, she could build an empire. She has the strategic mind of a general and the strength of a fine sword, but she knows that her beauty is her only useful coin in this world and she means to spend it as advantageously as she can. If you knew the saga of the Worthington clan, you would not judge her."

Aaron eyed the younger man silently. He seemed inscrutable, as cool and unconcerned as Michelangelo's *David*. Yet Aaron could feel the intensity radiating from the fellow. "What's this 'saga,' then?"

And without any more prompting than that, Cabot spilled the story.

"It began with the destruction of the manor, of course, fourteen years ago. One of the children playing with fire, it seems. Archie and Iris have a small but respectable income, a royal pension in fact—don't ask me the details of that, for I do not know—but it will never amount to enough to rebuild the manor. The estate itself is not large at all, and takes in few rents. Still, the family counted themselves lucky that everyone survived and moved into the London residence permanently."

Aaron thought of Worthington House, of the mad jumble of furnishings and treasures, and mountains of books. It wasn't a hoard, nor an accumulation of rubbish. It was simply all that could be saved.

"However, that night took a toll on Iris, who was expecting Miss Atalanta at the time. She'd had a very difficult time with the twins, as one could imagine, and she was greatly weakened by the subsequent children.

She nearly died giving birth to Miss Atalanta, and remained weak and ill for years afterward. Miss Calliope raised her tiny sisters herself. She was ten years old."

That explained a great deal about Attie. Aaron thought of little Elektra, who had been a mere five years at the time.

"However, Iris did recover eventually, and matters were calm for a time. Then Lysander went to war. A few months later, he was declared dead. That was when Iris began to truly slip away."

Aaron drew in a slow breath. "Only 'e's not dead."

"No, he yet breathes. Whether he *lives* remains to be seen. When he was finally properly identified, it was discovered that he'd been unconscious for several months in a war hospital, not expected to survive. Head injury, perhaps. No one actually knows. Papers mislaid, physician and nurses moving on. Wartime. However, he survived. He was simply asleep, and then one day, he woke up screaming. They sent him home, where he continued to scream for several months."

Aaron passed a hand over his face, thinking of Elektra, still in the schoolroom, losing her mother further by the day, listening to those screams resounding through her broken house. And Attie? Had she ever known anything but mayhem?

"Iris never quite came back to reality. Archie, though a loving father, is a rather ineffectual dreamer."

Aaron harrumphed. "And most of the rest of them 'aven't the sense to come in out o' the rain."

"But not Miss Elektra. She is far more acquainted with the realities of the world. Of course, what she truly desires is her family back, not social standing for herself."

"Aye, I'd gathered that much. But why should she think she's the only one who can fix them?"

"Because Elektra is the one who—"

"The one who what?"

Aaron started. Elektra had simply appeared next to them. *Are there secret doorways in this place?*

Cabot bowed deeply. "The one who will cap the match of the Season, of course. Your Grace."

Elektra did not look as pleased at being thus addressed as Aaron might have imagined. "Time will tell," she replied tightly. Then she turned a more pleasant expression upon Aaron.

"Mr. Hastings, I am possessed of a longing for an ice. Shall we?"

"Aye, miss." Aaron bowed her through the door, only too glad to leave Cabot's disturbing presence.

When he glanced back, he saw that eerie gaze following him, assessing him still.

"I don't understand how you can be so certain this will work."

Button looked up to see Cabot, carrying the tray that contained Button's afternoon tea, standing in the doorway of Button's office. This tiny room, mostly filled by a desk and chair, papered in sketches, piled with samples, was Button's mental storehouse, his inner sanctum, the flaming white-hot center of his creativity—where he'd been staring at a blank sheet of paper for over an hour.

Button sat silently for a moment, as if ruminating over Cabot's question, when in actuality he was wondering if he would ever get over that first little flip of joy when laying eyes upon the beauty and grace that was Cabot.

He'd once almost convinced himself that it was only the charming dew of youth that caught his eye, like admiring a long-legged colt, or an oversized pup running free in the park. Everyone liked to look at lovely, young things, full of life and glowing with energy, did they not?

And Cabot glowed more than most.

That lost young man, barely old enough to be called a man, ragged and starving, whom Button had caught robbing his little shop almost a decade ago, had spilled his bag of loot to reveal only the very best of Button's wares, unerringly selected with instinctive taste and style.

Button, being Button, had felt an obligation to sponsor such natural-born talent to its fullest fruition, and had taken in the skinny, frightened nineteen-year-old thief as his protégé. He'd only realized his own danger when daylight and bathing and a few good meals had removed the skulking, shadowed desperation to reveal that his new assistant was quite mind-bogglingly gorgeous.

Thus the theory of "youth as beauty" had been formed.

When years had passed and the effect had not worn off, Button was forced to admit that it was not simply youth, or even perfection of symmetry of jaw and cheekbone, although Cabot had that in shiploads.

It was, he decided in the end, simply the distilled Cabot-ness of Cabot. It was in the way he turned his head, in the way he lifted his hand, in the subtle casts of mist and storm cloud in his gray eyes, in his voice when he spoke only to Button—

All that ran through Button's mind, as it often did, in the blink of an eye, in the span of a breath, so it was the merest moment before he twinkled a mischievous smile at his assistant as Cabot set down the tray on a special small table next to Button that he'd long go ordered Button not to use for *anything else.*

Button looked away from the graceful competence of Cabot's long-fingered hands as his assistant arranged the tea set and spread his own hands wide with a confident expression. "Of course it will work! Why would it not?"

Cabot straightened and backed away a step from Button's expansive gesture. They were both so bloody cautious . . .

"Because Elektra is special," Cabot reminded him as he poured the tea. "Her life and her losses have taught her not just watchfulness, but suspicion. She sees around things. She has no patience with alleged coincidence and even less for the disastrous result of good intentions. If—when!—she sees through this—"

"She is but a child, Cabot!" Button laughed. "Truly intelligent and a manipulator-for-good after my own heart, but she is yet just a girl!"

Cabot gazed at him for a long moment. "Just because someone is young, does not make them an innocent, or an idiot. Just because someone has fewer years does not make them less of a person of substance and discernment."

Button knew that Cabot was referring to himself as

well as Elektra, but down that path lay danger to them both. So Button pretended, as he always did, that he had no idea of Cabot's true feelings.

"I daresay that Miss Elektra would be quite alarmed to hear it. She does work so hard to convince the world that she is nothing more than a pretty face."

He reached for the cup and saucer held in Cabot's extended hand, knowing it would be prepared as perfectly as if he'd done it himself, if not better. Cabot made sure everything in Button's life ran as smoothly as Chinese silk, the finely woven kind and not that nubby stuff from that inferior draper with the bushy mustache—

His fingertips stroked over Cabot's warm ones, quite by accident, in taking hold of the saucer. He jerked his hand away, breathless and shocked at the potent yearning that swept through him. Swallowing hard, he tried to turn the spasmodic movement into a casual wave at the little table. "Just put it there. I'll—I'll have it in a moment."

The dark flicker in Cabot's beautiful eyes lasted no more than an instant, a shadow passing before a silvery light of a distant lantern, but it stabbed Button like an icicle to the heart. If only. If only he were younger. If only Cabot were older. If he ever thought he could actually make a brilliant, beautiful young man like Cabot happy—

No, he would not take his assistant's gratitude and hero-worship as any more than it truly was. He would not take advantage of his position as mentor for his own satisfaction. Cabot was destined for greatness, perhaps even more so than himself! He would not hold him back. He would not hold him . . .

So he pretended not to see the pain and turned back to his blank sketchbook, hiding his pounding pulse and shortness of breath. "Now do let me concentrate, please. I must come up with some way to make the bodice of Mrs. Teagarden's opera gown play nicely with Mrs. Teagarden's bosom. A truly colossal task, I assure you!"

The tea tray rattled slightly and there came the merest brush of fabrics as Cabot turned away, but Cabot was a silently graceful person. Button carefully did not look up again until he was positive Cabot was gone. Then his gaze lingered on the empty doorway for far, far too long.

Chapter Seventeen

On the walk back to Worthington House, Aaron's mind was filled with the story Cabot had told him.

I can't give her what she needs.

He could only offer a title, attached to horrendous notoriety. She would honestly be better off with ordinary old Hastings than the publicly demonized Lord Aaron Arbogast. The marriage of a middling-high family member to someone of the lower classes might cause a whirl of gossip, but it would be short-lived. The new Mrs. Hastings, no matter who she'd once been, would fall from Society's sight like a stone into a pond. Ripples, yes, but ripples fade with time.

As Lady Arbogast, or even as the Duchess of Arbodean, she would live the rest of her life under the magnifying glass of Society's scrutiny. Everywhere she went, everywhere any of the Worthingtons went, people would turn their backs and whisper of poor Amelia Masterson, destroyed by Black Aaron, named after the tarnish on his vicious, depraved heart.

Aaron knew he'd never been forgotten. Even now, walking down a public London street, he kept his hat brim low and his eyes, quite properly as it happened, lowered. He dared not meet the gazes of any passersby on this fashionable street.

No, he could not do it to Elektra. He'd not realized it until this moment, but to ask it of any woman would be far too much. Not only would she be ostracized for the rest of her life, but so would her children.

His children.

God, he'd been so busy trying to turn himself about, to become the man he always should have been, to win back some semblance of approval in his grandfather's eyes that it had never once occurred to him that he would never truly succeed.

To Society in general, he would always be Black Aaron, the monster.

And he could never, ever reveal the facts of what had truly happened to Miss Amelia Masterson.

However, he could, and would, take his tarnished self as far as he possibly could from the woman at his side.

Just as soon as he knew she was safe.

Aaron began with pinning down each brother individually.

"What is your sister about?" he asked Orion. "Why is she so mad to land a duke?"

Orion lifted his gaze from the pages of the weighty tome on his desk. From where Aaron was standing, he could see detailed drawings of parts better left beneath the skin.

"I have no idea. I assume she knows what she's do-ing. She's more intelligent than people think."

That was all that was to be had from that source. Cas-tor was next.

The green-eyed man shrugged. "She's always been mad. I suppose she's a beauty, so she'll get by on that for a while. If she lands a title, she can stay as mad as she likes and no one will dare say boo to her." Cas fidgeted, eager to check on his lovely wife. "If you ask me, she'd do better to act a bit more like a lady, like Miranda."

Aaron regarded Cas's back sourly as he walked off. From what he already knew of Elektra, she could con-vincingly play a queen if it suited her. Who did her brothers see when they looked at her?

He didn't expect much response from Lysander, but asked anyway, being systematic. Zander surprised him greatly.

"She's in battle." Those three words seemed to come from some deep, strangled place within. Zander swal-lowed hard. "She's . . . a champion." Then he twitched slightly, shook himself, and walked away. Aaron stared after him with a frown.

Of course, it would be the maddest brother who un-derstood her best of all.

I understand her. What does that say about me?

Then Aaron turned his gaze upon the eldest, Dade. If there was anyone who ought to be looking after Elektra, it was he. Aaron wasn't going to leave her until he knew that someone—someone other than Zander the Undead!—knew what was truly happening inside that golden head of hers.

Someone who could help her, save her.

From herself.

He found Dade brooding in his study. The eldest Worthington looked up when Aaron entered, then frowned. "Yes, Hastings?"

It occurred to Aaron that Dade always spoke to him as if he were a servant. Elektra called him "Mr. Hastings" as if he were a guest.

He found himself irked by Dade's dismissive address, even though he himself called Hastings exactly that! For the first time, he wondered if that bothered Hastings—Mr. Hastings!—at all.

"It's the miss, sir. Miss Elektra, I mean. She's too thin." It would do for a start.

Dade blinked in surprise. "That's a tad on the personal side, don't you think, Hastings? Not really your place, I'd say."

Fortunately for Aaron, he was several rungs higher than Dade on the social ladder and therefore not in the slightest intimidated by such blather.

"Blather," he informed Dade. "Sir."

Dade's eyebrows rose nearly to his hairline. "I beg your pardon?"

"I take it back," Aaron went on. "You're right, it ain't my place, sir, because it's *your* place. You're the head of this madhouse. You don't look after her properly, I'd say."

Dade blinked, and surged to his feet in anger. Then he hesitated, doubt rising in his eyes, a look of regret crossing his face. He sank back into his seat and rubbed his eyes wearily. "I do try, you know. They are . . . unmanageable."

"Oy, I'll give you that, sir. A bigger bunch of maniacs were never born."

Dade drew back. "I didn't say that—"

"But that don't excuse Miss Elektra not eatin' proper."

Dade frowned. "I cannot help it if my sister is vain—"

"Vain?" Aaron sputtered. *Idiot!* "You're an idiot, sir! Your sister gives her meat to Miss Attie and her pudding to the expectant Mrs. Worthington because she fears they don't eat well enough!"

Dade stared at Aaron, his expression dumbstruck. "That—that can't be!"

Aaron folded his arms. "Then why did Miss Elektra tuck in like a farmhand on the road, then? And now she passes the roast meat right over her own plate and nibbles on bread and cheese? She's afraid there isn't enough to go around! All the while you louts eat like you're preparin' for your last battle."

Dade paled, not in fury at Aaron's tone, but in sudden realization. "That little idiot!" He rubbed his face with his hands. "It's my fault." He gazed at Aaron with guilty regret. "When she came to me for a dress allowance for her Season, I told her we barely had enough in the accounts to feed us all, much less throw away on fripperies that would be worn once and tossed aside."

"But it ain't true, is it?" Aaron scowled. "What'd you tell her that for?"

Dade blinked. "Because . . . well, she wanted *dresses*." He spread his hands, as if that explained everything.

Aaron shook his head sadly. "You're even more stupid than I thought, sir." He folded his arms. "Dresses ain't *dresses*! Dresses, for Miss Elektra, are *weapons*."

Even as he said it, he realized that it was true in so many ways. It was just as Lysander had said. Everything Elektra wore, or said, or did, was all part of her battle for the great glory of the Worthington family's future—for Attie's future, specifically!

Dade only looked confused. Aaron let out a breath. "I'm sittin' down, sir, because this is goin' to take a while."

"Cabot!"

The gown refurbishment for Miss Elektra had taken the greater part of Cabot's day. He was already approaching punctuality. Any more delay and he would be late—and he was *never* late.

Even so, Cabot stopped his fast pace and turned reluctantly. He knew that voice, though he'd not seen his friend Garrett in more than a year.

Slender, stylish, and supercilious, that was Garrett.

Garrett had been valet . . . er, *lady's maid* to Lady Alicia Lawrence before she had become the Duchess of Wyndham. Now Garrett served as chief gossipmonger and easily dismissed busybody . . . er, *spy* for that Liar's Club lot that Button had once been part of.

Garrett approached Cabot with a smile and a toss of his perfectly coiffed blond hair. "Cabot, you're looking very dapper today."

Cabot refused to allow himself to be charmed. It was only sunlight. it was only hair. He did not smile back. "I always look dapper. It is my job. Dapper is what I do. What do you want, Garrett?"

Garrett smiled, not put out in the slightest by Cabot's chilly greeting. That in itself was annoying. Everyone was put off by his aloofness. That *was* the point of aloofness, after all.

However, Garrett was a special case. He and Cabot had known each other long, long ago, when they'd both been street rats lurking on the edges of Bond Street, attracted by the fine togs and the possibilities available for a couple of handy pickpockets and petty thieves. Cabot had never been as deft as Garrett, but he'd been faster, so they'd both managed to stay ahead of the watch . . . at least, until Cabot had been caught by Button all those years ago.

Now Cabot was the assistant to the great Lementeur, gown designer to the rich and powerful and Garrett was little more than a snoop and a liar.

Well, a Liar, anyway. One of the that mingled pack of lords and louts that Button had once costumed for their forays into deception.

"How's the club, then, Garrett?" He might as well find out, for Button would want to hear the latest. Garrett was an acute observer and remarkably detailed tattletale. Cabot looked forward to repeating all the tastiest bits of news to Button. It might make his master smile.

In his own mind, Cabot was not afraid to admit that he lived for that smile.

But Garrett had other things on his mind. An offer.

"I need to talk to you about something. It's important. Come out with me, Cab. A wild night on the town, like the old days. There's a rout at Weatherly's, where there will not be single respectable soul in attendance. Or we can drink and dine at Mrs. Blythe's. You know she adores us. We are so very decorative."

Cabot remembered Mrs. Blythe very well. She ran a better-than-most establishment for naughty-minded toffs, but she treated her ladies well and her boys even better, so Cabot had no quarrel with the woman. In fact, she'd helped him out in the past, when he'd nearly run afoul of the law . . . but that was before Button.

Now he was an upright and proper citizen. He hadn't even . . . well, it had been years, to be truthful. And the gleam in Garrett's eye promised more than simply rambunctious companionship. Garrett was a generous and entertaining companion who was not inclined to get sentimental. If Cabot wanted to take the night off, Garrett would be the ideal playmate.

But how did one take the night off from love?

"I've duties to attend to," Cabot said stiffly. Garrett looked a little hurt, but Cabot wasn't too worried about his old friend. Garrett didn't lack for companionship, and he wouldn't stay hurt for longer than it took a squirrel to focus upon another nut.

Lucky Garrett.

It was the other offer, the stunning, outrageous, astounding offer, that he made next.

Cabot refused that one as well. He simply didn't think no would be an acceptable answer, not to the man who made the offer.

"Your loss, mate," Garrett informed him cheerfully. "You know where to find me if you change your mind."

Garrett ambled off, replacing his hat on his head with, of course, a jaunty tilt. For a moment, just an instant, Cabot envied him fiercely. To be free, to walk away from the constant ache in his chest, to turn love from pain back into play.

However, he had a place in the world. He had work, and responsibilities. He had Button's respect, and Button was obviously fond of him, in poor-orphan-boy sort of way.

Not precisely what Cabot had in mind.

Nevertheless, it was better than no Button at all.
Wasn't it?

At Worthington House, Cabot found Hastings first.
"Ah . . . sir. My master has a message for you."

Then it was the violet silk for Miss Elektra.

Hours later, in her bedchamber, Elektra gave herself one final glance in the mirror. Cabot stood behind her, hair ribbons still trailing from one hand, a vial of scent held in the other.

"I think this is the best I can do," Elektra tilted her head this way and that. "Do you think it is enough to win the Duke of Camberton's attention?"

"If he isn't looking at you, then he must be looking at me," Cabot said flatly. "You make me wish I admired girls."

Elektra turned to flash her dearest friend a delighted grin. "Cabot! That's the nicest thing any man has ever said to me!"

Cabot lifted a brow. "Wouldn't that send the eyebrows to the ceiling? You and I, stepping out together?"

Elektra's grin faded. "What's wrong? Something's wrong." She narrowed her eyes. "Tell me."

Cabot turned away and let the ribbons drift from his lax fingers to the top of the dressing table. "I think I may be going to the palace. The Prince Regent needs another dresser. It seems he broke the last one."

"Oh!" Elektra raised her hands to her cheeks in delight. Then, she let them fall. "Oh. Oh, dear."

"I do believe those were my exact words upon receiving the offer. Well, nearly, for I might have added a few harmless expletives."

Elektra bit her bottom lip. "Will you go? Will you truly leave him?"

Cabot turned back, but his gaze remained on his empty hand. "I believe the question is, will he let me refuse it? 'For your own good' and all that rubbish."

"But . . . he *needs* you," Elektra said delicately. "You know he does!"

"Does he?" Cabot looked up at last, and his lovely gray-mist eyes were the eyes of a man walking to the gallows. "Does he indeed?"

Elektra crossed her arms. *We shall see about this!*

Mr. Button was as dear to her as her own parents— but enough was enough! Her toe began to tap, rather in the fashion of her bossy older sister, Callie. When she realized it, she stilled the wayward foot, but forgot to erase the determined scowl from her features.

Cabot blinked and drew back slightly. "No."

"No what?" Elektra was still thinking furiously. When she got through with Button and his ridiculous notions of right and wrong and—

"No. No Worthington shenanigans! No outrageous plots involving mechanical geese or the twins clad as harlequins or some clockwork flaming phoenix!"

Elektra beamed her most innocent look at Cabot. "Why, how could I dress the twins as harlequins with Poll gone off to the Alps? Or has he reached Turkey yet?"

Cabot passed one hand over his eyes. "Just . . . just wait, please? I need to do a bit of serious thinking and I won't be able to if I'm worrying over a sudden delivery of a flock of monkeys!"

"It isn't called a flock, it's called a troop, or . . . well, I'll have to ask Orion. And anyway, it was only a single monkey and I only kept it for a day. Not at all nice, as I recall."

"Elektra? Promise me that you'll give me time."

"Well, there is this ball I must attend tonight. And then in the morning I expect I'll be receiving at least one important proposal. And then there will be my artfully but innocently worded acceptance to compose . . ." She let out a breath. "Very well. You have forty-eight hours. Then I will unleash the combined might of the entire clan upon his foolish head!"

"God." Cabot shuddered. "If I hadn't gone through a decade of impotent longing, I would almost feel sorry for him."

Elektra nodded shortly. "Confusion to the enemy, that's what Lysander . . . used to say."

She turned to gather up her fan and her shawl, already thinking about how to gain the stubbornly blind Button's undivided attention.

"Ellie."

She turned, startled. Even as close as they were, Cabot rarely used her family nickname. He stood there, with that slight crook in his lips that was the closest he ever really came to smiling, and then he bowed most formally. "You are brilliant and beautiful and your heart is more golden than you realize. You are more duchess than any duke deserves!"

Blinking back sudden moisture in her eyes, Elektra snapped her fan open flirtatiously before her face as she curtsied just as deeply. "Why, thank you for noticing, kind sir!" Then she stood and crisply shut her fan. "Now, a-hunting we will go."

Chapter Eighteen

In his own small room, Aaron tied the last knot in his cravat and turned slightly sideways to get a better look in the speckled mirror. "I haven't worn this kit before," he informed his observer. "What y'think?"

Where she sat on the floor, Atalanta Worthington stopped using Philpott's best shears to snip her brother Dade's third-best neck-cloth short enough to tie about her own neck and assessed Aaron's getup with an artistic squint. "You aren't fooling anyone, you know."

Aaron's belly did a little flip. He'd realized by now that sooner or later, Miss Elektra Worthington was going to discover his true identity. He was simply hoping he'd be safely miles away when that happened. Preferably in Scotland. Or maybe Finland.

Then his gut twisted slightly sideways at the thought of leaving Elektra miles behind him . . .

Pushing all that aside, he gave Attie one of Hastings's most mischievous smirks. "I'm foolin' everyone, all the time. Just like you."

Attie rubbed at the bridge of her nose. "Anyone can tell that you've dressed up like this before. I think you've been trying on his lordship's 'kit' behind his back!"

She'd wandered in after Aaron had donned everything but the neck-cloth, so she hadn't seen him struggling to button the extraordinarily fitted weskit. "Well, a valet's got to 'ave some all to do with 'is spare time!"

Attie lost interest in the cravat, now that she'd guaranteed a loud reaction from Dade, and crawled across the floor to where Aaron had laid out his coat over the chair by the fire.

"Get away from that with them scissors, you!" Aaron could move quite fast when necessary. He secured the shears on a high shelf and kicked Dade's ruined cravat underneath and out of sight. One almost fine cravat: noted. Another item to replace when he regained his inheritance.

And will you buy a replacement for Elektra's trust when someday someone points out the infamous Lord Anathema—formerly known as Lord Aaron Arbogast?

Someday wasn't today, thank heavens!

To his secret dismay, it seemed he was fitting in quite well with this mad bunch after all, for his primary tenet now seemed to be "Don't get caught."

As he turned to leave the room, Attie spoke again.

"Do you want to pollinate with her?"

Aaron closed his eyes. Damn. He was halfway into the hall. One more bloody second—

He inhaled deeply and turned to face one of his many personal demons—the shortest one by far.

"Why in the world would you ask that?"

Attie said, "Because when I say 'copulate' people tend to turn purple and sputter."

He might be turning a manly shade of puce but he most definitely was not turning purple! The sputtering, on the other hand, was unavoidable. "How do you even know that term?"

"Mama gave me a book about the reproduction process."

Aaron choked slightly. "Erk? Do you think it is appropriate to look at such things?"

She tilted her head. "It was mostly about frogs and bees."

"Oh . . . well. Bees ain't so bad I suppose . . ."

She shook her head at him in scorn. "You think I should know more about bees than I do about humans? But I am not a bee, so the information, while interesting, isn't terribly useful, is it?"

Aaron gazed about wildly for succor, but there was no one in sight to save him from this conversation. "I truly don't believe it is appropriate to be speaking to you about this!"

"About what?"

"About . . . bees!" With that he turned on one heel and strode away from the odd child.

She called after him, "You never answered my question. Do you want to pollinate with her?"

Aaron cringed and hoped the rest of the Worthingtons were out of range of Attie's reedy little voice.

It was only too bad that he couldn't also run away from the voice in his own mind.

Oh, yes. I want to pollinate with her.

* * *

As Elektra left her room, she could hear the babble of her family gathering in the front entry. She smiled at the excitement in their voices, but it was a wry smile. To them, this was simply more fun to be had.

Attie waited for her at the stairs, sitting on the top step with her elbows on her knees, her chin on her fists. She wore a strangely mutated cravat tied about her neck. Elektra realized that the knot was formed after a hangman's noose. She shuddered.

"Attie, may I have that cravat? It's just what I've been looking for to wipe my shoes before I walk into the ball."

Attie sat up and pulled the macabre thing over her head, handing it to Elektra wordlessly. Apparently it had accomplished its mission, which was most likely to give her older sister the willy-wiggins. It was a classic Attie-style protest. Translation: *I am tired of being the only one to stay home.*

Thirteen was difficult for anyone, more so for the youngest child. Elektra remembered watching her older brothers leaving for evenings out, dreaming of when she might attend glittering balls clad in beautiful clothes.

Strange how it all seemed much more like drudgery now, instead of that scintillating girlish fantasy. She might as well be a chimneysweep gathering his brushes for all the excitement she felt tonight.

Time to pay the bills.

So she passed Attie by with a swift caress to her little sister's braids and made her way down the curving stairs to the once grand entry of Worthington House. When she descended far enough, her family came into view. Dade looked golden and handsome, if a bit dour.

He knew it was his duty to escort his sister and cousin, but Elektra could see him twitching at the inconvenience. So many more important things to do, had Dade. She had long given up wanting to explain herself to her dismissive eldest brother. He couldn't help his preoccupation, for he was both father and mother to them all now, with Callie gone away to the Cotswolds.

Next to him stood Orion, rather surprisingly. Elektra wondered how Dade had managed to bribe his next-younger brother to accompany him. Funds for a new experiment, perhaps? Orion seemed willing enough to be there, in his distant way. Elektra took two more steps down. Bliss came into view.

Suddenly Elektra did not feel quite so resplendent. Her dress was just as fine, having come fresh from Lementeur's studio in Cabot's hands that afternoon. To be truthful, it was that bosom! Elektra couldn't help feeling that her quest would be so much more attainable if she were armed with that sort of man-bait.

In addition to her fine gown and her world-class figure, Bliss wore an expression of pleased serenity as she held out her arm to someone. Elektra descended another step just as a male figure in black stepped into view to Bliss's side. It was Mr. Hastings, clad in formal finery that a faraway part of Elektra's mind identified as belonging to her lost brother, Poll. Except for the rich blue silk waistcoat, which by the precision of the fit, had to be something Mr. Button had made just for him!

The precise color of the butterflies in the meadow.

Oh . . . my.

She had never seen him out of his rumpled, brown

suit, which was much the worse for all their adventures. In black and sapphire, he was as striking as Dade, if a shade less golden. His blond hair was as tawny as a lion, she decided, and his eyes—

At that moment his gaze rose to meet hers where she stood frozen halfway down the stairs, poised with her hand on the railing, feeling as if she wanted to vault the damned thing and then drift dreamily down like a feather into his arms, all the while holding that warm, gray gaze with hers.

Then he took Bliss's arm. Something spiked right through Elektra's middle, just beneath her bosom, just above her belly. She pressed one palm to that spot in alarm. What was that?

I should have eaten something, instead of spending my day preparing for the ball.

The ache didn't recede until Bliss slipped her arm away the better to adjust her perfect, pristine gloves. Elektra quickly lifted her own hand from the railing, which still gleamed from her recent cleaning, but she meant to take no chances. She refused to arrive at the Duke of Camberton's ball smudged!

Her brothers realized that she stood above them.

"Ellie, good God, it's about time!" Dade checked his pocket watch.

His impatience cut at her. She dared not fish for a compliment now. Her eldest brother already thought her selfish and vain. She wasn't sure when he'd formed the opinion of her worthlessness. All she'd asked for was proper Season, after all. And that, only in the last year.

Haven't you cost us enough?

Dade's voice rang through her mind. That's what he'd said when she asked for gowns, when he revealed to her that it was all they could do to afford to fill their plates. And he'd said it so wearily, as if she'd been begging treats from him for years and he was worn to a frazzle by it—except she hadn't, not really.

For the thousandth time in her life, she wondered what he saw when he looked at her.

She wanted to tell him that he needn't worry any longer. She wanted to tell him that she planned to fix it all.

How would he see her when she made the match of the decade? What would he think when she handed him the key to the front door of Worthington Manor someday?

Orion gazed at her evenly, with no more surprise at her appearance than if she were dressed in an ordinary gown on an ordinary afternoon. That was only to be expected. To interest Orion, one must grow wings, or a shell. Perhaps fins.

Only Mr. Hastings's gray eyes gleamed with appreciation. Elektra rewarded him with a smile. His lips curled slightly in response, and he shared an exasperated glance at her brothers. Elektra's belly warmed at his defense of her, as if he'd donned silver mail and challenged Dade and Orion to a joust in her honor.

What an unusual man.

Of course, then he ruined the moment by allowing Just Wonderful Miss Bliss Worthington to retake his arm. Bliss turned her attention to Elektra, all unaware of her cousin's sudden bloodthirsty gaze.

"You look very fine, Elektra. Shall we?"

"Oh, God, yes," breathed Dade. "Please, let us bloody go already."

Orion nodded. "I am sufficiently prepared, as well."

"Miss Worthington, please, lead the way." Mr. Hastings waved Elektra down the last stairs with his gleaming black silk hat, which also looked very Lementeur, adorned as it was with a perfectly matched blue silk band.

In fact, Mr. Hastings's sapphire-and-black could have been specifically designed to coordinate with Bliss's summer-sky-blue silk gown with silver braid trim at the neckline (really, why bother? No one was looking at the gown, not with that bosom!) and the dainty cap sleeves.

More bloody points for Bliss.

Bliss looked very pretty, indeed. She sat across from Aaron in the Worthingtons' elderly carriage, which held six easily. Mrs. Worthington was between the two younger ladies, facing forward, while Dade, Orion, and Aaron took the less desirable back-facing seat.

For a moment upon boarding the creaking contrivance, Aaron had wondered if the Worthingtons expected him to take a manservant's place up with the driver. At some point since this very morning, "Hastings" seemed to have graduated to something nearing gentleman's status in the household.

It hadn't been Elektra's doing, as he'd thought. She'd seemed entirely surprised to see him join the party, although thankfully not much bothered by it. Who then? Dade would just as soon "Hastings" fell off the nearest cliff—Aaron was fairly certain that the eldest Worthington sibling saw him as a harmless but annoying moocher. Orion might have enjoyed dissecting him, or stuffing him, or doing whatever it was he did in that den of horrors he called a study, but Aaron couldn't imagine him giving a damn whether Bliss had an escort or not.

In the end, he decided it must have been some impulse of Iris's, some half-formed thought of rounding out the party, which now she'd completely forgotten about as she chatted amiably with Bliss about Shakespeare and his farm animals.

Then Aaron ran out of inconsequential matters with which to distract his thoughts. His eyes slid slowly back to her, as if they were naught but steel balls and she, a powerful magnet.

She'd been beautiful when mud-stained and dressed like a boy. She'd been stunning when riding in the pony cart in a bright spring gown. But this . . .

There were words he could use. Exquisite. Flawless. *Incandescent.*

Those were all perfectly nice words. They were also entirely inadequate.

She'd floated down those frayed stairs like a heavenly visitation, come to urge them all up from their worldly cares. Of course, there would be no colorless debutante chiffon on a woman like Elektra. Her gown enhanced her slender figure, draping closely against hip and breast, clinging like water to her flesh while still managing to give an impression of modesty. The rich purple silk turned her skin to purest alabaster and her upswept hair to moonlit gold.

And in that shimmering pile of silky gold nested a handful of blue butterflies.

Her hand in his, her laugh in his ears, her smile

blinding his vision, as they ran through a whirlwind of azure wings.

Aaron had been born to astonishing wealth. He knew a fine gown when he saw one, so he knew that Mr. Button had quite outdone himself. The lads would be slavering and the ladies pining with jealousy.

But the girl inside the dress made the delicious work of art seem like no more than simple gown—especially when she smiled at him.

He'd had the most alarming urge to drop to his knees right there in the foyer, to rip the signet ring from his pocket, confess his many sins, and beg her to marry him on the spot.

The only thing that had saved him from such rashness, aside from the fact that she had hocked his signet ring to an innkeeper, had been the flash of hurt in her eyes when her brothers had behaved as if she were no more than an irritant, and this important evening nothing but a shallow, inconsequential waste of their time.

So he'd cheered her up with his mugging and his cheeky bow, and now he kept his gaze down so that she could not see the longing in his eyes. He hoped the house where the ball was being held was nearby, for he didn't think he'd be able to maintain his jocular distance for long.

When the carriage stopped, he leapt from it as if a sharp spring propelled him. Knowing how old those cushions were, it would not have surprised anyone if it had. They all seemed to take his abrupt exit in stride. One would likely have to behave very oddly indeed for a Worthington to take notice of it.

He took the opportunity to aid Iris from her seat and down the rickety carriage steps. Then he held out his hand to Bliss.

Because he feared he wouldn't be able to release Elektra's hand once taken, he continued to escort Bliss across the court and up the front steps. All the while, he was intimately aware of Elektra being helped from the carriage by Dade, who knew his manners, after all, while Orion escorted his mother inside the house.

Oh, hell. For the first time, Aaron looked about him. This was the city residence of the Duke of Camberton, a house Aaron knew nearly as well as he knew Arbodean itself. Neville, who was now the current duke, had once been Aaron's closest friend! They had played together as children, though they'd not crossed paths in fifteen years. Neville, who had gained his title at twelve years of age, had always been of a more scholarly bent. Aaron remembered a tall, thin, quiet boy who possessed a quick mind and a shy nature.

Once he'd become the boy duke, of course, he'd been far too above Aaron to spend summer afternoons rambling around the Camberton estate while their parents kept company.

Aaron admitted privately that the young man he had been would have been bored stiff by anyone who wasn't more interested in drinking and wenching than in books.

It was too bad. Neville would have been a much healthier companion than Wells, if only he'd had the sense to see it at the time.

Unfortunately, if he entered this house, his identity as "Hastings" would be punctured in approximately eight seconds. He was going to have to beg off, at once!

No, don't panic. He would not be announced as Lord Aaron.

Elektra seemed to sense his unease. She leaned close to whisper in his ear. "If you don't speak to the duke, and only bow, he'll never know."

Never know he was just a servant, she meant. Either way, he meant to take her advice. It was possible that Neville would not recognize him. He'd been away for a very long time, time which he'd spent filling out, changing, becoming a man instead of a feckless boy.

Then the second half of this revelation made its way into his consciousness. Neville, that weedy, thoughtful boy with a wild shock of black hair, was Elektra's chosen prey.

Oh, I am staying right where I bloody am, thank you very much!

Chapter Nineteen

Elektra had moved ahead of Aaron after the reception line. Aaron caught up with her and bent his lips to her ear. "Does this Neville bloke—?"

She pulled back to gaze at him with reproof. "You mean the Duke of Camberton."

Now he was taking etiquette lessons from a Worthington? "Aye, does this duke bloke know you're gunnin' for 'im? Seems like a lot o' young ladies here tonight 'ave the same idea. Some of 'em are right pretty, too."

"I take that as a backhanded compliment, Mr. Hastings." Elektra tossed her head like a prideful filly. "And yes, Neville will come to heel shortly."

She said it so effortlessly, with such ease of assumption that of course the aforementioned prey, er, fellow would fall instantly and permanently in love with her and beg her to wed him.

Aaron's gut went cold as he thought perhaps she might be right.

Of course, it would be a terrible match. With her

powerful will and her infectious madness, she would roll right over poor shy Neville, like a boulder dressed in white organza and pink silk dancing slippers.

Wouldn't that be better for her than some bloke who would try to control her or dominate her?

Yes, of course, but Elektra Worthington required much more precise handling. Elektra needed someone strong, someone who had come through the fire—someone who had learned from his mistakes. She needed someone who had spine enough to stand up to her, but was patient and tolerant enough to shore her up when she became frightened and angry.

Would absentminded Neville even grasp the depths of Elektra's fears? Would he be able to withstand the hot flash of her temper long enough to see the sensitive girl hiding behind it?

Now that he thought about it, he wondered how much Neville had changed in the fifteen years since assuming his title. What if all the wealth and power had corrupted the quiet lad, turning him into a tyrant or, worse, a deviant?

One never knew what lay beneath the surface of even one's closest friends. If he'd even for a moment suspected what Wells was up to, he wouldn't be standing here right now, lying his soul away to a beautiful girl!

As instructed, he didn't speak when introduced to Neville. His bow was low and swift and Neville wasn't looking at him anyway. He was just another bloke in the reception line.

Neville's gaze, like so many similar male gazes, followed Elektra.

It seemed that she had already attached His Grace's attention.

Aaron caught up to her once more. "How well do you really know this toff?"

Elektra pasted a serene smile on her face. "Don't say 'toff.' And I have met him on two previous occasions. The first time we spoke of our horrid names and swore to bestow upon our children names both short and common."

She smiled more sincerely at the memory. "Now that I think on the matter, I believe I was campaigning for Henry. The second time we danced at Mrs. Teagarden's ball at the assembly. It was only a country reel but I made him take note of me when I commented on the unusually early migration of the geese this spring. He fancies himself quite the naturalist, although not on Orion's level, of course."

Aaron stared at her. "What do you care about geese, then?"

"Nothing at all, I fear, but he does."

"You'd spend the rest o' your days pretendin' then?" He tilted his head to frown down at her. "That don't seem right, if you don't mind me sayin'."

Her chin came up. He'd stung her, he knew.

For a long moment, she fixed him with that beautiful green-blue gaze. Then she stepped closer, reaching a slender hand to run her fingertips through the hair at his temple. "Always so mussed, Mr. Hastings. Of course, you never stop to check the looking glass. Nor do you ever think twice before speaking your mind. What I wouldn't do to be like you, my dearest Mr. Hastings."

Her hand dropped away. He ached at the loss of her

warm, delicate touch, then ached further as the mask of formidability closed over her lovely features. She nodded at him in a distant fashion, then turned and left him there.

He should take his own leave now. Elektra was safely back in the bosom of her family and seemingly recovered from her bout of temporary insanity. With her sights set on a new target, one who hardly stood a chance as far as Aaron could see, she was well on her way to fulfilling her dreams. She would soon become a duchess, wed to a man so rich and powerful and respectable that no one would ever so much as whisper a derogatory comment about "those mad Worthingtons" ever again. Neville had ten times the wealth needed to restore Worthington Manor to its former glory. She could have everything she'd ever dreamed of.

As for "Mr. Hastings," no one but the two of them would ever know about how she'd climbed aboard him like a horse, wrapped her arms about him, and kissed him like *he* was the answer to her dreams.

No one but he would ever know that it was that thrice-damned kiss that haunted him, that played across his memory every time he saw her pink mouth, that woke him in the middle of the night with a granite erection and her name on his lips.

Yes, he truly ought to be on his way.

Just one dance. You'll never have another opportunity to hold her in your arms.

He would be on his way—after just one dance.

Elektra saw, across the room, the Duke of Camberton glance in her direction. He blushed when he caught her gaze. Neville was rather sweet, really. He clearly liked her. He was somewhat attractive.

Life with him would not be so very bad, would it?

Not that it makes any difference at all.

She let her eyes widen and her lips part slightly with "surprise." Then, with perfect timing, she slid her eyes coquettishly to the right, all the while tilting her lips in a secret little smile.

From his expression, he found this utterly bewitching. Heavens, men were easy. From the edge of her vision, she saw him bow slightly to the portly man he spoke to, then turn and start across the floor in her direction.

It was about time. She'd wondered if it weren't time to fetch a harness from the stable—he was too dense to follow where he was led!

"C'mon, Miss Elektra! You ain't dancin'!"

Strong arms swept Elektra into a waltz step. She had acted as practice partner for every brother since she was five, so her feet fell instantly into the dance, even as she drew breath to reprimand Mr. Hastings sharply for interfering with her machinations.

She looked up into his gray eyes and her annoyance faded instantly.

That in itself would have been even more annoying— but this was the man who'd flung himself into the river to save Bliss. This was the man who'd been a truly wonderful sport about being knocked unconscious, kidnapped, tied out in a hailstorm, and then forced to escort her and Bliss to London.

He'd even made friends with lonely little Attie, who rarely liked anyone who wasn't a blood relation. She could never embarrass him by fleeing his unconventional request. She owed him far too much.

You are publicly performing a scandalous dance with a man who is scarcely an appropriate or advantageous partner—

Oh, for pity's sake, shut it! I want to dance!

He was a wonderful dancer, a near-perfect partner. She relaxed into his lead, allowing him to whirl her about to the beautiful music, feeling safe and relaxed in his strong embrace, feeling light and happy.

Like an ordinary girl.

For no reason whatsoever, she began to laugh. He smiled down at her, obviously pleased by her pleasure. He wouldn't ask her why she was laughing. He always seemed to know those answers, without ever having to ask her tiresome questions. He simply *noticed* things.

I love that about him.

I love . . .

Oh.

Oh, she was so stupid, so blind, such a myopic, oblivious *idiot*!

I love him.

Overwhelmed by the sudden, irreversible, unforgettable knowledge—*oh, God, it hurts!*—she tilted her head away and closed her eyes while her body still flowed with his in the dance.

Something was wrong with her lungs. She couldn't draw her breath. The ache—that beautiful, agonizing, delirious anguish—that was love? It was unbearable. It was what she'd thought she'd never know.

It wasn't for her. *He* wasn't meant for her! He was meant for some pretty lady's maid, with a saucy smile and a good bosom, who would ruffle his hair and see through his blarney, catch him out in his bad-boy fibs and make love to him until they were both breathless and faint—

Sudden fury and hatred threatened to steal the stuffing from her knees. Fury at the pretty maid who would steal her beloved Henry Hastings away—and hatred at the rules and boundaries of their world, that would keep her from this wonderful, honorable, intelligent nobody, leaving her with no one but a wealthy duke to ease her eternal loss!

The storm of emotions was staggering. He felt her falter, for his hands tightened in concern. She wanted to tell him that she wasn't faint, she was furious! Except that her breath wasn't coming back and her vision was blurred by something—tears or dizziness?—and the music began to sound a bit hollow.

"Miss Elektra?" His steps changed tempo and his hold became more secure. "Bloody ballroom—can no one tell it's too bloody hot in here? Come on, there's the door."

Elektra heard the clasp of a door being snapped open, then felt a wave of cooler air on her face. She felt as though she'd been running for years, caught up in a race. What if she simply stopped?

She turned away from him, turning into the clean, pure darkness of the terrace. Her hands found the stone balustrade and she held on to it like a lifeline in a stormy sea.

Cold, hard stone.

I must be stone.

She might have managed it, if he hadn't passed the

back of one hand over her cheek, if he hadn't leaned close enough for her to smell his clean, waltz-warmed skin, if he hadn't once again seen right through to the very core of her.

"It ain't the heat, is it? You're shiverin'! You've 'ad a shock, you 'ave. What is it? What's upset you—"

She kissed him.

She poured it all into that kiss—how she truly felt, how she longed for him, how he woke up the other girl— the one who saw magical possibilities in a meadow full of blue butterflies.

It wasn't her fault. Something turned her head to find his face so close to hers. Something pulled her into his tall, hard body, something wrapped her arms about his neck, something sent her up on tiptoe so that she could kiss him as if he were her very own personal source of air.

Something made him kiss her back.

Oh, God. Aaron forgot everything. His mission, his goals, his very will. Her sweet, soft lips on his stole his very mind. There was nothing left of him but his beating heart, his hungry mouth, and his open, aching soul.

Her.

She filled the vacancy left by fleeing thought. The taste of her, the scent of her, the feeling of her body pressing to his, the strength of her fingers in his hair, clinging, pulling him down to her, stinging possession the like of which he'd never known.

Her.

Lovely, brave, determined Elektra—

Wanted him. Not the eligible Lord Aaron, but him— the lighthearted natural fellow he'd found within this façade of Hastings. The man he might have been, if he'd not gone astray so young. Miss Elektra Worthington, destined for a great match, born with INSERT NEARLY ROYAL TITLE HERE written on her ivory forehead, wanted *him*.

Now, if he was not mistaken.

He pushed her back until her hips pressed to the stone and his lower body met hers, heat to heat, hard to soft, his groin to her sweet hot center, his chest to her soft, giving breasts. The clothing between didn't matter. They were connected by far more than touch, far more than lust, far more than even simple loneliness.

He'd always known it, but her self-assurance had made him doubt that knowledge. Now she poured herself into his mouth, into his arms, against his hardening cock.

It wasn't like the first kiss, nor the second, exploratory one.

This was a larger deeper thing indeed.

This was a vow.

I will always, always . . .

No. No, not yet, not now! Not until you tell her the truth!

"Love you," she whispered against his mouth. "I love you, Henry Hastings."

"I—" *love you, Elektra*. But—

Henry Hastings was another man, a faraway fellow, of some forty years and vast, dubious experience. She couldn't love Hastings, for she didn't know him.

Nor does she know you.

On the far side of the brightly lighted ballroom, beyond the whirling gowns and flaring tails of the waltzing guests, a pair of pain-stricken eyes stared at the terrace door, the one that had closed after the attractive couple who had danced through it.

The fragile stem of the champagne glass in a fisted hand snapped. The fist tightened on the broken glass. A single drop of red splashed onto the pristine white marble of the ballroom floor.

Lord Aaron Arbogast!

"I have something I must tell you."

Aaron's throat tightened, cutting off the next words. He pulled her tight against him.

"Oh, yes," she murmured into his chest. "There is a great deal to talk about. We must think of some way to break this to my family that won't have you beaten to a pulp and tossed into the Thames. Not for being a man-servant, you know. For being male, for simply looking at me. After all, you are a guest in our house."

Aaron tried to swallow past the jagged knives of dread in his throat. "Elektra . . ."

She inhaled deeply, then stepped back and out of his arms.

"I had best make my way back to Iris," she whispered reluctantly. "We . . . you and I . . ."

She swept his heart away with the joyous smile she gave him at those words.

"You and I will speak more after we get back to Worthington House. Meet me in the library when everyone is off to bed." She went up on tiptoe to brush the softest kiss upon his lips. "I cannot wait," she whispered.

Then she turned and danced fluidly back across the terrace and through the half-open French doors, turning to close them—just an excuse to flash him one last wickedly innocent smile.

Aaron's throat tightened. Love. He was in love with a girl who didn't know his name. He turned away to lean on the railing with his head bowed, ashamed of his cowardice, awed by the sweet generosity of her heart. The cold stone of the balustrade felt like ice after her warm, supple self.

"Is she your next victim? Tell me her name, so I can instruct *her* brothers to kill you now, before you destroy her."

Aaron's first thought was, *at last.*

This moment had been ten years coming. The intonation was different, older, deeper—but the intent rang a bell of recollection across time from a day he would never, could never afford to forget. He turned toward the voice. "Hello, Carter."

A shadow detached itself from the darkness of the terrace. Carter Masterson, Amelia Masterson's younger brother. When Aaron had last seen him, he'd been a gangling boy of fourteen, furious and grieving, raging at his own youth and helplessness.

Carter stepped into the light streaming in from the ballroom. Aaron faced him squarely, but made no other move. This one was Carter's due, no doubt about that, and a long time coming, too.

"You ruined her, you bastard."

The first blow knocked Aaron's head back and forced his cheek into his teeth. He righted himself and spat blood. Still he did nothing but face the younger man down.

"You shamed her! You shamed all of us!"

The second and third blows came harder—a right to the jaw, a left to the belly. Aaron's breath left him in a rush and he tried to step back, just long enough to breathe—

The stone balustrade stopped his retreat. Cornered by the terrace railing, with a long drop behind him, Aaron had no choice but to put up his defenses at last.

"She died because of you! She couldn't bear it—she cried and cried! I heard her, all night long, night after night!"

Aaron blocked blow after blow, but as he took the punishment, more blows got through. Carter had a decade of rage behind him, a decade in which to prepare his body, to forge his fury, to count the days until he came within striking distance of Lord Aaron Arbogast.

"She took her own life, just to stop the pain, you evil—" *Thud.* "Foul—" *Thud.* "Vicious—"

He means to kill me. Right here, on this terrace, to-night—

If this had happened ten years ago, Aaron might have let it happen. Back then, Carter had been too weak. Now Aaron was too strong. He knew himself. He knew how far his own responsibility for Amy's death went and he knew where it ended. He'd accepted his own guilt and had done his best to make amends.

Those reparations, he realized, did not include dying.

Yet he couldn't bring himself to strike back. Carter was maddened, crazed with rage and grief held inside for ten years. The boy had grown into a man, but the soul inside had stayed, lost in that single impotent moment, stuck in the quicksand of memory and pain.

Aaron could feel the pain. It came off Carter in waves, in breathless grunts of rage, in near-sobs ripped from his lungs as he rained blow after blow upon Fate, Death, and Lord Aaron.

Aaron put his arms over his face, bent to protect his gut, kept the stone at his back, and endured blow after blow.

Carter's vengeful fury raged on.

Damn it, I'm going to have to—

Except that he'd waited too late. His face ran with blood, his eyes were swelling shut, his ribs lanced pain with every inhalation. His belly couldn't take another blow, but he couldn't straighten his body enough to turn—

Then came a shout and Carter disappeared, yanked backward into the darkness by a muscled arm.

Chapter Twenty

A few shouted words and the sound of blows penetrated Aaron's hazed consciousness as he slumped against the stone balustrade of the terrace. With his tormenter otherwise occupied, he took the opportunity to fall half over the railing and retch gratefully into the garden below.

"God, man! What the hell were you thinking? Why didn't you fight back?"

Aaron inhaled, wiping the back of his hand over his bleeding mouth. Then he blinked up at his rescuer. Dade Worthington. God, why couldn't it have been Lysander? The younger Worthington wouldn't ask questions!

Dade grabbed Aaron by the shoulders and propped him upright, leaning against the balustrade. Aaron tried not to flinch at Dade's grip on his bruised body. *I am going to be a map of the world—blue and green, with a few rivers of red.*

Dade wasn't being any too gentle, and it didn't take Aaron long to discover why.

"Lord Aaron Arbogast, is it? Black Aaron?"

Well. It was done. Just as he must have known, deep down, even as he dressed for the evening. *Too cowardly to tell her yourself? Let her find out in the worst possible way! Wonderful solution, you bastard!*

"You bastard!"

Oh, good. It was unanimous.

Dade's fury didn't run as hot as Carter's, it seemed. Aaron lifted his head to meet the cold, deadly serious gaze of the only serious Worthington he'd ever encountered. *Hellfire. I might actually die tonight, after all.*

"Worthington—" Aaron coughed. It hurt, but it didn't feel like any ribs were broken. Yet. "God, before you kill me, can you please—" His breath caught again. "If you will fetch me a whiskey . . . or three?"

The dying man's last request seemed to appeal to Dade. He turned and strode away, then stopped just at the ballroom doors.

"There is nowhere for you to run, your lordship. Nowhere in the world."

Aaron waved a hand in acquiescence, even as he slid down the stone railing to half sprawl on the stone floor of the terrace. He didn't—couldn't—run from this. She deserved better. She deserved to face him, to screech at him, to take one of those very large books and brain him with it.

The sweet music of her voice danced through his mind. *I love you, Henry Hastings.*

He'd thought himself in pain from the beating. That was nothing.

This was truly going to hurt.

The loving light in her green-blue eyes.

Oh, God. *Elektra.*

Aaron wasn't one to be intimidated by any man, even two or three men . . . but four large and angry Worthingtons were enough to send shivers up any man's spine. They loomed—great louts that they were!—over where he sat with his hands bound with rope in Dade's study chair, thinking he ought to have made out his last will and testament.

Furthermore, he deserved their scorn and fury. He'd entered their home under false pretenses and taken advantage of their generous hospitality. He was only glad they didn't know how many times he'd kissed their very pretty sister!

He knew Dade was only being a protective brother and Aaron admired him for it. The best he could hope for now would be to throw himself on their mercy and hope to survive it.

Orion, now, he could happily brain . . . but Elektra wouldn't like that. He turned his gaze from one implacable face to another. Cas shot him an especially bloodthirsty glare. Only in Lysander's tightened visage did he see even a glimpse of sympathy. Yes, Lysander knew of something of longing for redemption, or at least for a new beginning.

He took a breath and nodded to them all, one by one. "You have every reason to be angry. I have done the unforgivable in invading your home and lying to you all."

He cleared his throat and tried again. "I assure you

that I only came here to ensure Miss Elektra and Miss Bliss would arrive safely in your hands."

Dade frowned. "Ellie told me that you assisted them through some difficulty on the road. Now I am wondering if she told me everything. Wasn't she gunning for some earl?"

Lysander let out a small choked sound, but only Aaron seemed to hear it.

"I . . . er . . . came across Miss Elektra stranded near a ruined estate, which she informed me had belonged to you all."

"Still belongs to us, not that it's any of your business." That was Cas. He seemed possibly the most volatile Worthington male, but seemed willing to accede to Dade's leadership. Aaron wasn't sure if that was a good thing or not.

"Er . . . yes, well, she requested my assistance to return to the guardianship of her brother at a nearby inn. I was only too glad to help a young lady in need. Zander? Is there anything you'd like to add?"

Lysander only stared stonily back at his eldest brother, but Aaron saw the darker man's fingers twitch at his sides, his entire body tense with unspoken urgency.

"Hmm." Dade seemed to feel the same helplessness the rest of the family did concerning his war-torn sibling. He turned back to Aaron, a more acceptable target for his frustrated fury. "So Ellie got herself into a pickle and you got her back to the inn." Dade folded his arms. "Go on."

Aaron cleared his throat. "Well, Miss Bliss had arrived by then and Mr. Worthington was nowhere to be found . . ."

Dade scowled. "Yes, I am aware that he left his post. He was alarmed at Ellie's . . . er . . . disappearance."

It was then that Aaron realized that Dade did not know that he, Aaron, had been Ellie's intended "pickle" or that Lysander had been in on the kidnapping plot from the beginning.

And Lysander didn't want Aaron to tell him.

No, of course not. Telling Dade would only inflame him, for upright Dade would only see that Aaron had spent a night sans chaperone with his innocent sister and that would be cause, in the man's honorable viewpoint, to call Aaron out in a duel.

That would be very, very bad.

Aaron could not kill Elektra's brother in a duel, and, as much as he admired her, he truly did not want to die at her brother's hand.

So, the secret would be kept, forever. Even if his life were not in imminent danger of being snuffed out, Aaron would never dishonor Elektra by shaming her before her brother in such a way . . . well, not that Elektra was at all ashamed of her actions, which were perfectly justifiable, if one were an insane Worthington . . .

Do stay on topic, old chap. You're about to die, remember?

Dade straightened. "Perhaps you're right about the Thames, Cas."

Aaron leaned forward urgently. "Just . . . wait!"

Dade actually hesitated, then flushed angrily at himself for doing so. "Wait for you to tell us yet another lie?"

Aaron let his breath out slowly. "I am not lying. I only wished to see her safely home. After that, I only wished to stay to . . . to understand her a little better . . ."

"All the better to finagle your way in past her guard!"

Aaron sighed. There was no help for it. "All the better to finagle my way in." He shrugged. "So I will leave now. Thank you all for your hospitality."

He rose awkwardly, with his hands tied before him, and took a single step forward, hoping that they would simply part way for him. Such was not to be. The wall of Worthingtons loomed large.

"Black Aaron, known far and wide as the destroyer of young women. You seduced that Masterson girl, dishonoring her so that the poor desperate thing took her own life with an overdose of laudanum. Most honorable men would run you through with a sword, simply for casting shade upon their doorstep." Dade tilted his head and gazed at him with ice in his eyes. "Now you admit that you are up to your old tricks?"

Old tricks. Oh, hell. Aaron's heart sank, realizing that as far as the Worthington blokes knew, he was the same fellow who had ruined and abandoned Amelia Masterson all those years ago.

I can't believe I almost forgot that is who I am. Elektra had made him forget it, damn it. She had treated him like a human being for a brief time and he had begun to believe it himself.

"I'd like an answer to that one, myself."

At that steel-within-silk voice, Aaron's head whipped about. A delicate shadow stood in the doorway, just outside the pool of candlelight.

Elektra.

The study was cool at night without a fire, so Elektra had brought along a voluminous shawl and a candle stub. She curled up on the settee in the library and waited for Henry to join her.

They had a great deal to talk about. The future wouldn't be an easy one, for either of them. The world was suspicious of things that didn't fit. As a Worthington, Elektra had been born a misfit, albeit one tolerated by Society. As Mrs. Hastings, she would leave her world behind entirely.

Not her family, she was sure. At least, she'd like to be sure. Mama wouldn't care. Papa would likely quote *Romeo and Juliet* until they were all sick to death of it.

Attie wouldn't care, nor would Callie. Her sisters, she knew, would be at her side forever.

Lysander probably wouldn't notice. Castor had his own scandals to live down, along with his pregnant Miranda and his missing twin to worry about.

Orion? Elektra was certain that Society's whims meant less to him than the migratory pattern of starlings in northern Scotland. He would neither approve nor disapprove. Elektra wondered momentarily if she could interest Henry in biology to help win Rion over.

So the one she truly worried about was Dade, was it not?

Thinking about her eldest brother, who also served as a sort of unanimously appointed replacement father, Elektra felt that inner flinch once more.

Dade was not going to approve, for the very same reasons that she'd listed to herself last night after encountering Henry in the hallway and nearly kissing him.

Wedding "beneath her station," as the world would call it, would deal the family standing another blow, and they'd already had so many.

The loss of the manor, the damage done to Lysander's mind, Iris's permanent flight of fancy, the carelessly scandalous antics of Castor and Pollux, even Callie's shockingly quick marriage to that scarred hermit—who was a nice enough fellow once one got to know him, although Society eyed him askance.

Dade would not see a romantic tale of hearts united over the chasm of class. Dade, she feared, would view it as a betrayal of the family.

He would be right.

Is it so wrong that I long for something of my own?

And then the mantel clock, an ornate ceramic piece that would be valuable were it not hopelessly chipped, chimed two o'clock in the morning.

Startled, Elektra wrapped her shawl more tightly about her. So late?

Where are you, Henry?

Except that she was very much afraid that she knew. Dade had already found them out.

He and the other lads would take Henry to his study. All serious business took place in Dade's study. Elektra picked up her skirts and ran.

She skidded to a stop outside the study door to find her parents there, eavesdropping like naughty children. Archie turned his grizzled head to gaze at Elektra in vague worry, while Iris practically swooned in an excess of joy. Mama dearly loved a bit of drama.

Elektra paused to catch her breath. This would require a bit of cajolery. Blast it, how had Dade found out already, when she'd only discovered her own feelings a few hours ago?

Then, as her brother's angry words penetrated the

thick oak door of the study, her breath left her for an entirely different reason. Moving her mother gently aside, she pressed her ear to the door.

What she heard chilled her soul.

"Now you admit that you are up to your old tricks?"

"I'd like an answer to that one myself."

Elektra's voice came from the shadows outside the partially open study door. Even as Aaron's heart sank as he realized what was about to happen, she entered the room, breaking into the circle of light cast by the single candle.

This time her brothers did give way, stepping aside to allow an lane of entry so Elektra could face her almost-debaucher. Well, actually there was no *almost* about it.

She strolled through her guard dogs as if she strolled through a garden, with her hands clasped delicately before her and her expression serene. She stopped before him. "Mr.—? Not Hastings, I presume?"

"I am Lord Aaron Arbogast, Miss Worthington." He bowed. "I am pleased to meet you."

"How odd, my lord. I could have sworn we had already met." Her eyes flashed fury at him for a single instant, then her pose of serenity was again complete. "So this tale I hear that you are some dastardly defiler of respectable young ladies . . . is this true?"

Aaron had truly, truly been hoping she would not ask him that particular question. Yet even if he could break his word and tell her everything, it would not matter to the rest of the world.

And he could not break his word.

"There are many stories about what happened ten years ago," he said slowly, delaying the inevitable, as he had since he'd first laid eyes upon her in the ruin, not wanting the light of hope to extinguish from her gaze, that gaze that she kept carefully just for him, without letting her brothers see how much she wanted him to deny it.

Or perhaps he was a fool. Again. Perhaps she did not care for him. He was at best a liar and a disgrace. At worst, he was the worst a man could be and not hang for it.

At best, he was someone she ought to never trouble her mind over again, for her own sake.

"There is a great deal of truth in those stories."

It was the best he could do, for he could not bring himself to lie to her, not ever again.

He watched the ice form in her lovely eyes. Not the ice of anger, for Elektra's fury ran hot, not cold. No, it was the ice of desolation. It was the cold ache of betrayal. Damn it, he had done it again.

Then she shrugged and dropped her hands to her sides, looking anything but desolated. In fact, she looked the picture of barely impolite boredom. "Well, that was rather rude of you to come to stay in our house, now, wasn't it, what with two respectable young ladies in residence." She turned to Dade. "We didn't tell anyone he was visiting us, did we?"

Dade blinked. "Well, no, now that I think on it. He arrived in our carriage to the ball tonight, but I don't think anyone remarked upon it. We often show up with a crowd."

Elektra sighed. "Dade, we are a crowd."

Then she shrugged again. "Well, toss him out and let us speak no more of him."

Dade sputtered. "But he . . . he made eyes at you, and led us all to think . . . and he danced with you . . ."

Elektra rolled her eyes. "Dade, I danced with him to make the Duke of Camberton jealous! I certainly didn't care a whit for Hastings . . . er, Lord Aaron! I thought he was a servant, after all!"

Dade could not deny that. Aaron realized that Elektra had just neatly foiled her brothers' homicidal plans . . . or at least tried to. Which meant that despite her nonchalant act just now, she truly did care for him. Didn't it?

Cas stepped forward, rubbing his hands briskly. "You heard her, lads! Zander, wake up the old horses, will you? We'll need the carriage to do this properly."

Aaron peered around him, leaning hard to one side, trying to catch one last glimpse of Elektra. Did she care? *Could* she care for Lord Aaron the way she had for Henry Hastings?

Does she love me still?

Then Cas's words sank in and he gazed warily at the brothers crowding 'round.

I may not live long enough to find out.

Chapter
Twenty-one

Elektra moved numbly through the house, avoiding obstacles through long practice despite the roaring in her ears and the dull hollow thudding of her heart. At last, she reached the sanctuary of her own bedchamber, but it was an empty haven. A girl's room, festooned with the dreams of girlhood. There was no room for the brokenhearted here.

Her gaze flinched from the site of butterfly-blue ribbons still pooled upon her dressing table. She turned her back on it all—the lace, the ribbons, the silly novels she had studied to learn the art of love. Only the fire-blackened hearth did not make her twitch away.

Bliss found her sitting primly in the chair by the cold fire, her hands neatly folded in her lap and her spine quite erect.

"Cousin?"

"I'm sorry, Bliss. This is not the time."

"I see." Bliss daintily seated herself on the needlepoint footstool before Elektra. "His Grace was looking for you this evening. I believe you quite caught his fancy. I'm not sure that making yourself scarce was precisely the best mode—"

Elektra put her hands over her face, and tried to remember how to breathe normally. "Bliss, I don't give a petite pony's tail about the best mode."

"Language, cousin!"

Elektra giggled, a hysterical torn laugh that threatened to become a sob.

"Well, if you aren't upset about His Grace, then your distress must concern Mr. Hastings."

Elektra caught her breath. There was no point in turning her gaze away anymore. "I thought he was the only truly honest man I had ever met. I admired his ability to move through the world without caring what it thought of him. All lies. His name is not Hastings. He is Lord Aaron Arbogast." Say it all, say the whole thing, out loud. "They call him Black Aaron."

"Oh, dear." Bliss was silent for a long moment. "*That* Lord Aaron."

Elektra turned disbelieving eyes toward bliss. "You know about Black Aaron?" She threw out her hands in frustration. "How does everyone know about Black Aaron except me?"

"Some of us have learned to listen." Bliss's tone was gentle. "In addition, you seem to have been focused on other matters for some years now."

The husband hunt, she meant. The all-consuming meaning of Elektra's existence. "It was all I've ever cared about. I threw it away tonight, simply tossed it to the winds—all for a kiss from a heinous liar."

"Oh, I know why you threw it away. I simply wonder

why it consumed you in the first place." Bliss tilted her head, her summer-sky eyes as ingenuous as ever.

"Why?" Elektra stared at her cousin. "You know the state of the manor! You know the wealth it will take to restore it!"

"Yes, of course I do. But why must it be you who sacrifices yourself to rebuild the manor? Why not I? After all, I was just as responsible for the fire as you were."

"I—what?" It couldn't be. It wasn't possible.

It would explain everything. She shook her head, rejecting that thought. "I don't know what you speak of."

Bliss folded her hands in her lap, her pose mirroring Elektra's perfectly.

"I speak of you and me, playing in the drawing room. I speak of two curious little girls, encouraged in their curiosity, I might add—investigating the mechanics of a carriage lantern taken from the stables."

Elektra stared at her cousin with icy horror rising in her throat. She swallowed desperately, trying to rid herself of that growing realization. "I don't remember."

"Just as you don't remember me. Just as you don't remember what set you on this path of ruthless self-sacrifice in the first place."

"But the fire . . . It consumed everything, not just the drawing room."

"This may be hard for you to hear now, cousin."

"Tell me!"

Bliss sighed regretfully. "We did not alert anyone to the fire. We ran away and hid in the woods across the meadow."

The woods. Huddling in the great branching roots of an oak. Shivering, breathless fear. "I hate those woods. I would never go into them voluntarily."

"That is how you feel about them now. You used to like them."

Elektra shook her head violently. "I would never do such a thing! I would never run away and leave my family in danger!"

Those summer-sky eyes gazed at her with pity and understanding. "We were five years of age, cousin. We were infants. No one held us responsible for what happened. Except you, evidently."

Elektra's breath left her and would not come back. She covered her face with her hands and bent low over her lap. A shock-filled keen rose in her throat and stayed there, choking her.

It was me. It was always me.

I've always known it, haven't I?

It's all my fault.

Bliss leaned forward to gently pull Elektra's hands from where they threatened to tear her face. "It was an accident, cousin. Accidents happen. No one was to blame."

Bliss wasn't going to go away until she calmed herself. With every shred of iron will she had developed in this household of strong wills, Elektra forced air in and out of her lungs. She straightened in the chair and relaxed the fists still held in Bliss's grasp. "Thank you, cousin. Of course, you are quite correct. I understand everything now."

Bliss released her slowly. Her wide-eyed gaze might seem vapid, but Elektra had the feeling that her serene cousin missed nothing. However, she did nothing to refute Elektra's words.

"That is good news, cousin." She stood. "Now, if you will excuse me, I must be off to bed. I am exceptionally weary, for I danced every dance."

Elektra blinked. *I only danced one.*

The strange mad giggle threatened once more. Points for Bliss.

At the door, Bliss paused and turned back to her. "I know you are disappointed in yourself for succumbing to such a terrible man. However, he did save my life. I liked him, too. We all did."

"Except for Dade."

Bliss nodded. "Except for Daedalus. I expect that that is not so unusual."

Elektra used the very last of her self-control to offer some kindness back to Bliss, who was not who she'd thought. "I appreciate your thoughtfulness, Bliss. You have been very charitable to me. I'm sorry I misjudged you."

Bliss blinked. "People often do. I imagine you know how that feels." She turned to leave once more, then turned back again. "As does poor Lord Aaron, I'm sure." Then she was gone, leaving Elektra in her chilled pit of turmoil.

I have done so much damage in my life—and I am only nineteen! Please, someone stop me before I rain down the end of the world.

She would trade that world for one opportunity to fix what she had broken. She would go back in time to that single moment, the moment when she knew she had passed the point beyond which there was no return.

When was that? When you started the fire, or when you first kissed Lord Aaron?

Aaron's body hit the rippling surface of the Thames with hardly even a splash to give away murder in the act. Not that there was anyone near at all. Cas had directed the brothers to a stretch of riverbank off Vauxhall Gardens, currently deserted at this near-dawn hour. Too late for the respectable to be out, too early for the dishonorable to be awake.

As his head slipped beneath the icy, muddy water, Aaron wildly wondered how the Worthington twin had known precisely where one might dispose of an inconvenient soon-to-be dead body.

There would be no rescue, of course. If anyone in London knew what transpired, they would likely gather 'round to watch the death of Black Aaron, nibbling on candy floss and cheering when the bubbles of his last breath rose to the surface.

His wrists were bound with rope, as were his ankles. Feeling himself roll in the water, he flexed his body violently back and forth, fighting for the surface. He'd taken one last good breath as they'd tossed him from the bank, but he'd lost half of it in shock at the freezing water.

Panicking now, he struggled senselessly, his body taking over for a mind frozen with impending doom. He simply writhed in protest, in soundless vehement protest that it wasn't yet his time, that he didn't want to die. Twisting and rolling, he lost track of up and down, of surface and distant, filthy bottom.

Then, like a miracle accompanied by angel song, the

ropes about his wrists simply parted and fell away. He clawed his way up and up—at least, he prayed it was up!—until his head broke the water and he sucked in a great gasp of fetid river air.

Beautiful.

He kept himself there for several seconds, taking in one great lungful after another of lovely, dank air. Then, he held his breath once more and let himself roll beneath the lapping waves to tug at the ropes around his ankles. They, too, fell away like magic.

No, not like magic. Like a trick knot. The Worthingtons knew their knots, after all. It had been Lysander who had taken the rope from Cas to tie Aaron's hands in the house, and again to tie his ankles in the carriage.

As Aaron stretched out to swim to the bank in long, powerful strokes, he pondered that notion, but he could think of no other explanation.

Silent, mysterious Lysander, it seemed, was on Black Aaron's side.

Aaron was quite sure he was risking another dunking—or worse!—by going back to Worthington House, but every time he considered the alternative, he saw her face in Dade's study—her chilled, proud expression that in no way hid the slight tremble of her bottom lip.

He had to tell Elektra . . . something. He couldn't tell her the real truth of Black Aaron, obviously. He simply couldn't bear to part ways with her thinking that he'd lied and finagled and kissed her—

You did lie and finagle and kiss her!

Yes, but not for the reasons she thinks!

Those reasons mattered to him. He only hoped they would matter, a little, to her.

Besides, those Worthington louts had kept his horse.

So after he'd climbed out of the revolting river and squeezed out his clothing, he set out. He crossed the section of London between the Thames and Elektra on foot. By the time he found his way, the sun was well up. Thankfully, his clothing was mostly dry by then.

As he approached the house, limping in the shoes he'd borrowed for the ball the night before, cursing all the Worthington males to the fires of hell, he saw the old family carriage waiting out front. The gray-muzzled team drooped resentfully in the traces, and the clear morning light was not forgiving to the tarnished brasses.

He'd thought his old carriage had been a collection of sticks and varnish, but this one had to precede his by a couple of decades! Cas and Lysander appeared. Aaron stepped back into a shadowed doorway on the other side of the street.

The Worthington lads lugged a battered, strapped trunk between them. When they hefted it carelessly onto the carriage's baggage rack, the entire conveyance shook like old kindling.

Then Aaron saw Elektra exit the house. She wore a mint-green gown, topped with a dark green spencer and a bonnet trailing hunter-green ribbons.

Her eyes must look like emeralds, wearing that.

Her lethally fashionable ensemble, along with her natural grace, made her look like a princess among the peasants. Her brothers could dress well when required, and Cas's formal weskit last night had been either fashion-forward or delusional, but today they wore nondescript browns, rather like his own third-best suit.

Then Iris and Archie appeared. Archie was stuffed into the same fine, if slightly shiny-in-spots suit that he'd worn to the ball the night before. Iris wore layers of blue diaphanous fabrics that trailed behind her and fluttered about her so that Aaron got the distinct impression of medieval banners flying. It would have been rather impressive had Iris not wandered dreamily into the street and required Cas's quick reflexes to snatch her back before someone ran her over.

The whole clan emerged from the house, including Attie and Bliss, and even Philpott, who looked remarkably lucid. Then again, it was early yet. Iris and Archie, along with Elektra, distributed kisses and hugs and then boarded the carriage. Lysander listened to some murmured instructions from Dade, then climbed easily into the driver's seat. The rickety carriage rolled away with a clatter as the crowd on the walk waved good-bye until it was out of sight.

Aaron drew back into the shadows. A journey of some days, by the looks of the trunk. This could be very good. There would be only one Worthington lout between him and Elektra. If he could discover their destination, he could easily reach it on Lard-Arse before they did.

He didn't want to cause trouble. He only wished to speak to her for a moment. To apologize, to explain, to beg her forgiveness . . .

That was all. Truly.

Until Dade put his arm around a sulky-looking Attie. His deep voice came clearly across the street.

"She isn't getting married quite yet, Attie. She has to accept the proposal first. They are simply going to the Duke of Camberton's estate to work out the details. She'll be back in a week."

Aaron's jaw hardened. Despite Dade's words, Aaron knew a formal engagement was as binding as a wedding vow. If Elektra actually accepted the duke, she would have to marry him or be socially destroyed.

Neville, if you sign that betrothal, you will be signing your death warrant. I will never let you touch her.

Well, then. Perhaps he wanted to do a bit more than talk.

Some minutes later, Aaron had slipped into the stables behind Worthington House. He found that his abductors had thrown his small valise into the stable for Lard-Arse to trample, roll upon, and otherwise violate.

Aaron gratefully changed into his own boots, then saddled the recalcitrant Lard-Arse, who like his new home just fine, thanks for asking. The rangy bay gelding snapped big yellow teeth, managed to step on Aaron's foot more than once, and delivered annoyed kicks to the crumbling wooden wall of his stall. Aaron cursed the beast quietly and hoped that the Worthington household would merely think Lard-Arse was being his usual obnoxious self.

There were a few close calls as he tried to lead the horse out of the stables into the alley behind the house. Lard-Arse seemed to realize that Aaron meant for him to leave his beloved Bianca behind.

Finally, mounted safely beyond the range of those teeth, Aaron kicked the furious beast into a gallop. For once his luck seemed to be turning, for he made his getaway without anyone the wiser.

Or so he thought.

From the shadowy rafters of the stables swung a pair of skinny, pale legs with scraped knees and boots too large that threatened to drop right off.

Attie chewed the end of one of her many braids and gazed thoughtfully at the open stable door. If she told Dade, then he would ride Icarus out at great speed and stop old Pasty Hastings from ruining Elektra's betrothal to the duke. Or she could *not* tell Dade, and let matters develop as they may.

Elektra would surely be furious if her betrothal were mucked up.

Attie lay back on the wide, dusty rafter and chewed a piece of straw. Once upon a time, she had liked nothing better than to enrage Elektra. That was before Callie had left to marry that mad hermit and Attie had begun to realize that her siblings could actually slip away from her.

And it wasn't as though she disliked Hastings, or Black Aaron, or whatever his name was on Tuesdays after breakfast. Actually she liked him quite a bit, mostly because she detected evident liar and ne'er-do-well about him. She did have a fondness for a fellow mischief maker.

Unfortunately, she had recently come to suspect that this Hastings fellow had nefarious designs upon Elektra's spinsterhood.

How else did one interpret the way his eyes had followed Elektra around the room? How else to explain the way his hands twitched as her sister walked by, as if he wanted to reach out and brush his fingers across Elektra's skirt as she moved past him.

There was no possibility of Atalanta willingly giving up another sibling to marriage. She had already proven her determination in that regard. She'd tried projectile weapons, but that had not gone well at all. Poor Callie! Attie's thoughts shied away from the memory of her beloved eldest sister lying bloody on the moor.

She'd even tried poison, which had gone awry. Callie still lived far away with her rotten Sir Lawrence Porter!

When her darling twin brothers Cas and Poll had fought over a pretty widow, Attie had then attempted benign interference, which had made a bit more progress. That strategic counter-matchmaking, aided by her good friend Button, had gained her a new sister and an incoming niece—which did not precisely even her score but at least did not entirely lose her a brother.

It was all so stupid! No one needed to grow up. No one needed to go away. And certainly, most very definitely, no one needed to go start new families of their own. They were Worthingtons! They had a family—the family that belonged to her.

The very fact that she was gradually being left behind, by sister after brother after sister, was enough to give Attie wakeful nights and lonely afternoons, wandering her swiftly emptying house and considering her options.

If her options in this case meant a choice between some stupid, stuffy duke or good old Black Aaron as a future brother-in-law, at least she knew that Aaron could handle the Worthington world. And even—a fact she admired greatly—sometimes get the upper hand in it!

Chapter Twenty-two

Even as Attie was deciding not to interfere in Aaron's quest, another set of eyes widened at the sight of the infamous Black Aaron, bruised almost beyond recognition, wearing a filthy rumpled version of formal attire, erupting from the mouth of an alley mounted upon a large, ugly bay horse.

Carter Masterson, on his way to urge Daedalus Worthington to join him in his quest for brotherly vengeance, reined his horse about and took off down the London streets after his enemy, the embodiment of all evil, Lord Aaron Arbogast.

Elektra chose to ride in the driver's seat with Lysander. It was a lovely summer day and although a duchess would never do such a thing, she wasn't a duchess yet, was she?

Furthermore, Archie and Iris were feeling frisky. Elektra could tell by the way her father kept stroking her mother's wrist above her glove and the way her mother kept flipping her shawl fringe at him in mock reproach.

The poorly padded driver's bench was a far more comfortable place to be at the moment.

Love was the last thing Elektra wanted to think about. The heavy weight of her sadness fair to stopped the carriage horses in their tracks. Her poor little beginner heart would be stunted forever, bound in wire, forced back into the shape of Elektra-that-was.

Thank heaven for her brothers, discovering that miscreant in their house before she'd done something irreparably silly, like run off to Gretna Green for a quick, shady ceremony!

It's lovely there this time of year.

Oh, shut it.

Thank heaven for her brothers. She only hoped they hadn't been overzealous.

She cleared her throat. "Zander, what did you do with him?"

He did not look away from the road. "Thames."

Elektra lifted her chin. "Ah." Then, because she couldn't be sure, "You tied him up before threw him in, didn't you?"

Lysander didn't respond.

Elektra turned to pin her brother in the full force of her gaze. "Zander, you *did* use the trick knot, didn't you?" It was the twins' favorite scare tactic for fellows who owed them winnings.

He didn't answer for a long time. But even Zander wasn't immune to her stare. She was aware that her eyes were an unusual color, and their focused intensity could be unnerving to some. It was most useful doled out sparingly, so she saved it for the direst of moments.

He gave a short, tiny nod, his gaze dropping to his hands.

Relief swept her. She had no issue with giving that liar a good fright, but, for a moment there she'd feared her dear brothers had actually killed him on her behalf.

Then, Zander, quietly. "Dade told me not to."

Elektra nodded and swallowed. "I see."

How close you came to death, Black Aaron. I hope you learned from the experience.

I certainly have.

The journey continued, as uneventful as one could wish. They stopped in a small village for the purchase of wine to add to packed basket luncheon Philpott had provided for the journey. Since Camberton lay a short distance into Sussex from London, they expected to make it easily by nightfall.

The elderly team had other ideas. Progress was also slowed by the left rear wheel, which had begun to wobble unless adjusted regularly.

Night had fallen fully and they were still on the road. The old carriage lanterns cast a little light, enough for the horses to follow the road, but the moon was a mere sliver in the sky.

Nothing like the night she'd held Lord Aaron prisoner in the manor ruins. That night, the clouds had parted to reveal a perfect silver globe that glamoured the rubble in fairy light . . .

"Stand and deliver!"

Highwaymen!

For a fraction of a second Elektra felt a jolt of true fright. Lysander reacted instantly, pulling the old family dueling pistol from within his coat.

Then the familiar timbre of that voice penetrated Elektra's surprise. *Oh, for pity's sake!*

It seemed Black Aaron intended to live up to his name. However, he had to know that robbing the Worthingtons was an exercise in futility.

He isn't after money. He is after me.

The fact that her heart leapt like a deer at that thought only meant that she was her mother's daughter after all. Romantic nonsense! Lord Aaron Arbogast wasn't going to fight his way past her armed brother to sweep her away into the darkness!

Except that was precisely what he did.

Zander stood in the seat, pointing his pistol into the night from whence the voice had come. Suddenly a dark shape surged up behind him, knocked his pistol hand high, and felled him with a single mighty blow to the jaw.

Elektra jumped up. "Zander!" But her brother only slumped limply on the seat.

The assailant stood above Zander, shaking out his hand. A white grin sliced the night. "I enjoyed that! I've been wanting to hit someone for days!"

Elektra knelt next to her brother, checking him with quick hands. It wasn't too serious, no more than a knot on his skull. She glared up at Lord Aaron. "Was it necessary to hit him so hard?"

Lord Aaron paused in the act of appropriating the heirloom pistol to point down at Zander in affront. "He hit me first!"

Elektra stood and folded her arms in disapproval. "Men!"

She wanted to say, *Boys!* But the dark, broad-shouldered figure before her was no lad.

Without another word, he stepped toward her. She drew back but there was nowhere to go. Leaping down from the high top driver's seat—in a gown!—was not an option.

It did not even occur to her to call for her parents. What could Archie do that Zander could not?

When the strong arm of Black Aaron swept her from the carriage and deposited her in the saddle of his tall, leggy horse, her heart pounded with mingled fright and delight. *I am doomed!*

This man did not alarm her.

It was of herself she lived in mortal fear!

With a decidedly middle-aged grunt, Archie lugged his unconscious middle son into the carriage seat opposite Iris. "Good news, pet!" he gasped. "Our Lysander has put on a bit of weight!"

Iris leaned forward, her eyes bright. Her hair was a bit mussed and she'd not quite managed to set her diaphanous layers right again after her little . . . ahem . . . *nap* on the wide carriage seat with Archie.

"We could toss a bit of cool water in his face," she offered. "I've seen that done in plays."

Archie settled on the seat beside her, his arm draped over her shoulders. "Oh, let the lad sleep. He looks so peaceful."

Then he leaned to peer through the carriage window. "Are you sure I ought not to go after them? What if this Aaron fellow means her harm?"

Iris waved a languid hand. "And interrupt the most romantic moment of her life? She'd never forgive you." She snuggled into his side. "Bliss vows that he is entirely gentlemanly and heroic. Besides, Elektra can handle herself. Remember when she tricked Cas into the linen closet and locked him in there for hours for dipping her braid into hot candle wax?"

"It was Poll, and it was because he put liver cheese into her best shoes."

"It was both of them, and the girl who can outsmart our clever twins is more than a match for Black Aaron!"

Archie chuckled and relaxed, pulling Iris closer. "Beauty and brains! She takes after you, my goddess."

"Well, I had worried that she had hardened her heart, poor little thing. If this fellow cracked that shell, he is made of superior stuff. Worthington-worthy stuff!"

"Ah, yes." Archie let out a satisfied sigh and leaned back, propping his feet up next to his son's limp body. "We've done well, haven't we, my fairy-queen? Eight wonderful children, all unique, all exceptional. No ordinary dullards among the lot!"

"That's all due to your genius, my warrior." Iris fluttered her eyelashes at her husband and let her shawl fringe trail over his wrist.

Archie lifted her hand and kissed the inside of her palm. *"Come, madam wife, sit by my side and let the world slip: we shall ne'er be younger,"* he quoted huskily.

Iris sighed blissfully. *"The Taming of the Shrew*, Induction, Scene Two," she breathed. "Grab that lap blanket, won't you, my love? I saw a grassy patch a few yards down the road."

In the kitchen of the Green Donkey Inn, chambermaid Edith laid a piece of fine linen over the brass tray—the one saved for only the finest guests—and set about fixing his lordship's tea. It was her way of ensuring that Lord Aaron got his medicines with none the wiser at the inn.

"He wants a special blend," she told Cook. "Don't you worry none. I'll do it for you."

Cook was just as happy to hand over the chore, though she gave Edith a knowing look. "Take care not to be foolish, girl. Don't be looking above your station. That just gets a girl in trouble."

Edith only shook her head and continued to serve his lordship. She was only doing her duty, for if one had the healing Knowledge, one was bound by duty to use it to help others. That was the only reason for her constant attendance upon his lordship.

Any other thoughts were utter nonsense. As if a man like that would have eyes for a plain little sparrow like her! He was grateful for the nursing, that was all.

So when the tales of evil Black Aaron reached the Green Donkey Inn—shiveringly good gossip of seduction, treachery, and doom that made all the folk belowstairs nod their heads as if they'd spotted the bad'un from the first—Edith had no call to feel betrayed.

So why did her heart feel torn to breaking?

Whether or not his lordship had seduced and destroyed that girl years ago was no concern of hers, now, was it? Edith's mother had tended the good and the bad, all equal.

"Let God sort them out," she would say. "I've got me hands full."

So Edith steeped the tisane of medicinal herbs, just as she always did, and she carried the tray up the stairs, just as she always did.

However, when she set the tea on the small table

kept just outside the chamber so she could knock and turn the latch, the shaking of her hands had everything to do with Lord Aaron.

And no matter how she scolded herself, she could not help but suck in her breath at his welcoming smile.

What business did a lord have, smiling like that at a poor serving maid? He had to know he was handsome and fine! To make a girl's heart flip in her chest, to tempt and tease nonsense dreams from a mind that should be set on more practical matters—why, it was nothing short of cruel, it was.

How glad she was that she'd learned of his true nature, and could now see him as he was! Jumping for joy, she was.

Except that her eyes stung and her heart ached worse with every beat and her hands shook so that she spattered the boiling tea on herself like a silly, credulous cow!

His lordship noticed at once, so keen was his predatory gaze. "Now, now! Take care for yourself, little one! Have you burned your hand?"

False concern! Bait for the trap!

Kindness. Goodness beneath the veneer of badness.

Oh, which man was he?

She looked up to see that he'd thrown off his covers and climbed out of his bed. Even in the nightshirt and bare feet, he was a fine-looking fellow. His dark hair was tousled and a bit too long so that it fell over his brows. His color was much better today, his skin flushed and tanned once more. His snapping blue eyes were bright and fixed upon her as if she actually mattered to a man such as him.

She could see how that girl in London could make

herself mad unto death over him. Edith thought she herself might very well have caught a similar malady.

You've seen this ailment before. Rapid pulse, shaking hands, dry mouth, and ready tears.

Oh, she had a right case of it all right.

Love.

He came close, reaching his big square hands to take the tray from her. "Give me that. Sit down, little Edith." He set the tray aside and took her unresisting arm to lead her to the chair by the fire. When he'd seated her as if she were made of finest porcelain, he eased himself to kneel at her side and take her hand in his.

"Tell me what is wrong? Are you ill?" The concern in his sapphire gaze seemed entirely sincere. She despaired of her own thudding heart. Fool!

She must be as a frozen pond in winter. Nothing of her inner turmoil must show upon her surface. One might be fool enough to fall in love with a rotter, but one needn't let on!

Carefully, she withdrew her hand from his large warm one. Though she craved the feel of his fingers wrapped around hers, she would not show it.

"You're not a righteous man, are you?" She folded her hands in her lap. He could have her sacked for such disrespect, truth or not. Nonetheless, she refused to keep her peace. She looked him in the eye. "I ought to have known you for a deceiver. You're always smilin' at me, callin' me your little Edith. Me, of all people! I thought you were lonely, maybe, stuck up in this room on your own. I thought you were only playin' at flirtin' with me."

He blinked. "A deceiver, you say. What do you mean by that?"

His confusion seemed real, except that a wary shadow had come into his eyes. His gaze shifted to the side a bit.

The habit of a liar, methinks.

Her heart broke. She shook her head. "You're a cruel, cruel man. Just another scoundrel, taking advantage of those weaker than yourself. If you've no care for a lady's honor, you certainly have no thought for a humble girl like me!" She pushed her shaking hands against the arms of the chair and stood. She felt slight and weak next to him, but she would not show it.

"I may be poor and plain, but I'm no fool, Black Aaron." *Oh, I am such a fool!* "You'll hoodwink me no more!"

"Black Aaron?" He stood and paced away from her. For a long moment, he stood with his back to her, gazing out the window.

He was quiet for so long that Edith began to worry. She'd said unpardonable things to the highest-ranked guest the inn had ever served! This was a good place, one she was lucky to have. The innkeeper and his family kept a respectable business, where the maids were safer than most and could even put a little by if they worked hard enough.

No matter how she treasured her employment, she wouldn't take back a word she'd said. Still, it might be good to make herself scarce for a bit.

She could move in silence if she chose, after long years of practice in her mother's sickroom. Abandoning the tray, she slipped quietly to the exit. Just as she put her fingers on the latch, a large hand flattened itself on the door before her eyes, pinning it shut.

Heat shimmered across her back as warm breath stirred the tiny curls on the back of her neck. He was so close she could have leaned back against his wide chest without taking a step.

Helpless against his size and strength, shaking with her own fruitless longing, Edith simply closed her eyes and waited.

"Ye might give a bloke a chance to explain, li'l one."

His voice was a deep rumble that set her very core to vibrating in response. Then, the change in his words and tone brought her head up and her eyes open. She turned in the tiny space he had left her, tilting her head far back to gaze at him searchingly.

A devilish grin flickered across his mouth. It was a smile she'd not seen before, but she recognized the chancer within him again. Amazed, she drew in a slow inhalation. "Liar," she breathed. It was an accusation. It was a revelation.

Warm fingers stroked up her arm. "Ye found me out, my Edith. I'm just like you. Just someone alone and afraid in a big world, just a man who went astray and tries to make amends—an ordinary man. I ain't no more Lord Aaron than ye are a princess." His touch moved to drift along the coil of her ear. "Though ye look like a queen t'me."

"But—but the fine clothes! And your manservant!"

He chuckled and she knew it at last for his true laugh. "That weren't no servant. That were Himself."

She pressed her fingers to her lips. "The innkeeper sent him to sleep in the hay!"

He shrugged. "Do 'im good, the mad toff. He's not so bad, really."

"But why the lyin'? And you were truly ill. I know enough to know that!"

"Oh, aye." He smiled down at her as if she were the finest of treasures. "I would be yet, if it weren't for you, m'lass. You've a gift, sure enough."

Alarmed, she drew back slightly. "You mustn't say, please. It'll go easier for me if no one knows."

He chuckled. "Now who's the liar?"

Pricked, she lifted her chin. "I never lie. But I come from far away, and am regarded suspicious on that alone. There are them that think healin' is witchery. They might—" She shuddered.

He took her into his arms, pulling her close to his large warm body. "Now then, ye needn't worry. I wouldn't let anyone harm ye, my sweet Edith. My tired, worldly heart is smitten, it is."

For a single moment, she let her forehead rest against his broad chest. Oh, to have someone to reach out to again—someone who knew her, who treasured her! *I've been alone for such a long time.*

And you're alone still. He might not be Black Aaron—but he is more a stranger than ever now!

Cold alarm threatened to squeeze her throat closed. She put both hands upon his hard chest and pushed, just a little. He released her at once, which was reassuring in itself. All the better, he backed up a few steps. He seemed to understand her withdrawal.

"Miss Edith, my name is Henry Hastings." He bowed. When he straightened, his blue gaze was most serious. "You are right about one thing. I am not a righteous man. I am a liar and a gambler and I won't say I've never been at odds with the law—but I would never press a lady!"

She believed him. After all, she'd been alone with

him in this room for hours on end and he'd never even spoken anything untoward. She must have been holding her breath, for it eased out of her now in slow relief. "Thank you, sir. That does make me feel a sight better."

Then she bit her lip. "Oh, but if you aren't his lordship—"

He spread his hands. "Then who's to pay the cost o' the room?" He rubbed a hand through his thick hair, disarranging it.

Edith's fingers twitched in longing to smooth it back for him.

He sighed. "That's a pickle, for certain. I haven't a farthing left. Himself will be a rich man someday—I hope—and he's the sort what pays his debts, but in the meantime I couldn't travel and he couldn't pay."

Edith lifted her chin. "Meanwhile the hosteler turns away paying custom while you lie up here like a lord and eat up his living. For shame, Henry!"

He looked ashamed. "Now, Edith, I wouldn't've done such a thing were it not needed."

She wrapped her arms about herself. "And you've made me party to it! Oh, you've gone and made a deceiver out of me after all!"

He drew in a breath. "Now, don't say that. I ain't askin' ye to lie for me!" He began to move about the room, a bit unsteadily but with purpose. She watched him grab up his clothes and his shaving items. When he bent to drag a battered valise from beneath the bed, he staggered just a little.

In a flash Edith was there, under his arm, supporting him back to the bed. "You're mad, you are! You cannot go from your bed to the road in an hour!"

He turned and took her face gently between his large hands. His rakish grin turned into something so gentle that it stole her breath clean away. "My queen, I would fling myself into the river so as not to cause you further pain."

It wasn't his "lordship" voice, nor was it the confident tones of the chancer. This tender avowal gave his voice a resonance from another time altogether. She saw the glint of silver armor and flying pennants in his gaze.

Honor, his gaze said to her. *Truth.*

Faithfulness.

When his lips touched hers in the lightest kiss, it was a promise that she dared to believe despite anything the world might think of him, her handsome chancer.

Then he pushed her from the room. "You go and tell the innkeeper everything, my true-heart. I wouldn't have it any other way." Then, with a tender smile, "And you ain't plain, my girl. Never say it." He shut the door with a decided click.

Edith stood outside the chamber door for a long moment. From inside the room she could hear movement, the opening and closing of the wardrobe, his halting step as he packed the valise.

She was an honest woman. She would go to the innkeeper and tell him her suspicions of the man in the finest room.

However, there was no real hurry, was there?

After supper would do.

Chapter Twenty-three

Upon Lord Aaron's horse, they rode far into the night. Elektra lost track of distance, lost track of time. At first she'd tried to lean away from his big body, but eventually the difficulty balancing sidesaddle in a saddle not made for such riding took its toll and she leaned back against him.

His encircling arm tightened about her waist. She felt the warmth of his breath against her ear. Had he just dropped a kiss upon her hair?

She leaned farther into the shelter of his hold and turned her cheek to rest against his chest. He was large and strong and she knew in the depths of her feminine heart that she was in no danger from him—had, in fact, never been safer in her life than she was in his embrace.

Lord Aaron—Black Aaron—held her as if she were the most precious item in the world, and he, the only one who could protect her.

The hoofbeats of the big bay gelding thundered

down the dark road. When enough distance had been covered that Aaron believed them safe from pursuit, he slowed Lard-Arse to a trot.

On the long-legged horse, that gait was a punishing one. After another mile, Aaron was forced to slow to a walk. It likely didn't matter, for he had no destination in mind. In fact, now that he had Elektra alone, he had no idea what to do with her.

That was a lie. He had many ideas. None of them were good ones.

Now that the breath wasn't being jounced out of her, Elektra sat stiffly in the saddle, carefully not leaning into him. It was clear that she expected an explanation for his lies.

Unfortunately, he could not offer that to her.

Finally, she reached out to wrap her fingers around the reins. She pulled Lard-Arse to a halt before Aaron could stop her. Then she turned to sit sideways in the saddle so that she could face him directly.

"Well?"

He wasn't ready. He hadn't thought it through. He had no idea what to say to her.

"Fine then. I shall start." She drew in a breath, and Aaron clearly heard the shaky sound of it. Even inches away from him, he could feel that she was trembling. Though she might toss her head, and behave with the utmost confidence, he knew something that the rest of the world did not know.

Elektra Worthington was just as much of a fraud as he was.

Aaron let out a short laugh. "You have no idea what to say, either!"

She pressed one hand over her mouth, but a panicked giggle made it through. She let her hand drop and shrugged. "After that dramatic rescue, everything I think of sounds like a bad melodrama."

Aaron was silent for a moment. "Rescue," he repeated thoughtfully. *And here I thought I was kidnapping you.*

Hope stirred within him. If she felt her engagement to Camberton was something to be rescued from, did that mean that she might feel what he felt?

Although it was quite dark, with only the slight smile of the moon to guide them, he turned his face away lest she see the longing in his expression. Then his gaze sharpened on something just ahead.

Squinting, he saw a strangely shaped shadow on a hilltop. The scrap of moon gave just enough light for him to realize what it was.

It was no Green Donkey Inn, but it would do. He turned suddenly off the road, giving Lard-Arse a kick to run him up the hill. Elektra squeaked and clung to his waist.

He pulled the leggy gelding to a stop before the white marble façade of a stylish Grecian-temple folly, no doubt part of some wealthy man's nearby estate. The little building was no more than a room with arching windows looking out over the fields beyond, built from gleaming stone and placed artistically among the plantings to give viewers the impression that they'd discovered a secret, magical place.

On the saddle before him, Elektra sat quietly for a moment. Then she turned her head until he could see the ivory oval of her face in the moonlight.

"My lord, how long have you planned this particular portion of our adventure?"

He regarded the silly splendor of the folly with a smile. "For approximately thirty seconds."

She shook her head. "I don't believe you."

He grinned down at her. "If there are cushions and blankets within, I won't believe me, either."

There were neither, but there was a fireplace. Upon the mantel, Aaron found an old-style tinderbox. Elektra took it from him and struck a spark with a practiced motion.

Then Aaron returned to Lard-Arse. After removing the gelding's tack and setting it inside the folly entrance, he used a certain river-stained length of rope to tie the horse out to graze. A picturesque little rivulet had been redirected to chuckle its way past the folly. Lard-Arse whickered grumpy contentment and bent to the burdensome chore of removing every blade of grass within the perimeter of his stake.

As he went back inside, Aaron bent to retrieve the bundle that had been tied behind the saddle. Elektra knelt before the small fire she'd begun in the hearth. She looked up as he entered the round, domed "temple" portion of the folly.

Aaron didn't take another step for a moment. "Do you know, when I first saw you in the manor, you brought to mind a goddess." His voice came out husky and tight, not light and teasing as he'd intended. "Now to see you sitting in a temple, keeping the eternal flame . . ."

She blinked at his rusty compliment. "It isn't eternal. In fact, I don't think we have enough wood to last the night."

"A practical goddess. Here, then. A practical offering."

He let the bundle drop at her side. She glanced at him curiously, then bent to untie the cord binding it.

After unrolling two thick woolen blankets, she discovered a corked glass bottle full of country red, a loaf of hearty brown bread, and, wrapped in waxy paper, a wedge of creamy golden cheese. "A feast!" Then a troubled frown crossed her brow. "But you have no coin. Did you steal this?"

He nearly laughed, but the distrust in her gaze went much farther than believing that he'd nicked a loaf of bread. "Did you not see the abbey we passed this afternoon? Apparently the church has no issue with the brethren pressing grapes, nor with playing at dice with passing travelers. I had a bit of time to pass. Your team is so slow I wondered if perhaps they spent every third hour pacing backward." He bowed with one hand over his heart. "I vow I did not even cheat."

She hefted the bottle with a critical eye. "Oh, I don't mind cheating. Anyone foolish enough to gamble ought to expect it."

Aaron sighed. "Worthington ethics are an education in themselves."

Further education was afforded him when she slid the hem of her gown up to reveal a small embroidered knife sheath strapped to her shapely calf. She removed the shimmering little blade and began sawing competently at the cheese.

Aaron was so stunned by the glimpse of secret skin and rounded flesh that for a moment, the presence of the knife floated just outside his ken. Then he blinked away the haze of lust that had seized him. "You carry a *knife*?"

"You do, too, I imagine."

He did, in fact, keep a small, wickedly sharp blade inside his right boot.

"Of course." He shook off his stunned stupor. "However, I have traveled the world, including places where there is no law, nor even the slightest mote of civilization."

She smirked. "And I live in London. I believe I win."

He opened his mouth to argue further, but then he thought of the other London—the one where the chandeliers did not glow over ballrooms, where dining tables did not groan with plenty, where a lady might have need of a razor-sharp blade.

He pointed at her with one finger. "You are not to leave the house. Ever."

She laughed at him then, a sweetly chiming giggle that only ended when she ripped off a bite of bread with even, white teeth.

Then Aaron had another thought. "I just kidnapped you and ruined your betrothal to a duke. Why aren't you trying to kill me with that?"

Her smile faded as she chewed and swallowed. "I don't know." She held up her hand, turning the knife to catch the firelight. "Lysander gave me this before he went to war. I was Attie's age. He said it was just in case, since he wouldn't be able to protect me for a while. I've always been closest to him of all my brothers, though the twins are nearer my age—but Zander was special. He was different, not pure mischief like Cas and Poll, not brilliance like Orion, nor the steadfastness of Dade."

A look of dreamy recollection took over her expression. "Lysander was laughter and effortless kindness, just because he liked to make people smile. He was always Iris's favorite. We all knew it and we didn't mind. He was our favorite as well."

Frankly, Aaron couldn't imagine it. From what he'd seen, Lysander was more likely to empty a room with his lifeless stare than to fill it with joy.

Elektra's expression hardened. "Then he left us. I think he went to war because the house was so maddening. So many of us, and all our treasures, crammed in tightly together." She let out a slow breath. "So that is laid at my feet as well."

"You?" Aaron moved forward to kneel beside her. "That's nonsense. You were a child when he joined the military. How could you be responsible?"

She lifted her gaze to meet his. "Have you ever made a mistake so large, so far reaching, that the ripples just go on forever?"

His belly went cold. "I know something of regret, yes."

"I feel gray inside, as if all the color has been squeezed from my being. I feel like a shadow." Her green-blue gaze fixed on his. For once, her lovely face was without artifice or even normal reserve. Her raw state made him ache. He had longed to pierce her haughtiness. Now he felt as though he'd stripped the wings off an angel.

Here, he thought wildly. *Put them back on. I'm sorry!* "What is it that you did, to feel so responsible?"

"It was my fault, you see. Everything. All of it was due to me!" She swallowed and turned her face aside. "I burned down the manor." Her voice was a horrified whisper, as if she hardly dared say it aloud.

"You—" *Wait a moment.* "Weren't you an infant?"

"I was five years of age," she said flatly. "Old enough to ruin everything."

He began to laugh. He couldn't help it. "Precisely how powerful do you imagine yourself to be, Miss Worthington?"

He fell back on the blanket, laughing until he felt her silence like a weapon about to fall upon him. He rolled his head and grinned at her, still chuckling. "The all-powerful goddess Elektra, raining down vengeance at the tender age of five years? Don't you think that is a touch on the arrogant side? When I was five I think I might have caused the sea to rise when I tinkled on the beach—but boys will be boys."

He sat up and leaned forward to take her furious, confused face gently between his hands. "You cannot blame yourself if you weren't properly supervised. Would you blame Attie for the book avalanche? Would you blame Bliss for the dunking in the river?" He shook her head gently. "Sometimes. Bad. Things. Happen."

She gazed at him, her eyes shadowed. "Like what happened to that Amelia girl?"

Aaron drew back, releasing her. "I cannot talk about that," he said tightly.

She pursued the question, leaning forward, her gaze sharp on his face. "I will ask you three questions." She narrowed her eyes. "It doesn't matter if you tell the truth or not, for I have a bit of experience with lies. Five brothers, after all."

Aaron stood. "This is nonsense."

"What is your second name?"

He gazed at the domed ceiling of the folly. "Michael."

Then he looked back down at her in triumph. "I would have told you that anyway, so you wasted a question."

She only smiled tightly. "Mine to waste. Second question: Was Amelia Masterson in love with you?"

Aaron stiffened. He looked away. "Yes. Desperately."

For some inexplicable reason, her smile broadened. "Third question: Do you have a brother?"

He flinched slightly, but met her hard stare evenly. "No."

She smiled at him, a lovely bright smile that took his breath away. "Bliss was right all along." She shook her head. "I suppose Dade never bothered to ask you about the past. He's quite good at spotting outright lies—but he sometimes forgets how tricky assumptions can be."

Aaron frowned at her. "What are you talking about?"

She patted the blanket next to her. "Sit down, my lord. Let me tell you about yourself."

Mesmerized by that inviting smile, Aaron found himself sitting. When she pressed bread and cheese into his hands, he found himself eating.

"You are Lord Aaron Arbogast, heir to the Earl of Arbodean. When you were younger, you had a friend. You were as close as brothers, which is why you appeared to be lying, even when I knew you told the truth about not having one. You thought of him as a brother." She handed him the bottle and he numbly drank, washing down the bread and cheese as she went on.

"Amelia Masterson was in love with someone, according to all reports, but it certainly wasn't you. You're a terrible liar, especially when you are being Lord Aaron. I suspect that the real Mr. Hastings, whoever he is, is a rather good liar. When you played Hastings, you were much more difficult to read."

"My manservant," he said absently, even as his mind raced. How could she know so much?

"Now, I know a little something of the bond between brothers. I know that if one brother gets himself into a pickle, the other brother will do anything he can to get him out of it. So this friend of yours—"

"Wells," he told her, automatically filling in her pause, then locked his jaw shut. How had she done that?

"Wells caused poor Amelia to fall in love with him. Perhaps he loved her as well?"

Aaron held absolutely still.

Elektra smiled slightly. "Infatuation, at the very least. However, Wells had a problem. After compromising Amelia, he found himself unable to marry her. Was he already married?"

Aaron didn't dare to breathe.

"Hmm. Engaged. To someone he didn't dare disappoint. Some highborn girl, with a titled papa who might not find it amusing that Wells changed his mind?"

His vision was going a bit gray. He didn't dare inhale. She was a witch!

He heard her pause for a bite of bread and cheese. Finally, he allowed himself a change of air in his lungs. She leapt into the breach.

"You stood up, didn't you? Offered to take one of the ladies off his hands? You're an heir! What papa wouldn't prefer you?"

Wells's voice, begging. *"You're the heir! He will go much easier on you!"*

"But something went wrong, didn't it? Amelia's papa would have been fine with your alternative proposal—but she wasn't, was she? She was in love. *Desperately* in love, just as you said!"

"Please . . . stop."

"There's something that doesn't fit," she mused. "If he loved Amelia, and Amelia loved him . . . why didn't you simply offer for the other girl instead?"

God, he'd kept the secret for so long.

Chapter Twenty-four

Aaron fought years of silence and the dark, desperate burden of a truth he'd never dared speak aloud.

Tell her! She already untangled the worst of it!

"Serena," he muttered. The truth was gravel in his throat. "Serena is my . . . my cousin."

Elektra gasped. Part of him was gratified to spoil her little moment of superiority. "Oh, heavens! Then the angry papa—"

"The earl is her grandfather as well." This time the truth came out a little more easily. He felt . . . lighter, somehow.

"So there was no possibility of him disappointing Serena in favor of Amelia! Oh, that *idiot*!"

Aaron cleared his throat. "He was twenty-two. All men are idiots at twenty-two."

She was silent for a moment. "It would have worked, wouldn't it have? If Amelia hadn't been such a silly thing, she could have been a countess someday, with no one the wiser."

Aaron breathed deeply. His lungs seemed to be working again. "Do you think she was silly for being disappointed that she could not wed the man she loved? That she would see him wed another instead?"

Elektra sighed. "Oh, no, my lord. She wasn't silly for wanting to be loved. She was silly for wanting to die instead!"

Aaron shook his head. "It wasn't suicide. That was the gossip, because it made for a marvelous story, but I know it was an accident. She said she couldn't sleep for crying. She told me she couldn't give me an answer until she'd managed to have a bit of sleep. I went away, thinking I'd ask again on the morrow. The next day she was gone, an overdose of laudanum."

She drew in a long breath. "How sad! Oh, the poor girl!"

"I should have pressed for an answer. I was an idiot for dawdling, for being reluctant to make it right when it wasn't my doing. I was glad for a reprieve, glad to walk away. I got drunk that night, because I was a twenty-two-year-old idiot, and told someone—I honestly don't remember who—that I refused to marry out of duty. Empty words—but much repeated, after Amelia's death became public. A truth here, a surmise there, and everyone suddenly believed that I had seduced and then disappointed Amelia unto death."

"Why didn't you tell the truth?"

"The truth has very little to do with what 'everybody knows.' It would only have involved Serena in the sordidness—and her child. She was already expecting when she married."

She was very quiet. A quiet Elektra was a dangerous Elektra. Aaron turned to look her way.

By the fire in her tropical-sea eyes, he knew she was furious.

"I don't believe I like your friend Wells very much. We are going to have to discuss your tendency to misplace your loyalties."

A small laugh burst from deep within Aaron's pain. "It's a bit late for that, I fear."

She gazed at him, her eyes suddenly sorrowful. "The truth can never come out, can it? Despite Wells's actions, Serena and her child don't deserve scandal, and Society never forgets."

"Serena has two children now. A boy and a girl. I hear they are exceptional. I have never been allowed to meet them, of course. Wells, I fear, did not prosper. Guilt, I think. His indulgences overcame him. He died seven years ago, racing his horse while drunk."

"And the earl? You could have told him, at least."

Aaron tried to smile at that thought, but he feared it didn't come out quite right. "The earl is not a tolerant man. Wells knew he'd be driven off instead, and Serena was already . . . well, it seemed better at the time. The damage was done due to the gossip, and I knew I'd played my part with poor Amelia—"

"You didn't do anything wrong!"

He shook his head. "I think perhaps a girl might like to be proposed to properly, not offered a reluctant hand, don't you? I did a poor job of it. I blamed her for putting Wells into a fix, thereby putting me into a fix by association. I'm sure I didn't hide it well." He shrugged.

"And I knew that Wells was engaged to Serena, but I thought he was only flirting with Amy. Just having a bit of fun before tying the knot. I was too wrapped up in my own pleasures to see what was going on beneath my very nose. I could have stopped it so easily, if only I'd bothered to pay attention. Amelia needed protecting, but I failed her."

"You weren't her father, or her brother! Besides, if I truly wanted to sneak away with a man, no one could stop me. You carry so much guilt—why, when you've done nothing wrong?"

Wonderful, mad Elektra. After knowing him for less than a week, how could she possibly have that sort of belief in him, when his own family had not—even Serena?

He smiled sadly at her. "It is harder than you realize, to remember yourself when you have forever lost the good opinion of the world."

Their gazes met and held for a long moment. Aaron hadn't felt so light in years. The relief was amazing.

Unfortunately, it changed absolutely nothing.

Suddenly he saw her beautiful eyes fill with tears. She lifted her chin and looked away.

He returned to her side, kneeling on the blanket. "What is it?"

She brushed the back of her hand over her eyes impatiently. "It is nothing."

Aaron reached for that hand and kissed away the dampness there. "I have split open my soul, Elektra. Time to pay the piper."

A small laugh cut damply through the tears. "I miss Hastings! Isn't that ridiculous?"

"I am right here."

She turned to regard him. Her gaze was unflinching. "You are a stranger to me, Lord Aaron."

He gave her a Hastings smile. It did not feel false upon his face. "That didn't stop you from kissing me before in the ruin."

She laughed again, albeit reluctantly.

Encouraged, he brushed a strand of golden silk away from her face. "Elektra, I think you are wonderful."

She looked down at her hands. "Hastings didn't think I was wonderful." She sniffled. "Hastings thought I was a spoiled brat."

"Hastings—I—thought you were a complete bed-lamite, actually. I also thought you were beautiful and fascinating—"

"And complicated."

He tipped her chin up with one finger and smiled at her. "You say that as if it is an insult. I shouldn't like you nearly so much if you were simple—if you were Bliss."

The smile that broke out then was reward enough for days. Then she reached out with one finger and gave him a challenging poke in the chest. "Be careful, my lord. Bliss is a Worthington!"

Aaron vowed to himself to never, ever bring up Dade in conversation.

"Now you know everything about me," he said softly. "So you must realize how alike we are. I know precisely how you can want something so much that you will turn yourself inside out to make it happen."

Elektra gazed into the warm gray eyes of the most astonishing man she'd ever met. How could he know what he knew? How could he understand what she barely understood herself?

He might be impressed with her little game of deduction, but Elektra knew she wasn't brilliant like Attie, or capable like Callie, or even good-natured like Bliss. She wouldn't even own the title of family beauty much longer, not with Attie growing up so quickly.

What she was, the only gift she knew was truly her own, was her strength of mind. Her determination to repair her family. Now that she knew the source of that purpose, she was more resolved than ever.

She could not part with that goal, not for anything. Not for anyone.

Not even for love?

Instant terror swept her. Love?

She could not love him! She could never fall in love with him!

Lord Aaron Arbogast was everything she'd ever wanted, and everything she never wanted. Wedding Black Aaron would not bring the Worthingtons up from their disreputable reputation!

Aaron could not make her a lady of Society who was accepted wherever she went. Aaron could not legitimize her quirky family, nor whitewash their eccentricity. Aaron would only add further gossip and scandal to a family reputation already checkered with madness and chaos.

No. Elektra needed the Duke of Camberton. She needed him to turn her family's status to the finest sterling, to wipe the tarnish from the Worthington history, to end the chatter and gossip and chaos once and for all!

I need Camberton . . . but I love Aaron.

I want to be selfish. For just this one moment, I want to be as selfish as people have always believed I am.

Very slowly and with great purpose, she removed the pins holding her chignon. Ignoring Aaron, although she could feel his eyes fixing on the fall of her hair, she began to unbutton her spencer. She laid it aside. Then she stood and reached behind her. With the ease of a lifetime of looking after herself, she swiftly undid the long row of tiny buttons on the back of her gown.

Only then did Aaron seem to rouse from his hair-induced daze.

"Elektra? What—"

When her gown slid from her shoulders and pooled at her feet, she turned to face him at last. He was staring at the pile of mint-green muslin on the blanket. She watched as his eyes rose slowly and his gaze passed over her pearly stocking-clad calves, over the mint-green ribbon garters tied above her knees, over the hem of the chemise that brushed halfway down her thighs, to the twin points of her nipples, chilled with excitement—and yes, a bit of fear!—and not very well concealed by the filmy, finely woven white batiste.

Then, with obvious effort, he forced his gaze to her face.

"I—" He swallowed thickly. "I don't think this is a good idea."

She lifted her chin. He wanted her. She could feel his desire emanating from him. She thought of the kiss—she thought of each kiss separately. There was the first one, when she'd been so surprised and pleased at the thought of feeling such attraction for her future husband. Her pulse increased at the memory.

There was the second kiss, when she'd believed him to be a servant and was sure her perfect plan had been ruined, when she'd felt the compulsion to retrieve one good thing from the mess, even if it remain just a memory forever. Her lips parted, her breath coming faster.

Then . . . then there was the third kiss, the kiss of a girl in love against custom, against rank, against everything she'd always assumed to be valuable.

Her heart melted. Her body throbbed in time with her speeding pulse. Her hands began to shake. Her knees, already weakened by the memory of his mouth on hers, gave way. She knelt before him on the blanket, facing him—offering him . . .

Everything.

Chapter Twenty-five

Elektra watched Aaron swallow hard again. He blinked, started to speak, then halted. Then, incredibly, he drew back, practically scrambling backward on the blanket. She bit her lip.

How sweet. He was trying so hard not to give in. He was trying desperately to remain a gentleman, though he wanted her so badly he seemed beyond speech entirely.

"Aaron?" she murmured. "What are you going to do—mount your horse and ride away?"

He stopped his retreat. "No." His gray eyes went dark then. All gentlemanly reticence slipped away, rolling off him like water, leaving him larger and darker and far more intimidating.

He reached his long, muscled arm out and caught her about the waist. In one powerful motion, he pulled her tightly to his body. They remained there for a thrilling, breathless moment, on their knees, chest to breast, hard to soft, caught on the cusp of no return.

Then he rolled her beneath him on the blanket. She

gasped at the weight of his big, hard body on hers. His two days of beard set her skin to tingling and sent shivers down her neck when he pressed his hot mouth to her throat, sucking and nibbling at her most tender spots. Her lips parted in a gasp. His mouth sought hers.

He took her mouth hard, with all the passion he'd kept so well hidden since the ruins. She willingly let him in, let him dive his tongue into her, let his firm lips mold her softer ones. She wanted him hard, wanted him to want her as fiercely as she wanted him. She'd felt his gentleness. Now she wanted his shadows as well.

His knee pressed between hers, pushing them apart. She spread her thighs willingly, welcoming him coming to rest with his muscled thigh hard against her mound. Her hands clung to him, moving over him, tugging at the buttons of his weskit, at the studs of his shirt, then wonderfully, miraculously, over the bare hot skin of his back.

He pulled her chemise off in one motion, leaving her in nothing but stockings and garters. Pulling away from her for a heart-stopping moment, he came back stripped of his clothing, hot and hard and naked against her.

He began to enter her. She squirmed above him, and he realized after a moment that she squirmed with discomfort. Not precisely how he would prefer her to squirm.

"Sh. Wait." He withdrew from her, although it made him ache to leave even this small amount of her warmth that he'd enjoyed. He kissed her softly. Then he rolled over, pulling her on top of him to sprawl across his chest. As her golden hair fell in a veil around them, he decided he liked this better anyway. She pressed against him invitingly, soft yet lithe and strong.

He pushed the hair back from her face and smiled up into her scowl. "Don't worry. Nothing has to be perfect, my darling. We are here to touch, kiss, and to love. You don't have to get this right. You don't have to be perfect." *Even though you already are. Born perfect*, he thought. Perfect for him.

His chest ached with the expansion of his heart as he watched the concentration and worry ease from her expression. She even gave him a small rueful smile, an easing of the tension she wrapped herself in like a suit of armor.

"I don't know what to do."

He could tell she hated admitting any such thing. It was incredible how well he could read her eyes and the tilt of her head and the lift of her chin. The language of Elektra. He wanted to spend the rest of his life reading and rereading this book.

"Do whatever you wish to do."

Aaron slid his hands up smooth thighs and wrapped them around the curve of her hipbones, which fit into his palms as if they were made just for him. With a single gentle tug, he positioned her in a straddle with her hot damp center pressing his aching erection down on his belly. She gasped in surprise, and then sighed with pleasure when he tilted his pelvis to slowly slide his cock along her slick, aroused slit.

She had braced her palms on his chest, and now her hands tensed. Aaron moaned at the bite of her nails on his skin and the heat of her on his cock. It took every thread of concentration he could summon to keep his movements slow and careful. As much as he wanted to possess her, to lose himself in her, he wanted even more to please and satisfy her.

What man would not want such a delicious creature to come back for more?

He watched her eyelids drop as she took over the rhythm from him, arching her body to attain even more contact as she slid faster against him. He slid his hands up her waist and ribs to cup her full breasts in his palms. "Yes," he urged softly. "Feel my hardness."

Elektra lowered herself down onto his erection, feeling his hardness pressing into her. How could someone be so hard and so gentle at the same time? She paused, her breath catching as she stretched painfully. This was it. If she did this, she would have done something irrevocable.

Worthingtons weren't terribly respectful toward the irrevocable. Worthingtons believed it was better to apologize than to authorize.

Abruptly, she lost patience with herself. She lost patience with this gentleness and this tenderness. Blast it, she lost patience with her fear!

Taking a deep breath, she drove her body down onto his. Ignoring his gasp, ignoring the burning of her own body its most tender point, she bloody well got it over with!

The pain was actually rather shocking. Her breath left her completely in a ragged gasp. Beneath her, Aaron writhed. "Oh, you little fool," he gasped. "Why did you do such a thing?"

He tried to withdraw from her, but even in her dis-

tress Elektra could out-stubborn any male of the species. She gripped him with her knees and fisted her
hands in his hair and held him tight as the uneven gasps
tore from her throat.

Giving up on wresting her impaled body from his
erection, Aaron settled for wrapping her tightly in his
arms and pulling her down to his chest. "You're entirely
mad, Miss Elektra Worthington!"

She shook her head, rolling her cheek against the
hard plates of his pectoral muscles. "Me?" she panted.
"I'm the sane Worthington! Ask anyone!"

Aaron gave a resigned sigh. "A question of relativity,
I assure you."

Elektra hid her smile beneath her fallen hair.

Then, just like that, her body took over. She melted
around him, relaxing, wrapping him snugly within her.
The fullness made her want to move, to slide up the
hard rod of him, then slowly ease back down.

She had the rhythm of it now. She rose and fell on
him, each slide taking him deeper, each withdrawal
teasing her. She made it last. The world might think
her impetuous, but she had an instinctive knowledge
that if she hurried it would be over too soon. She moved
slowly and purposefully until he moaned and bucked
and sweated beneath her.

He didn't speak, didn't urge her to go faster. She understood that he liked it, that he wanted to be teased to
an unbearable level. She waited until her own body began to ache and long and shudder. She could not bear it
any longer. She had to know what was at the top of this
mountain!

She dug her fingers into his biceps and she rose and

fell on him in a rhythm as old as time. He held her breasts in his hands and called out her name as his body convulsed between her thighs. She felt him as he hardened even further and enlarged even more inside her, throwing her from the heights into a final tailspin of ecstasy.

Aaron had lost thought, had lost all shred of civilization. Without restraint, he plunged deeply into her. She was everything he'd ever dreamed. Her ardor moved him, driving him higher than mere sex, than mere satisfaction. There was no other woman like Elektra. She was a creation of fire and spirit that he'd never known before.

She met him, gasp for gasp, thrust for thrust. Her hands slid around his back, tightening on his shoulders, her fingernails digging deep, driving him higher. Her sighs blended with his moans. One breath, one body, one heart.

God, how I love her.

He could not tell her that now, not while he was deep inside her body, not while his release built within him and the blood left his brain and there was nothing in the world but sweet, wild, hot, slippery *Elektra*.

He considered her wary heart and knew she likely wouldn't believe him anyway.

So he loved her as best he could—with his hands, with his mouth, with his open heart and his every thought. *I love you*.

She cried out, calling his name—his real name. Then she came around him, her body tightening around his cock, pulsing her ecstasy around him. His release overwhelmed him, and he exploded inside her as a deep, choked roar was torn from his throat.

The mad pleasure vibrated through Elektra, exploding the very center of her outward, sending light and heat and chills throughout her entire body. She knew that she made noises. She could hear her own animal cries but she could not control them and furthermore she could not care about them. At last she slipped and fell, and fell.

And then drifted like a feather down to lie upon his chest, sweating and panting and finally truly understanding what it was. The great mystery of taking a man inside her wasn't just about skin and flesh and hardness and softness.

This man inside her, this was the man she loved.

Aaron wrapped weary arms about his woman and held her close. He had thrown it all away for this single moment with her. There was no going back now to that man who first stepped upon this shore but a week ago. That man could think of nothing but regaining the past.

Now all Aaron could see was the future, his future. A future full of fire and light and love and sweetness and arguments and more relatives than he could count, because they seemed to be increasing.

There was no other in woman in the world but Elektra. Even as she relaxed upon him, his body between her thighs, her forehead resting on his shoulder, his face buried in the damp sweet-smelling crevice of her neck, fear grew within him.

What if she didn't love him?

What if she never loved him?

He rolled with her in his arms until she lay limply beside him, her head upon his chest, her long legs tossed over him coltishly, her hair a tangle that blocked his vision. His expanded heart beat a new rhythm, with a resonance that shook into his soul.

Elektra sleeping was a wonder of softness and sweetness and pliancy that anyone who had bounced up against her razor-edged exterior could not imagine. At least, he would not have imagined it if he had not seen her gentleness with her little sister or the delicate respect she had for her mother.

Elektra was not insensitive. If anything, she was too aware of others. She cared too deeply for their good opinion, even more when those others dared judge her mad family.

This scheme of hers, this quest for the Perfect Bachelor, was merely her way of trying to protect that bunch of deliriously lovable oddballs—Aaron allowed a single exception to that lovability in the person of Orion, who clearly possessed nothing even resembling a heart!—but now he hoped that they could put the matter of the Perfect Bachelor behind them. He would die to keep her—but losing her would kill him as well.

Aaron slid his arm beneath her head and rested his cheek on the silky pile of her hair, which in typical Elektra fashion had taken up more than its share of the blanket. He smiled in sleepy desire to fight her for the blankets for the rest of his life.

He closed his eyes and breathed in the sweet damp scent of satisfied Elektra. Fine. He was a dead man. But what a way to go.

Chapter Twenty-six

Aaron stretched languidly. His feet came to the end of the covers and emerged into the chill air. He shivered, his eyes still closed, and pulled them back in. The bed was a bit short.

The bed was also a bit hard. Actually, it was as unforgiving as a marble floor!

The marble floor of the temple folly . . .

Folly. Blankets.

Elektra.

He reached a sleepy hand to one side. She was so beautiful, so soft and giving, so fiery and passionate—

She was not there. Aaron opened his eyes, blinking and squinting against the morning sun pouring into the many windows of the folly. Bright sun, blinding white marble, and a single graceful shape in pale green standing in the open doorway, looking out.

"Someone's coming."

Alarm shot through him. Aaron stumbled to his feet, realized his nakedness and grabbed up his trousers.

Donning them quickly, he joined her at the door while shoving his arms into his shirtsleeves. "Who is it?"

The road stretched out beyond and below them. They could see for a mile in either direction. Alone on the road, approaching the way they themselves had come, a lone rider trotted a weary horse.

Elektra tilted her head. "That isn't one of my brothers. He's too fair to be Zander or Orion and too thin to be Dade or Cas."

Aaron smiled down at her. "Not every rider to come our way is going to be a Worthington."

She slid him a playfully sour glance. "They have been so far."

He chuckled. "Fair point."

The distraction of her golden hair flowing down her back, shimmering corn silk in the morning light, dragged at his attention. Her lovely pale skin, like alabaster by candlelight, like finest ivory by day, made him want to run his hand over her cheek, down her graceful throat, into her bodice—

"He has seen us."

Ahem. Right. Even after the passion of the night before, Aaron had no idea how Elektra would respond to his touch. Turning back to the view of the road, he beat his lust into submission and tried to focus his vision on the rider.

The horseman had kicked his horse into a gallop. The pale oval of his face beneath his hat definitely appeared to be turned in their direction. Aaron tilted his head, thinking idly that there was something familiar about that lean stature.

"I don't think I know him," Elektra mused aloud.

"Although he seems to know us—and to be in a distinct hurry to reach us!" The rider had turned off the road and was urging his mount up the hill toward the folly.

Suddenly Aaron knew where he'd seen that person before. His last view of Carter Masterson had been when the young man had been pounding the pride out of him at the ball. One didn't soon forget an encounter like that.

Aaron backed into the shadow of the doorway, tugging gently at Elektra's hand. "My sweet, would you please put on your shoes? No, don't bother with the blankets. We need to leave. Now."

Elektra didn't question him, thank heaven. She scurried to her things and pulled her shoes on, then stuffed her arms into her spencer. As he tugged his own boots on, Aaron spared a moment to wonder how many times the Worthingtons had needed to move along at a moment's notice.

They were too late. A shadow stepped into the open archway. "Lord Aaron!"

Aaron pushed Elektra behind him when he saw the pistol in Carter's hand.

"That's mine!" Elektra hissed from behind Aaron's back, and he saw that it was indeed. *I left it with Lard-Arse's tack, like a fool. Just a little harvest-fair prize for an intruder!*

"Shh!" He positioned Elektra directly behind him. If Carter fired, the old pistol would not have enough kick to send a ball through him to strike her . . . he hoped.

"Help!" Elektra squeaked. "Save me!"

"I'm trying to save you," he muttered over his shoulder. "Hush!"

Carter raised the pistol. "Get away from her, you rotter!"

Aaron went very still. He could see Carter's hand shaking from nerves strung too tightly. The idiot could fire at any time without even meaning to.

Elektra drifted away from Aaron. He saw a flutter of mint green from the corner of his eye. What the hell was she doing?

She staggered to a point halfway between Carter and Aaron, very nearly in the line of fire. Then she halted and, unbelievably, pressed the back of one hand upon her forehead in a ladylike cue to faint.

It worked, by God. Carter lowered the pistol long enough to lunge forward to catch her. His inbuilt gallantry, finely honed by a probable lifetime of romantic music and lurid novels, proved more than he could resist.

Elektra delivered a stellar performance, timing her faint to perfection, draping herself across his rescuing arm as if it were a move rehearsed a hundred times. Knowing her, she had probably practiced on her brothers. In a mirror.

Since a gentleman did not hold a pistol like a brigand in one hand and a fainting lady in the other, Carter was seemingly unable to retain his aim on Aaron.

So far so good. Aaron decided to stay very still and follow Elektra's lead. "She's mine," he growled with what he considered to be the perfect level of insane lust.

From where she remained artistically blocking Carter's ability to aim, Elektra rolled her eyes at him.

Aaron blinked. *Too much?*

She shut her eyes briefly and shook her head fractionally. *Putrid. Really.*

"Miss Worthington, have you been harmed?" Carter held the pistol straight out to one side, but Aaron was too far to rush him before the man could repair his aim and fire.

"Miss Worthington?"

Elektra inhaled deeply, then opened her eyes to flutter her lashes dramatically at Carter. "Oh, I had the most awful dream—" Then, realizing that her dream was indeed true, she shrieked appealingly and turned to cower in Carter's hold. "Oh! Oh, we must flee! You must take me away from that terrible, dreadful man!"

Aaron fought to keep his expression from souring and continued to project a bestial leer. *Take care not to run out of synonyms, my love.* He'd been Black Aaron for far too long. He didn't care to play this part any longer.

"What have you done to her?" Carter gazed at Aaron with the purest hatred. "Bastard! Blackguard! Scoundrel!"

Aaron gritted his jaw. *We have moved into nouns.*

"I knew you were up to no good! What other reason could you have for returning to England but to despoil more virtuous women?"

Well, I had worked my way through every female in the Bahamas . . .

Unfortunately, Aaron could not bring himself to mock Carter. Although Carter was an idiot, he was a righteous idiot. The young man had every reason to want retribution for his sister's senseless death.

"How—" Elektra clung to Carter, her voice wispy with distressed innocence. "How did you find me?"

Carter sneered. "I watched him stealing away from

your house in London. I was on my way to warn your
brothers, you see. I had no idea you were not safely
within your home, so I followed his ugly horse for
miles." Outrage took over Carter's expression. "Then I
saw him steal you directly off your own carriage!"

Elektra could barely breathe with the stranger's arm
wrapped about her ribs. She needed to think, quickly!

First of all, who was this idiot? Aaron seemed to
know him. So who would hate Aaron so much he would
feel compelled to follow him halfway across England?

Well, Black Aaron had killed Amelia Masterson—
according to gossip!—so this must be a Masterson.
Brother, probably. Younger, definitely.

She twisted a bit, trying to expand her lungs. He
gripped her more tightly to his side. "Don't worry, Miss
Worthington. I have you. I will take care of you. I fear I
cannot undo what this maniac has wrought, but I will
repair your reputation as well as I can. We will ride directly to Gretna Green. I traded for a fresh horse just
this morning. I calculate we can be married by supper!"

Elektra panicked. *Marvelous. Everyone wants to
marry me—except the one man I wish would ask!* "But,
sir—we do not have a ring!" She heard a strangled noise
from Aaron's general direction.

"Furthermore, this morning I posted a letter to the
Earl of Arbodean about your activities! That will fix
you, you bastard! I would kill you myself right now, but
I would not deprive Miss Worthington's brothers of their
right to vengeance!"

"Oh!" Elektra fluttered her lashes at young Mr. Masterson a bit more. He did not seem tired of it yet. "I long
to see my dear brothers! Please, let us go from here!

Leave him behind—my brothers will see to his dastardly hide!"

Mr. Masterson gazed down at her. "Yes, you have been through too much. However, we must assure that he does not follow us."

"Tie him!" *Don't sound too eager.* "If you think it would be best, of course." *Flutter.*

"I haven't any rope."

Heaven help her. How had he survived to his twentieth year all by himself? *So this is how it feels! Trying to talk sense to him must be what it's like for an ordinary person to talk to a Worthington!*

She pasted a worshipful expression on her face. *Flutter.* "Rope? Oh, you are brilliant, sir! The rope he tied his horse with, of course!"

Mr. Masterson looked torn. She could almost see the gears turning slowly in his head. Very. Slowly.

Elektra filled in the blanks for him. "Yes, I will fetch it for you. Anything for you, my rescuer!"

She slipped out of his arm before he could wrench her back and scuttled to the exit. Once outside, it was a simple matter to set Lard-Arse free and return with the rope.

"Miss Worthington, you must hold the pistol upon him while I bind him."

Elektra staggered backward, etching a horrified expression on herself. "Oh, I could never touch that awful thing!" She took the rope from him quickly. "I shall tie him while you protect me. I know you would never let him hurt me!" *Flutter.*

She tied Aaron very well indeed, using miles of rope and creating large unwieldy knots that would convince

Mr. Masterson even at a distance. It wouldn't do for these two to get within arm's length of each other.

Poor Aaron was at his breaking point, she could see. Alarm for her, fury at his helplessness, and just plain anger at Mr. Masterson's assumptions called up storm clouds in those gray eyes.

She reassured him with a squeeze of his fingers when she was sure Mr. Masterson couldn't see, then finished tying him. She tried not to look too practiced and efficient, but she also wanted to get this idiot as far away as she could from Aaron before something detonated!

Returning to Mr. Masterson, she shyly took his unarmed hand. "Please, let us leave this horrible place." *Flutter-flutter.* "He is bound and his horse is gone. He cannot follow us now!"

If she could get him on the road, she was sure she could extricate herself from his presence quite easily. She managed to get him as far as the open archway. Unfortunately, Aaron rushed matters just a bit. Men! Before she could stop him, he burst from the folly to fling himself bodily upon Mr. Masterson.

That was the trouble with the trick knot. It was simply too easy to get free of, once one had learned the way of it!

Elektra gazed down at the bound and furious Mr. Masterson. This time her knots were unassailable.

She folded her arms in exasperation. "He's so earnest and noble. How exhausting!"

Aaron glanced at her. "I didn't realize you knew Carter Masterson."

"I don't. I simply recognized the species. I believe it

is *Gullible idiotis.*" She rolled her eyes. "Easily identified by total lack of humor and immunity to irony. Natural predators include Castor and Pollux Worthington—and anyone else with a brain and an agenda. Spare me, please."

Aaron gazed down at Carter, who nursed a black eye and a decidedly resentful humor. "It isn't his fault. He's hardly more than a boy."

"He must be twenty at least!"

"Twenty-two," Carter muttered bitterly.

"There, you see what I mean?"

Elektra and Aaron spoke simultaneously. Aaron stared at Elektra. "So . . . how old are you?"

She tossed her head. "Nineteen. Why, how old are you?"

He rubbed his face. "Mumble-mumble."

Unfortunately, Elektra was fluent in Mumble—probably due to close association with those five miscreant brothers. She gaped at him. "You're thirty-four?"

"Is that a problem?"

She blinked. "Ah. Well, no. It is only that Archie is precisely fifteen years older than Iris. And . . . they wed when she was nineteen."

"What does that mean?"

She shook her head quickly. "Nothing. A coincidence, I'm sure."

Aaron felt a strange tingling sensation on the back of his neck, the sort of feeling one gets when being watched—or being conspired against!

Carter lifted his head. "If you two are finished comparing birthdays, I think you should either untie me or kill me, for you both sicken me!"

Elektra scowled at Carter. "Pardon me, but we were happily minding our own business when you insisted on inviting yourself in."

"Happily?" Carter sneered. "He doesn't deserve happiness! Amy deserved happiness! He deserves to be lying cold in the ground, not her!"

Elektra knelt beside him and put her hand on his arm. "I'm so sorry. I forgot about your poor sister for a moment." She was enraged at Carter but also heartbroken for him. She knew what it meant to watch one's family fall apart.

However, he was far too mired in the past. Instead of enjoying his own careless youth, he remained obsessed with his own helplessness while his sister crumbled, too young at the time to help her, too young to challenge Aaron to a duel, too ignorant to help his parents survive the tragedy.

Mired in the past? Does that sound familiar?

Elektra tried to shut that thought away. She was entirely focused on the future.

Really? While wearing the key to a moldering ruin about your neck?

Carter pulled away from her touch. She looked up at Aaron, biting her lower lip. "Can't you—?"

"No," he interrupted her. Then, because Carter's pain was so obviously raw, "I wish I could, but it would only cause more pain."

"More pain?" Carter turned his hate-filled gaze upon Aaron. "Do you know what you did to me? To my entire family?"

Elektra reached to comfort him again. He scuttled violently away from her hand.

"You are a fool to trust in him," he snarled to her. "He'll only betray you, too!" He pointed out the door with his chin. "Go, look in my saddlebag! I was bringing my sister's diary to prove this bastard's worthlessness to your family. Read it! You'll see his relentless, heartless seduction and his vicious attack on her innocent heart!"

Elektra glanced at Aaron. "Hmm."

Aaron narrowed his eyes. "Elektra," he warned.

She raised a brow. "Do not take a tone with me, my lord. I will read what I like."

In moments she had the leather-bound journal in her hands. Poor Amy Masterson's diary had only a few weeks of entries. Elektra supposed the girl had never had a secret before in her life—until she met a handsome, flirtatious fellow at a ball.

Furious, Aaron stalked from the folly. He couldn't bear to watch Elektra read Amy's words. Would they contradict his tale? He thought they must, if Carter Masterson had read it and still believed in Aaron's sins.

Although he'd spent the night in her arms, Aaron still wasn't completely sure how Elektra felt about him. She spoke nothing of love. Didn't women speak endlessly of love?

Damn it, she had finagled her way into his lonely, dark heart, his mind, and his soul. He could not bear to see her turn away now!

Would she keep faith in him, even in the face of Amelia's words? Would she join the world in its poor opinion of him?

In the end, who would Elektra believe?

* * *

Elektra read quickly but carefully. Once, when Carter Masterson began to speak to her, she held a finger absently to her lips. "Hush!"

He actually obeyed her. It was refreshing, that's what it was.

The pages were full of a young woman's fancies come to life. The moment she had met "Him." Their first kiss, the description of which caught at Elektra's heart. She firmly squelched her own romantic flight of fancy to continue reading.

Amelia and "Him," making love for the first time. Elektra swallowed hard, reading the diary's frank description. She could not rationally feel superior to "silly" Amelia any longer. She now knew the pull of male to female, the bond of heated kisses and tender touch, the wild sensation of skin to naked skin, the way a man's body fit into hers.

Then came Amelia's realization of her lover's failings—her disillusionment, tangled with the love she still felt, confused by her passion and jealousy. She'd been shattered—entirely devastated by "His" desertion.

Finally, Elektra reached the last entry, the final words of Amelia Masterson.

Lord Aaron came to me today. His lordship's words left me cold, my heart frozen and alone, my life an interminable winter.
The winter must end. I must convince Lord Aaron that I am willing to end it.
I must sleep.

The girl's words left Elektra chilled and aching herself. She could see how Amelia's family must have interpreted the final sentence.

However, if one read it with the knowledge of Aaron's conversation with Amelia on her last day, one realized that the dire-sounding "I must sleep" meant precisely that. They were the words of a girl exhausted by her grief, who recognized that she was weary beyond the ability to make reasonable decisions.

Elektra closed the diary slowly and pressed it to her lap.

"Well, now you know the truth about your lover." Carter Masterson's voice overflowed with bitterness. "You must realize that you are simply another Amy, on your way to ruinous disappointment."

Elektra didn't look at him. "Mr. Masterson, was your sister a mannerly girl?"

"Why—I know you think her wicked from her diary, but she wasn't!"

Elektra closed her eyes. "I am trying to ascertain if she were inclined to the proper use of titles and rank."

He sputtered. "Well, yes, of course! She was most genteel—until he debauched her!"

Elektra opened the book to the last page and held it out for him to see.

He flinched. "I've read it! I couldn't bear to read it again!"

She moved closer. "Pray, take note that your sister refers to 'Lord Aaron' and 'his lordship' when speaking about Aaron's visit that last day. A visit, I might add, in which he offered her his hand in marriage and she refused him an answer."

Carter snarled. "So he claims. Of course, he would say anything to absolve himself!"

Elektra resisted the urge to smack him firmly with the diary. "Mr. Masterson, my point is that your sister, even on her darkest day, did not forget to properly refer to him as 'Lord Aaron' and 'his lordship.' Do you concur that that was characteristic of her?"

"Yes." Then, more quietly, "She was exceedingly well mannered."

Elektra sat herself down, tailor-fashion, before him and held the diary in his view. "Yet, see here, and again, here—she refers to 'He' and 'Him'—not 'his lordship.'"

Carter blinked and peered at the pages where she indicated. "I . . . I did not take note of that before."

Elektra regarded him with sympathy. "Would she have refrained from doing so for weeks, then, in the last entry, suddenly change her address?" He remained silent. She leaned forward. "Sir, don't you see that whoever it was that seduced her and broke her heart, it was not 'his lordship'?

"Further, here she states that 'He' is due to marry another in a matter of weeks. Yet Lord Aaron has never been engaged, nor married."

Carter stared down at the diary. "But—but everybody knows it was him!"

Elektra shook her head. "Sir, hundreds of years ago, 'everyone knew' a ship could sail off the edge of the flattened earth!" She drew in her temper. "Amelia was not accusing Lord Aaron in her last entry. She was simply recording his visit, and his offer—and her own desire to sleep on her decision."

He swallowed hard. "If that were true, why take her own life?"

Elektra put her hand on his shoulder. "I do not believe she did. I believe that 'the winter must end' means that she was determined to put her heartbreak behind her, to see to her future." She closed the diary and set it next to him. "She was exhausted and careless with the laudanum. That is all."

He stared down at the journal, helpless to wipe at his dampened eyes with his bound hands. "It was just an accident. Oh, my God. Oh, Amy . . ."

Then he lifted his head to gaze at Elektra. "Black Aaron—Lord Aaron knows who it was, doesn't he? He knows who ruined my sister! Why else would he offer for her, unless it was to save someone he knew?"

Elektra remained silent for a long moment. Carter was still caught up in retribution, unwilling to release his role as his sister's avenging angel.

"Carter," she said quietly. "What if I swore to you, upon my word, upon my name, that the one who Amelia loved has long since joined her in the grave? Would you take my word? Would you let her go, and live your life the way she would wish you to?"

Just outside the folly archway, Aaron leaned against the outer wall and listened to the utter faith and belief in Elektra's voice. His heart expanded with every breath.

Oh, my beauty. You make me believe again.

Carter's breathing was ragged. "I—yes, I would believe you, Miss Worthington."

* * *

When Carter Masterson climbed back on his horse and rode slowly away, Elektra watched until she could no longer see him on the distant road.

There was a lesson to be taken from her encounter with Carter.

She simply wasn't sure which one it should be.

Let the past be in the past. The future awaits you.

Or possibly—*Putting your family back together is the most important thing you can do.*

While she had watched over Carter's departure, Aaron had retrieved Lard-Arse from his wandering. The rangy gelding was saddled, and their things were tied neatly on board.

Aaron turned to her as she approached. "I ought to take you home now, but my grandfather—his health is most delicate, and I fear that Carter's letter may well destroy him."

Elektra nodded. "Of course. We should go at once."

He shook his head. "No, I will escort you back to the last village, where you can contact your family to come get you."

She folded her arms. "Oh, will you? And what will you tell your grandfather about Carter's claims? That they aren't true?"

He blinked. "Of course."

Elektra narrowed her eyes. "But they are true. Entirely. Completely. True."

He opened his mouth to protest. Then his eyes widened. "Oh, hellfire."

She nodded sagely. "Indubitably."

Aaron rubbed his hand through his hair in dismay. "So . . . now I truly *am* Black Aaron!"

She smiled slightly. "It looks good on you."

He shook his head. "No, I must still see him—if only to apologize, to try to repair something." He sighed. "My inheritance is lost, I realize that. However, I need him to know that I—that I never meant to—"

Elektra couldn't bear it any longer. "Oh, for pity's sake, my lord. Put me in the saddle and let us go explain ourselves to your grandfather!"

Chapter Twenty-seven

Button cleared his throat. "Well, lad . . . you'll have a fine time at the palace. What a marvelous opportunity for you!"

Cabot paused for just a moment, breathing deeply, allowing the pain to move through him and then disperse.

Except that it never did, not really.

Button stood in the doorway to Cabot's bedchamber. One hand was braced casually on the frame; the other held a hanger of freshly stitched cravats made from exceptional opalescent silk—his farewell gift.

Of course, he did not venture farther into the room than the doorjamb.

Cabot continued in his methodical packing. He had many fine suits after his years with Lementeur, and he packed each with the care it deserved. Each layer of superfine or silk had a sheet of linen laid between it. It was an exacting job, and Cabot took care to do it perfectly. Such attention to detail kept the pain at bay.

Except that it didn't, not really.

Now he turned to Button and gazed at him levelly. "I will be done shortly. If you do not mind the wait, I will bring your tea then."

Button waved a careless hand and smiled. "Nonsense. I managed to make my own tea for most of my long life. I can manage it again."

Another reference to the difference in their ages. Did Button even recognize his tendency to utter such things anymore, or had it become such an ingrained habit, a way to keep Cabot at a distance, a way to remind himself?

Cabot had never understood it, not when he felt a hundred years older than his puckish, playful master. Not years ago, when he was much younger than he was now, and Button had taken a mentor's role. Not now, when he was a master himself, as fine a designer as Button himself, if a bit less outrageous.

It hadn't worked, in the end. All his striving for perfection, secretly believing somewhere inside him that by gaining artistic equality with Button, it would somehow cancel out Button's fixation with Cabot's lesser years.

Now he had achieved the pinnacle of success. He'd been called into service by the Prince Regent himself, to add his genius to the Royal Wardrobe, to bring his talents to bear in dressing one man, and one man only.

And Button would not even allow him to make the tea, one last time.

Cabot turned back to the trunk he was currently filling. As he spread out the fine linen, he listened carefully to the brush of the cloth against his skin. For all these years, he'd longed for the touch of something other than fabric.

Now, with a tightness in his throat and a piercing ache in his chest, he was releasing that dream.

It was time to walk away from love.

The Earl of Arbodean sat in his grand hall, on a fine carved chair, by his massive stone hearth, and gazed sternly at Elektra for a long moment. "Worthington, eh? The name is familiar."

She had done her best with the mint-green gown, and her hair, with the few minutes she'd been allowed to freshen up in a guest chamber. She was a bit less mussed, a bit less dusty, and on her very best behavior.

Aaron watched her face. She did not seem at all intimidated by the grandeur of Arbodean.

His grandfather had yet to look at him. Aaron supposed that he ought to be grateful to have been allowed within the ancient doors of the hall. A slender woman entered the hall, carrying a tray of tea and cakes.

"Grandfather, let the girl sit." Serena had a light, musical voice, but time and motherhood had given her a tone of command.

Sourly, the earl waved Elektra to a chair opposite his. Then he slid a glance toward Aaron. "You. Wait outside." And to Serena as well. "You, too, pet. I wish to hear Miss Worthington tell me why Aaron is not a blackguard."

Aaron felt his face heat, and for moment he held his ground. He wouldn't leave Elektra alone if she felt at all uncomfortable.

She smiled easily at him. "It's quite all right, my lord. The earl and I will become better acquainted."

Aaron remembered who it was the earl was dealing

with and nearly laughed aloud. As he left the room, he heard the earl speak.

"I met an Archimedes Worthington, a very long time ago. Odd fellow, but clever."

Aaron was still smiling when Serena caught at his arm. "Aaron! When I told you to stay away, I didn't mean for you to run away with someone's daughter."

Aaron stiffened. "From you, Serena? I thought you of all people understood the truth of matters."

She blushed and released his arm. "I do . . . now. I admit, when Wells finally told me, I thought he was just in his cups again. Then I realized how it all fit together. I knew what you had done for me—and for my children."

Aaron shook his head. "I never meant for you to know at all. Wells made a mistake, but it was his mistake, not yours."

Serena lifted her head. "My mistake was in not trusting you when you told me to keep my distance from him."

He looked away. "Well, I may not be the best person to give advice on making wise choices."

Serena's gaze sharpened. "She's very pretty."

Aaron sighed. "She's astonishing. And exasperating. Clever. Brave. Quite possibly insane. I cannot bear to lose her."

His cousin bit her lip. "Oh, dear. It's like that, is it?"

"Oh, yes. Entirely like that." He rubbed his hand over his face and admitted his greatest fear out loud. "But I am not what she wants."

Serena snorted. "Perhaps she is not as clever as you think her, then."

Aaron shook his head. "I will always be Black Aaron,

Serena. I will always be the uncle that people whisper about behind the boys' backs. If I were to have children of my own, they would always be known as Black Aaron's get. How can I ask a woman to wed herself to that?"

Serena put her hand on his arm, but she had no comfort to offer that would erase the unavoidable. She left him there to linger in the hall, wishing he could hear what went on behind closed doors.

Then those doors opened and he saw Elektra being ushered out by the earl's own gnarled hand. "Thank you, dear," he heard the earl say. "Send the boy in now, if you will."

Elektra spotted him lurking in the shadows and wiggled her fingers at him. "It is your turn to brave the lion's den. Go on. He's a sweet old dear, isn't he?"

Aaron tilted his head. "Not my first choice of description, no." Then he took her hand, grasping her fingers in his. Her skin was warm, her grip steady. She was frightened of nothing, it seemed.

"What did you tell him?"

Elektra blinked. "I told him everything."

Aaron swallowed. "Ah . . . everything?"

She grinned at him. "Do you fear that I corrupted his innocence? Yes, I told him everything—from the first time I saw you in the inn-yard at the Green Donkey to the moment we sent Carter Masterson packing. He seemed greatly interested in the slightest of details."

Aaron looked down. "I vowed to Wells that I would keep his secret forever."

Elektra waved a hand. "Oh, he already knew all about that. Lady Serena told him the truth just today, when he got that ridiculous letter from in the post from Carter and nearly dropped dead from the shock."

Aaron sucked in a breath. "She did not say. That . . . that is unexpected indeed."

Elektra rolled her eyes. "Oh, I'm going to strangle that boy. Do you know that he described me as 'naive beyond sense'?"

Aaron couldn't help smiling. "How dare he," he said mildly.

She turned him about and gave him a bossy little push. "Go on. Don't keep him waiting. He's likely to expire any minute. I've never in my life met someone so old."

When Aaron opened the door to the hall, he was still laughing.

When he saw the grave expression upon the earl's face, his merriment faded away like mist before the midday sun. He bowed. "My lord. You wished to see me?"

The earl waved him in from his seat by the fire. "Sit down."

Aaron sat opposite him. The earl regarded him in silence for far too long. Aaron fought the urge to fidget like a boy.

"I sent you away."

Aaron met his grandfather's narrowed gaze. "Yes. I recall it quite clearly."

The earl picked up a sheaf of letters from his side table. "These letters of recommendation—are they real?"

Stung, Aaron kept a tight hold on his temper. "Why do you not correspond directly with the men who signed those letters, if you do not trust my word on it?"

The earl waved a hand. "Don't be so touchy, boy."

Aaron sighed. "I am not a boy, my lord. I have spent

a decade trying to make up for something terrible that happened, but in that time I have realized that my portion of the blame is not large enough for the punishment I was served. I was a youthful idiot. I was not gentlemanly when it would have served everyone for me to remember my honor, but I did not ruin that poor girl. This you already know, apparently, so why do you still treat me like a liar and a criminal?"

The earl leaned back in his chair. "Well, you've certainly learned to hold your temper when prodded. That alone was worth sending you away. You were always such a touchy little sod."

Aaron seethed, but kept his tongue.

The earl went on. "That girl—she's a pretty little thing, and not half clever! She told me a tale that made me laugh, it did!"

Aaron frowned, confused. "I'm glad you found it amusing, my lord, but—"

"But I didn't believe a word of it, of course! Kidnapping *you*! Ha!" The earl kept chuckling while he sipped his tea.

Aaron sat, his confusion mounting. The earl always made him want to check his weskit for stains. The old man was as straight as a stick, and as conservative as any white-haired statesman could be. Yet he'd enjoyed the company of the most irreverent, subversive woman Aaron had ever met.

The earl sipped his tea, still chortling. "Lard-Arse!" *Snort!*

Aaron frowned at his grandfather. "He is in your stables. You can meet him if you like."

The earl shook a teasing finger at Aaron. "Ha!"

Finally, the chuckles subsided and the earl put down his teacup. He turned his bright gaze upon Aaron. "So it was Wells all along, eh?"

Aaron didn't speak. Others might, and be quite within their rights to do so, but his own vow kept him silent. The earl frowned. Wrinkles folded on wrinkles.

"Oh, relax, boy! You've got your place back! You must disregard that Black Aaron nonsense—a man is who he is inside with no regard for the opinions of outsiders. They used to call me Wild William in the day. I was a lad bent on sin and indulgence!"

Aaron blinked at that. "My lord, my imagination fails me completely."

The earl snickered. "It was a good woman who settled me down. Your grandmother took a rolling pin to my head once! Crack! Knocked the sense right back into me!"

He became quiet for a moment, gazing into the fire. "She would have done it again, you know, the day I sent you off. She would have reminded me to listen to my own opinions—not to let gossip rule my actions."

He turned his gaze on Aaron, who was stunned at the sadness he saw there. "Do you know why Serena never told me the truth until today?"

Aaron shook his head, although he had a fairly good notion.

The earl went on. "She said she feared I would send her and her boys away as well. Why would she think a thing like that of me, eh? Because she'd seen me be a stiff-necked fool already, that's why!"

Aaron suddenly realized what his grandfather meant by having his "place" back. "Are you saying—will I inherit everything after all?"

"Hmph!" The old man glared at him. "Yes! Did you take too much sun on those islands? You used to be quicker than that!" He waved a hand imperiously. "Now fetch Serena. I'm tired."

Aaron stood and delivered an admittedly automatic bow. His thoughts whirled in a hurricane. It was over? He would have the means to care for Arbodean? For Serena and her children?

He felt his "place" settle back upon him, like a suit of armor—heavy, but strong. It fit better now than it ever had.

As he left the room, his grandfather called him back. Aaron turned. "Yes, my lord?"

"That Worthington girl? She must be madly in love with you, if she would tell a great porky-pie to my face like that. She reminds me of your grandmother, you know. If I were your age, I wouldn't let that one get away."

"Yes, my lord."

Unfortunately, Aaron was honor-bound to do exactly that.

Aaron found Elektra on the terrace, gazing out upon the vast starlit gardens. Although her mint-green gown had seen its share of adventure, it remained as elegant as the beauty who wore it.

Elegant and sad. He could see it in the arch of her proud neck and in the sad slope of her graceful shoulders. *I have cost her so much. I cannot take any more from her.*

He couldn't bear to think of her spending her life regretting the day she'd seen him in the inn-yard, regretting that she'd had her dreams stolen by a highwayman in the dark.

He opened his mouth to speak, but nothing came out. He cleared his throat and tried again. "It is not too late, you know."

She turned to smile sadly at him over her shoulder. "I was just thinking the very same thing."

Her expression was so full of melancholy that it broke his heart. "Neville's a good sort." Something twisted tight and hot in his chest, but he forced himself to go on. "I always liked him."

She turned fully to face him, leaning her hands behind her on the balustrade. "I like him, too."

That was like an arrow through his already aching heart. He swallowed, fighting himself, battling the urge to sweep her away again, to gallop off into the night on a horse named Lard-Arse.

She watched him, waiting.

He drew in a tight, painful breath. "No one need know about . . ." He had to clear his throat. "Your family wouldn't breathe a word, of course. And Carter is so embarrassed about getting it all so wrong—he just wants it to go away."

She leaned her head back to gaze up at the stars. "I suppose I will have to explain to Neville why I am not a virgin. Do you think he'll mind?"

How could he tell her that a man would forgive her anything for a smile, a laugh, a flash of love in her aquamarine eyes? "I think he'll be reasonable about it, if he truly loves you."

She pointed upward. "There's Orion." She smiled slightly. "See? My family will always be with me. Do you think Neville will like the Worthingtons?"

"Ah." *Only if he never actually meets them.* He

cleared his throat. "When he protests, you could simply pour him some of Philpott's tea."

That got a smile. She turned her gaze to him at last. "Now, there's a plan."

"You can still have everything you want. Neville can help you rebuild your manor. His wealth and standing will make your family simply eccentric, instead of notorious."

She nodded slowly, but her smile faded. Her gaze never left his. "Yes, that would be good for Attie."

Aaron cleared his throat again, but he couldn't disperse the choking knot that fought his next words. "Marry Neville, Elektra."

"I suppose I have to marry someone, eventually." She walked slowly toward him, her hands clasped behind her back. Each step brought her closer, until her bodice nearly touched his weskit front. "May I have a kiss good-bye, my lord?" Her whisper danced across the skin below his ear.

Even though her agreement proved that she had never truly loved him, even though his heart felt as if it were bound in white-hot wire, he had to. Just one last taste . . .

He closed his eyes in grief and bent his head to hers.

She whispered something against his lips. "Stand and deliver, my lord."

The cold, steel barrel of a pistol pressed to his jaw. He drew in a sharp breath as his eyes flew open to see her dangerous smile.

"What—"

"I'm kidnapping you, Lord Aaron Arbogast. We will ride directly to Gretna Green." She smirked. "I traded for a fresh horse. I calculate we can be married by supper!"

"But—" He couldn't believe he was protesting the fulfillment of his deepest dream, but he had to give her one last chance! "What of my reputation? It will not help your family to be associated with me!"

She shrugged carelessly. "The Worthingtons have survived being odd for many years. They'll survive a little longer."

He suppressed a smile at that. "But—we do not have a ring!"

Elektra reached into her neckline and pulled out the ribbon that hung there. Alongside the ornately worked key to Worthington Manor hung something else. The gold of Aaron's signet ring gleamed in the torchlight.

"How—?"

Her eyes narrowed slyly. "I lifted it from the inn-keeper's pocket before we resumed our journey that morning. You were so upset about parting with it."

His heart freed itself from its last torturous binding with an almost audible snap. Aaron raised one finger to carefully avert the pistol from his head. "Well, there's no need to be quite so forceful about it."

She kept the pistol raised, but pointed slightly to one side. "I am taking no chances this time. I stole you away once and you managed to talk me out of it then. Silly man." She smiled at him, a wild, wicked Worthington grin full of danger and laughter and love. "Don't you know? Worthingtons always win in the end."

My goddess Elektra.

Aaron pulled her close and swept her lightly into his arms, pistol and all. He spun them both in a circle of joy as he laughed aloud. "I must be a Worthington, then!"

Epilogue

"Ah, Mr. Hastings! Won't you join us for a spot of tea?"

Iris Worthington was holding court in her drawing room—which was, quite literally, filled with drawings. *Shakespeare and Octopus. Shakespeare and Duckling. Shakespeare and Shakespeare*, the great man looking at himself in a mirror. If one looked closely, one could count five ears.

Attie perked up at the name, but when a strange man entered, she went back to her own drawing. Her mother had asked her to bring some color to the walls, so she was adding an undersea scene.

Hence the octopus.

The man sat down with Iris and poor brokenhearted Button. Button was sad because Cabot had left. Attie was a little bit mad at him for letting Cabot leave, but mostly she was sorry because he was so terribly sad.

Tea and sympathy, that's what Iris had said. Attie didn't think the tea would help much. It wasn't even Philpott's special tea.

"Are you going to join dear Aaron at Arbodean, Mr. Hastings? I'm sure he'll expect you."

"Only long enough to collect me back pay, missus. 'E don't need me anymore."

Attie began to make circles for the suction cups on the tentacles. Lots and lots of circles.

"It must have been so romantic! A midnight dash to Gretna Green. Our Ellie is so impulsive!"

Ellie had married that other Hastings, run off with him in the night and everything. Attie was a little bit mad about that, too. Lots and lots of circles.

"I'm bound to do somethin' like that meself."

"Ah. Romance!" Button was trying to be his old bubbly self, but it wasn't working very well.

"Aye. There's a girl I know, a little Cornish maid named Edith. She won't be expectin' me to come back, but—"

"But you simply cannot stay away!" Iris sighed. "Isn't love wondrous?" She poured more tea for Mr. Button, who was drinking rather a lot of it. "I think it all worked out rather well, don't you?"

Mr. Hastings raised his teacup in salute. "I couldn't have planned it better myself, Lady Iris."

Iris giggled. "Shush. We mustn't upset the children."

The three of them leaned close together. "Now," Iris whispered. "About Orion—"

Attie listened so hard she stopped breathing, but she didn't hear any more.

Mr. Hastings finished his tea and went on his way. A moment later Dade and Orion entered the drawing room. Dade tugged on one of Attie's braids. "Nice tentacles, Attie."

She grunted. She was a little bit mad at Dade. She forgot why.

Dade bent to kiss his mother on the cheek in greeting. "Who was that fellow who just left?"

"That was Henry Hastings, dear."

Dade made a noise. "Not another one!"

Attie looked up. "I liked him!"

Dade closed his eyes. "Oh, God."

Orion narrowed his eyes. "I can see we will need to be more thorough next time."

Attie gazed up at Orion. He was one of her favorites, for he was nearly as intelligent as she was. Should she warn him that Iris and Button had him in their match-making sights?

Or should she wait to see what happened next? She smiled to herself as she went back to her drawing.

She had always been a most curious Worthington.

Look for these wonderful romance series from
New York Times bestselling author
CELESTE BRADLEY

The Wicked Worthingtons
When She Said I Do
And Then Comes Marriage

The Runaway Brides
Devil in My Bed
Rogue in My Arms
Scoundrel in My Dreams

The Heiress Brides
Desperately Seeking a Duke
The Duke Next Door
The Duke Most Wanted

The Royal Four
To Wed a Scandalous Spy
Surrender to a Wicked Spy
One Night With a Spy
Seducing the Spy

The Liar's Club
The Pretender
The Impostor
The Spy
The Charmer
The Rogue

**AVAILABLE FROM ST. MARTIN'S
PAPERBACKS**